TETHERED FEATHER

LIZ TOLEVSKI

ISBN: 978-1-7640904-0-7 (ebook)
ISBN: 978-1-7640904-1-4 (paperback)
ISBN: 978-1-7640904-2-1 (hardback)

Cover Design by Murphy Rae

For all my loves:
my love,
my lady love,
and my littlest love.

Without you, I never would have believed in myself

*Netted prey lurk in darkened corners to capture night-time essence
in jars-
Others, like the light of a firefly, shine a small welcoming beacon-
then head towards a blinding light.
-No true love story is ever ordinary-*

PRESENCE

Kara Collins once heard her father say it was 'better to be not present and not there than to be present and not there'. This riddle would challenge her ideas about the management of her own time. It also meant Kara's ideas could be dismantled, reprocessed and compartmentalised. Their relevance depended on her presence.

The presence Kara recognised was fractional and lingered like a thief waiting in the crevices of her tempered thoughts. It appeared desperate. It tried to fill the void left by the love she thought she had, and it left her to pick up the leftover pieces to bolster itself.

Time was something that presence appeared to have no concept of. It rid itself of all temporal elements, mimicking eternity. It presented Kara with wonders and beings that acted like saviours to tormented liars. It burrowed into her mind, leaving her grasping the possibility of belief. If possibility had a colour, it would be desperate red, covering everything with its crimson lies. Presence wandered into Kara's memories, deeming some parts unnecessary and condemning them, shining light on moments that needed to be remembered.

Presence situated itself within five-year-old Kara's memories.

It tainted the foggy in-between years of before – appearing like segments on a camera reel filtered through sunshine and laughter. No one ever truly remembers what happens during those formative years. They flash past momentarily, narrated by the people who were present at the time. And somehow, with each retelling, the original stories become more complex and convoluted. But those memories can also be clouded and cluttered by the past, obscuring moments we would rather forget to never be burdensome.

Kara remembered her earliest childhood memory. She was with her mother and father in the car, and she looked at her mother like she was a real-life princess. Her mother was the prettiest woman she had ever seen, and her father was the prince who rescued the princess from trouble. It was a sweet fairy tale that allowed her to believe in the innocence of love. Kara wanted her world to centre around a love like the one her parents shared simple, pure and uncomplicated.

It was early morning, and the rain had left a sheen on the bitumen, creating misty swirls that touched dawn's heat. Kara was fascinated with the ribbons of smoke that rose from the floor. They looked like they were dancing in the lane, leaving the road little time to retire from the night-time heat. There would be no reprieve from the scorching morning sun.

The hot air stifled breathing in the confines of the car. Kara's dad had an old Ford Escort that was most likely past its use-by date. It didn't have anything modern inside because he claimed he never needed it. 'Wheels and a reliable engine. That's all you need to get to where you're going,' he would say. So, although the windows were fully open, there was no respite from the summer. Kara's mother would turn around from the front seat and extend a hand out to tickle Kara's toes, distracting her from the suffocating warmth. 'Not long now, Karina,' she would say. 'The ocean will cool you down, *principessa.*'

Having never seen the ocean, Kara wondered how it would cool her down. But it didn't matter; she would giggle at the thought like it was the funniest thing she had ever heard. Kara would copy her mother, sticking her hand out of the window, trying to capture a moment of wind to cool her down. Her legs were drenched from where they touched the hot vinyl, and she would squirm, moving in the seat to escape the stickiness.

Her father was always stoic behind the wheel. He navigated corners through clutches and gears as he cruised the Great Ocean Road. His hand would stray from the steering wheel to his wife's knee. She would beam at him, carefree, as if it was the only place on earth she wanted to be. Her hair would whip the side of her face, the strands caught in her smile. Often, she would turn the music up loud, saying, 'I love this song,' then sing broken, made-up lyrics with abandon.

Kara's dad would talk about landmarks Kara had no comprehension of. She didn't know what the Apostles were but felt excited they were going to see them. He would slow down and say 'Hang on' as the turns got sharp. The car would slowly grumble through the corners, leaving a vapour of burnt fuel in the already-hot air. The smell was inescapable. If they rolled the windows back up, the heat would be too intense inside the car. So, they left them open, making summer a memory of corners, hot wind and the smell of petrol stuck to their clothes.

The cliffs nearby rolled down to the ocean, where the waves crashed along the side in angry washes of white. It scared Kara to think this was the ocean her mother told her would cool her down. She didn't want to be near the edge where the rocks were; she worried the car would slip from its spot and slide down. It was such a long way up, close enough that Kara felt like she could touch the sky.

Kara's dad pulled over then looked in the rear-view mirror. 'I hope we haven't lost them.'

'I'm sure he's being super careful with his new car,' her mother reassured him.

'That's why he needs one like this,' he reminded her, patting the dashboard.

'So they too can wilt in the sun.' Her mother laughed back at him. 'Maybe Karina and I should bail and go with them. Leave you so you can enjoy your car.' She laughed so hard, that it made Kara giggle as well. It was a welcome distraction from the unrelenting heat.

'There's Nick!' he yelled when he saw them approaching, waving his arm out the window.

Kara liked Nick or, as she called him, Uncle Nick. He was married to a woman whom she knew as Aunty Lou, and she was always happy with a sweet disposition. She had a crinkled smile that reached her eyes, unlike her seven-year-old twin sons Eli and Noah. Their soured faces scared Kara, and they made it their life's mission to never be nice to her. They would pinch her under the table when no one was looking or hit her across the head when she walked past. If she ever said anything about them to her parents, it was met with a look of disbelief. So, she had to fend for herself when they were around.

Weekends would usually revolve around visits to each other's houses. The adults would stay up laughing, drinking wine and playing cards with pretend money. The music would blare through the radio with a competition to see who could sing the loudest. Meanwhile, the children would be left to their own devices. This usually meant sitting in front of the television, gorging themselves on salty chips and sweet fizzy drinks. As the hours passed and no one would pay any attention to them, Kara and the boys would eventually tire with heavy eyes on the lounge. The presence of their parents allowed them to sleep safely through the night.

But not all the memories Kara had of their visits were fun. She remembered a time when Eli came and sat beside her. Before she knew what was happening, Eli pinched her hard on the leg and ran off, sitting back next to Noah. They continued to play their handheld games as if nothing happened. Kara held back the tears that were threatening to spill, rubbing her leg trying to ease the pain. As if on cue, her mother came over to see what they were doing. Noah looked up at Kara and made a gesture across his neck with his finger. Heeding the warning, she lied and told her mother she was upset because she tripped.

She remembered how her mother would sit with them for a while, playfully warning Alex and Noah with a 'Boys!', which they paid no attention to. She would stay and play mediator for as long as she needed to, her suspicious smile letting everyone know she was very aware of what was happening.

When things seemed to settle, she would look at Kara, silently asking for permission to leave. She would lean over and kiss Kara on the cheek, whispering, 'Behave, principessa.' Kara remembered smiling back at her mother, watching her leave and waiting until the boys were distracted before she walked into their bedroom. The boys had a tub full of cars and trucks, which they cherished. Peering over her shoulder once more, Kara got to work. She relished in her destruction, eventually walking out with her pockets bulging with the mangled leftovers of their beloved toys. Emptying her pockets into the rubbish bin, she walked back into the room where the adults continued to play cards.

Kara sat in her mother's lap and stared at Aunty Lou as she held the cigarette to her mouth. She scraped the rigid wall of the packet of matches, the smell of phosphorus lingering for a second. Aunty Lou inhaled, and Kara was sure that the smoke swirled in her lungs before she blew out the stub of the match with her smoky breath. Aunty Lou relaxed into her exhale, talking through the grey, white plumes.

'Would you like a drink, Karina?' she asked between puffs.

'Yes please,' Kara replied with her best manners.

It was a memory that had her smiling in the back seat.

They drove for what felt like hours, only stopping to fill up her dad's thirsty car. When they finally arrived at a place called Warrnambool, the air seemed to change with a cool breeze that tickled Kara's skin. The relief was welcomed by everyone as they got out of their cars.

'Last one to the maze stinks like Karina,' Alex taunted.

'Don't be rude,' Aunty Lou yelled after them.

But the boys paid no attention to anyone, heading straight for the big hedge, where they soon disappeared. Kara secretly wished they would never be found so they wouldn't bother her again. She often had bad thoughts like those and knew she had to keep them to herself.

She waited for her father to finish talking to Uncle Nick so he could take her to the park. It didn't take long for her father to notice her waiting impatiently. He grabbed her under the arms, swung her around and headed towards the swings, Kara giggling along the way, feeling like she was flying.

Her mother was never too far behind them. Being outside made her happy, and she would smile towards the sun. The only time worry etched her face was when Kara was pushed high on the swing yelling, 'Higher, Daddy! Higher.' Kara would dismiss her mother's fears, swinging her little legs up and down, allowing the wind whooshing past to catch her giggles.

'Are you ready, Karina?' her father asked. 'Do you want to go to the ocean?'

Kara's movements on the swing slowed down enough so she could jump off into the orange bark. She didn't want to go near the ocean she remembered as white and wild, a place that hit rocks over and over relentlessly with no remorse. It terrified her to think her father would want to take her somewhere like that. She wondered how they would get back up when they fell.

Crouching down to where she stood, he lovingly pushed her hair behind her ear to soothe her. He leaned in close so no one would hear and whispered, 'What's the matter, Karina?'

'It's such a long way down. I don't want to go,' she told him.

'What do you mean it's a long way down? It's not far from here at all.'

'I don't want to go.' She pulled back, not wanting to go any further. 'The ocean looked angry, and I don't want to go off the cliff.'

Her father laughed with a rumble that made his chin shake.

She was instantly embarrassed as heat coloured her chubby cheeks.

'Do you trust me?' he asked her.

Not wanting everyone to know how scared she truly was, she nodded her head and took her father's hand.

It was the sound that caught Kara's attention first. The waves were crashing by the shoreline, but they didn't look as angry. Here, a calmness washed over her, and she found herself inhaling the salty air. It filled her lungs with the smell of newness. The vastness of the ocean was intimidating, and she wondered if it ever ended. Where would it stop if it took her? Embarrassment stopped her from asking in case the boys would hear so, like she often did, she kept her thoughts to herself.

Noah and Eli ran past them, kicking up sand along the way. They paid no attention to anyone, especially Kara, who felt intimidatingly small standing there in awe of the ocean.

'Do you want to dip your toes in the water?' her mother asked.

Kara hadn't noticed her mother standing there watching her and her father the whole time. It was as if she was waiting for Kara's unsure moment to pass. When it did, Kara grabbed both their hands, like she was the luckiest girl in the world.

Walking closer and closer to the waves, the coldness of the water began to tickle her toes. A moment of terror seized her, and she pulled back, wanting to run to the shore. She was worried the wave would get bigger, and she would end up washed up on the rocks. Her father held her hand firmly, smiling over at her mother and silently telling her what to do. She squeezed Kara's hand and let go, taking a few steps back.

'I've got you, Karina,' her father said. 'Want to go a little deeper?'

They walked hand in hand until the water level reached her knees. She found the cold refreshing, the saltiness replacing the sticky stench of the trip.

'When I say jump, we jump high, alright?' he instructed.

An ominous-looking wave headed Kara's way, and sheer panic took over. She only wanted her toes to feel the water, and she knew she couldn't run, especially while her feet kept disappearing beneath the surface.

'Jump!' he yelled, as the wave reached past her knees, wetting her hips.

Kara laughed, thinking about how silly she felt about it all earlier. There was nothing for her to fear when her father was present. She looked up to see his cheeky smile, and he winked in reassurance.

They stayed jumping waves for what seemed like hours. He would yell 'ready', and together they would jump and laugh as if nothing else mattered. Kara could see her mother standing on the shore, smiling at them. She would clap, looking at Kara like she was extremely proud. Her father let go of her hand, giving her tiny bits of independence so she could jump on her own.

Meanwhile, Noah and Eli kept running in and out of the ocean, pushing each other underwater. It terrified Kara to watch, but she knew Uncle Nick wasn't too far away and would never let anything happen to them.

Her father was laughing at the boys and didn't notice that Kara had taken her eyes off the ocean. The wave came quickly and without apology, lapping just past her shoulders. She found herself unsteady then under the water. She felt a hard pull on her arm to lift her. But it wasn't the spluttering of water that came from her mouth and nose that worried her. It was the pain that radiated in her arm down to her fingertips. She screamed in agony. Her tears instantly mixed with the salt on her face. Picking her up, her father carried her back to the shore, worry etched in the lines of her mother's face.

'Karina, what happened?' she yelled.

'We didn't see that one coming. I had to pull her up,' her father said.

'Where does it hurt principessa?' she asked.

The pain was intense, and she felt like she was unable to form words, so she pointed with her finger to where it hurt.

'Your elbow?' he questioned.

Kara tried to lift her arm, but the movement made pain shoot down it. Looking up at her dad, she saw worry settle with a paleness on his face. Guilt lifted in his lips, and it made Kara want to cry harder. She didn't blame her dad; Noah and Eli were the reason she was distracted. When they came back and saw Kara sitting, holding her arm, they started to laugh. Uncle Nick was quick to give them a swift slap across the head. He said something to them in a language Kara had vaguely heard before but didn't understand, then ushered them away.

'I think we should go to the hospital. Karina, can you try and lift your arm again?' her mother asked.

When Kara tried again, she screamed in agony, scaring the seagulls that settled around them.

'It hurts,' Kara cried.

Scooping her up like she was completely broken, her father carried Kara back to the car. Uncle Nick said he would drive them because he had air conditioning. Aunty Lou said she would drive the other car with the boys, who grumbled something about how the other car was old and smelly. Aunty Lou's whisper threatened the boys about if they didn't listen, and it was overheard by everyone. The boys followed, kicking sand along the way.

The hospital wasn't very far. The doctor's presence was calming as he told them that they needed to take some scans to rule out a fracture. Paling and unable to form coherent words, Kara's father could only nod. Not long after the X-ray, the doctor informed everyone that there was no fracture, but there was most likely a small sprain. He reassured everyone that it would get better over the next few days, and it wasn't anything to worry about. Forgiveness and Kara's smile allowed colour back on her father's face.

The doctor gave Kara some medicine to help with the pain and, not long after that, she fell asleep only to wake in a strange bed. Her arm had a funny white bandage that was wrapped in a white cloth, and she clutched it to her chest. Using her other arm to push herself out of bed, she went looking look for her parents, who were nowhere to be found.

She could hear muffled noises outside, so she drew the curtain on the window aside to see and hear a little better. Her father was pacing while her mother stood there with her hands on her hips. She was yelling at him about something, and Kara hoped it wasn't her.

As if they sensed her staring from the window, they stopped yelling, and her father walked towards her mother. When he got there, he pushed her hair away from her eyes, differently from how he did it with Kara, and rested his hand on her cheek. She could see him mouth the words *I love you, you are my everything* and lean in to find her lips. They kissed for a while. When they stopped, he rested his forehead against hers. Kara closed the curtain, slightly embarrassed that she had seen them kissing.

In that instant, she knew that one day she wanted to find a love like that: a love where forgiveness could purify the deepest parts of her soul. Kara knew she wanted someone to look at her the way her father looked at her mother where, if hate tried to surface, love would guard with its undeterred presence.

She walked back towards the bed, smiling. She didn't care if her arm still hurt, or that her time with the ocean was terrifying. What mattered to her most at that moment was that her parents were there. Her mother had found her real-life prince, and hopefully one day Kara would too. Her parents loved her and chose to be present in her life. At least, that's how she remembered her earliest memory.

2

IMPRESSIONS

Kara's path led her to the people she met. It reminded her that although the destination was the same, the means of arrival were different. She tried to balance her way, especially with people she befriended.

Some strangers left impressions on her soul, lasting impressions that swarmed with fluttering kisses on her heart, while others passed through with the speed of a shooting star. These people were remembered but claimed little time and space in Kara's memories. Every now and then, someone would unexpectedly enter and shift the fragile balance of her reality and Kara would deem their presence significant.

Now in her late twenties, Kara tried to forget her childhood memories. She embraced changes in her life with a mixture of fright and excitement. She was now in a position to be selective about the people she met; some came and went with little or no regard. Others however, like her friend Michael, took up permanent residence in her life. During the few years she had known him, he had seamlessly inserted himself, making an impression in her life.

Michael Farrino was the kind of person who needed no time to get ready and less time to ask questions. Their friendship was unconventional. Like Kara, he didn't care what other people thought about him.

He had three means of communication: silence, encryption and honesty. It wasn't that he didn't want to speak to anyone, but he believed music and songs filled the space better. His fluency with words were often heavy and needed translation. But it was his honesty that she most appreciated. His transparency was real and unfiltered. He portrayed himself as a person with no walls who shared only what mattered to him.

Michael had the type of personality that came with no expectations. Kara questioned sometimes whether others wondered how they maintained their friendship without crossing any boundaries. The answer: they never gave unnecessary details to anyone and kept their private lives to themselves.

Not long after they first met, she had tried to push the boundaries of their friendship. Buoyed one evening after a bottle of wine, Kara threw herself at Michael with an expectation that he would share her feelings. Instead, he smiled at her like a brother would and laughed at how drunk she was.

'I'll accept your drunken version of flattery,' he said. 'But that will never happen. I'd rather we keep things the way they are.'

'Oh,' Kara replied, sobering up quickly. 'I'm sorry.'

'There's no need for an apology. I love our friendship. There is no need to over-complicate things. And, to be honest, I'm not looking for anyone right now.'

'Is it because you like men?' she asked, realising the answer when she heard Michael laugh.

'No,' he replied, his laughter eventually dying down. Then his face was solemn as if trying to find the right words. 'No, but I'll never cross that line with you. This is all we we'll ever be.'

She never threw herself at him or questioned their friendship again. The more time they spent together, the bigger the impression he made on her life. Michael felt like a long-lost relative she never knew she had. He called her regularly to see how she was faring. Kara's current phone conversation with him was no different to any other.

'Turn that obnoxious television down so we can have a decent conversation,' he demanded.

Kara looked towards the television screen: **Man's body found floating in Merri Creek**

'Wait,' she told Michael. 'I just want to hear this. Something has happened not far from my place.'

'Something always happens not far from your place,' he laughed.

'Shhhhh…'

'Police said a passer-by found the body of a man floating in the waterways of Merri Creek early this morning. The victim is Attius Barno, who police say was shot execution-style. Mr Barno was also known to police. He was out on bail and due to appear in court later this month for a list of convictions that included aggravated assault. Mr Barno was most recently seen leaving the home of the late Aldo Cartelli's son, Domenic Cartelli, the notorious gangland leader. Detective Peters told us at Channel Seven that while Mr Cartelli was earlier taken in for questioning, he has since been released. Detective Peters also told us they were concerned with the rising number of gangland-type crimes in the area and are looking to investigate the connections.'

Kara remained silent long after the news-reporter finished. Her guts somersaulted with uneasiness. The name 'Domenic Cartelli' had made her mother once shiver when she heard it, but anything else about Dom Cartelli had been lost to Kara's past.

'Hello,' Michael blared down the receiver. 'Are you still there, or have I lost you to the news? You should turn that incessant noise off.'

'Sorry. It's off,' she told Michael, still staring at the blank screen. 'And you have my undivided attention.'

Kara could hear Michael talking in the background, but something churned in the pit of her stomach at the name

Domenic Cartelli. She tried to brush it off, dismissing the nagging feeling, as if it were nothing more than a coincidence.

'Chicanery,' Michael continued, oblivious to her internal peril.

'In a sentence?' Kara asked.

'The surname he gave exemplified dishonesty, therefore you knew who he was.'

'So what you're saying is beware of the person telling lies.' She laughed.

'Perhaps. But also beware of trickery,' he said, with a matter-of-fact tone.

Michael's words were always some sort of warning or premonition to remind Kara to stay guarded around others.

'Be careful out there tonight. You never know who you'll run into,' he heckled over the phone. 'And remember…'

'Only ask what is necessary.'

'And why is that?' he asked, as if she was a child.

'Because we only need to know so much about the people we meet. Especially the transient ones. Is that right?'

'Exactly.' He chuckled. 'Now go, you little miscreant. Have fun, but not too much fun without me.' He hung up the phone.

Their conversations often ended cryptically and, while she would never admit it, there were times it unsettled her. However, Kara dismissed those feelings as nothing more than Michael's overprotection.

Kara enjoyed her time alone but wasn't as reclusive as her mother. Often, she would find herself out late at night drinking in bars, talking to strange men, enjoying the attention, then leaving once she felt they had served her purpose.

She thought she was comfortable with her seclusion. She convinced herself that nights out were to escape her world. She could be whoever she chose, entertaining herself along the way. She didn't believe it to be a double life. But it was how she wanted her life structured, so no one could see what she believed the real Kara to be.

Responsibility was something Kara was loathe to accept. Especially given that she didn't have to work. Unbeknown to her, while she was growing up, her father had been putting money into an account for her. She remembered when her mother came in with the envelope on her eighteenth birthday, holding it out without saying a word.

'What is it?' she asked, taking the envelope. Her name was written on the front in writing she didn't recognise. There was no return address.

'It's from your father.'

'I don't want it,' she said, trying to hand back the envelope as if it burnt her hand.

'It doesn't matter if you want it or not. It's yours.' Her mother looked at Kara with sympathy in her eyes. 'He wants you to have it.'

'How do you know what it is?' Kara asked, suspicious. 'Have you spoken to him?'

'No. But I've known about this for a long time. Or I should say I assumed I knew about this a long time ago. Just open it.'

Kara opened the envelope with shaky hands. Inside was a note:

For you. Happy eighteenth birthday.

Behind the note was a cheque for an obscene amount of money, one that meant she could live her life without worrying about working. It was a large sum of money that Kara intended to waste, every last cent. He owed her more than what was written on the cheque, and it angered her that she wondered if this was his way of buying her happiness.

She tried to give the cheque to her mother. She wanted her to have it, but she shook her head, misty-eyed, telling her, 'I have enough blood money of my own that I don't touch. I don't need your father's charity.'

Kara had never asked her mother what she meant by that. She knew she wouldn't give her the answers she truly wanted.

So, Kara used that money to fund her lifestyle. She used it to impress people who fell for the avatar she created. That money paid for her apartment, and the car that she hardly used, and her wardrobe for nights out in bars, like tonight. So, with painted lips and stiletto heels, she kissed her little mirror goodbye and went in search of the perfect martini.

Melbourne's sounds crashed into her like a familiar friend. If she closed her eyes hard enough, she could pretend she was hearing everything for the first time, the sounds amplifying the longer she stood still. Cars honked and tyres screeched on the crowded roads. The ticking of the pedestrian crossing sent people from one street to the next. It smelled like spring mixed with cigarettes. It was the weekend in the city. Young adults walked through the Melbourne alleyways looking for night-time solace. Their joy was intoxicating and contagious. Everywhere she turned, life was continuing with a frenetic beat. People were walking around looking for somewhere to be welcomed, a space with the prospect of fantasy and escapism.

Before heading into New Gold Mountain, a strangeness settled into Kara that she had never experienced before. It was as if someone wanted her to know she had been noticed. Unable to shake the feeling, Kara looked around the alley to see who was making her uncomfortable.

But no one in the alley stood out, and no one looked like they were paying much attention to the woman standing near the door. She looked to the street again and noticed a black car idling with its indicator on, but they soon pulled into a spot.

Kara felt uncomfortable and unusually on edge. She wanted to call Michael, but she stopped, reminding herself that she was being silly. There was nothing to worry about. She was heading into her favourite bar, and her wild imagination was making itself known.

The bar had a quaintness that matched how the tourist guides described Melbourne. The hidden door was only noticeable because of a pushbike hanging from the wall. The alleyway leading to it smelled of urine, soured beer and vomit. Graffiti coloured the once-brown brick walls. Unidentifiable tags were scattered across one side, with half-drawn pictures on the other. The colours dripped along the edges, making it look as if the artists were in a rush to get away.

Walking up the rickety stairs to get to the first level, Kara looked at the mosaic mirror on the wall. Hundreds of images reflected her rouge-noir lips. She winked at herself before she picked off another piece, putting it in her handbag. Impulse told her to do it every time she was there. Once home, she would carefully glue it so it could join the others displayed on her lounge room wall.

The bar wasn't as crowded as it normally was on a Saturday night. The lights were dim, and the booths on either side were occupied by lovers seeking privacy. The music swayed around the room. A woman's sultry voice whisper-sang something about being in love. It was evocative and sensual, adding another layer of seduction to this already private place. Frankie smiled at her from behind the counter.

'What about a little new thing I've been working on?' they asked.

'Surprise me,' she said, winking.

'I call it "paying my tuition", a play on the porn-star martini. Fitting, don't you think?' Frankie laughed.

Someone snickered, and she turned to her right. There was a well-dressed man she hadn't noticed earlier sitting one barstool away. He stared at her and shook his head. Returning a polite smile, Kara pretended to be unaffected, reaching into her bag to pull out her phone as her martini arrived.

'I'll get that,' the mystery man told Frankie.

'Thank you, but you don't have to,' Kara said.

Deep down, she felt no remorse about him paying for the cocktail. Her thanks were as fleeting as his chivalry. A strange man buying her a drink in a bid to get under her skirt wasn't new. It certainly wasn't the first time she had been tempted through intoxication. But she never let herself get that far. Two martinis were her limit then she would leave.

'Think nothing of it. I admire a woman who can drink martinis. I don't know how you do it.' He opened his wallet and gave Frankie his card.

'If a cocktail is good, then it's all worth it. Frankie's are the best,' Kara said.

'Indeed,' he said raising his wine glass. 'Cheers.'

'Cheers, and thank you again.'

He was handsome. The first thing she noticed was a small dimple in his left cheek. His nose was slightly crooked, as if it had been hit a few times and never re-set. It added a certain character to his charm. His accent was barely noticeable and she wasn't sure where it came from. His dress sense came straight from a men's magazine. The suit was impeccably moulded to his body, the top button of his shirt undone. He oozed sexy self-control. He looked like he had left a wedding, but there was only a ring on his right hand. No wedding band.

But it was his eyes that left the biggest impression. His soul was captured in their scorpion-brown depths. They came with a piercing intensity that scattered all rational thought. For the second time that night, Kara felt unsettled.

No one ever looked at her that way - a combination of satisfaction and curiosity. Her heart pummelled in her chest, wanting to escape. Wrapping her hand around the stem of her martini glass, she twitched with an unfamiliar nervousness. She knew his game ... she had played the vixen before. But never had anyone tormented her so with a simple glance. He looked like he was hunting and she was his target.

Avoiding further eye contact, Kara hoped he would be gone by the time she finished her drink. The booth on the other side of her emptied, and she took her drink to the quiet corner.

The barstool he sat on moved back, and Kara inwardly groaned as he headed her way. His strides were unhurried. When he got to Kara, he casually pulled out a tub chair from the table off to the side and sat directly opposite her. She laughed and thought how very cavalier of him, then that Michael would be proud she had thought of such a word.

But, behind his bravado, she thought she saw a moment of hesitation in his eyes, as if he was harbouring some secret that should stop him from being there. Whatever it was, it was fleeting.

'Do you mind if I join you?' he asked.

His voice sounded smooth, like chocolate wrapped in velvet. He didn't wait for her reply, smiling at his cheekiness. The lone dimple she saw earlier now appeared on both cheeks. Temptation had her wanting to reach out and touch them, but she stopped herself and simply answered, 'I believe you answered your own question.'

'I don't want to sound cliché, but are you waiting for someone?'

Kara wanted to appear disinterested, but something told her he had already read her.

'I am,' she told him. 'Or I was, but I think I've been stood up.' She bent the lie a little.

The reality was, nobody was coming for her and she wasn't waiting for anyone. Kara regularly sat in the bar while Frankie made a martini. She would listen to the music then leave.

'Well,' he said, 'I guess it's his loss.'

'What makes you think they are a he?' she said, deadpan.

'Oh,' he stumbled. 'I beg your pardon. You're right. That was rude. Her loss, then.'

'I'm messing with you,' she said after watching him squirm for a while. 'I was here to meet a friend, but I don't think he's going to show. It's a long story.' She grinned knowing she had stretched the truth a little further.

'*His* loss, then,' he said.

He appeared not to care that she may have been meeting another person. Part of her wanted him to ask about who she was supposed to meet so she could elaborate on the lie. She wanted to mess with him, but she also had a feeling that he was not the type to be messed with. Right now, his eyes were zeroed in directly on her. They hadn't strayed, not even back to the bar, where two beautiful well-dressed women sat. His intensity made her feel like she was the only person there. His stare simmered comfortably along her skin like it belonged there.

He sat back in his chair, crossing his right ankle over his knee. Watching him take a sip of his wine, Kara was suddenly envious of the glass.

'I'm Val,' he said. 'Valerio Kavalenko.'

She didn't want to hear anymore. He had destroyed Michael's number one rule. According to him, Kara already knew too much and should immediately leave.

Time played with her inner reality, crystallising her version of the truth. He was making an unwelcome impression, one that Kara feared would leave a permanent imprint.

He had her twisting in her chair with a combination of deliberation, fear and anticipation. It was an unexplainable joy, but she knew it also came at a price. She asked herself if she wanted to dredge her heart through the torment of it all. As soon as the thought arose, she chastised herself for having it about a man she had just met.

'Kara,' she said smugly over the rim of her glass.

'Short for?'

'Nothing. Just Kara.'

'Do you have a surname, Just Kara?'

Michael's voice came into her thoughts, reminding her to never give away more than she had to. But it soon disappeared. Kara was always adept at lying, thriving in situations like this. But she didn't want to lie to this man. He was different. He was intriguing. And, she had a feeling that this Valerio was harbouring a secret of his own. It shouldn't have mattered. But there was a pull, a thread, something that she knew she wanted to explore. It saw her straying from her norm, accepting something closer to honesty.

'Collins,' she blurted out truthfully. She had now broken a

very significant rule. It was privileged information, now he could find her after she walked out of there.

'Kara Collins.' The name rolled off his tongue, her name finding beauty in his lips. His slight accent accentuated each syllable in her small name. 'It's a pleasure to meet you.'

The word 'pleasure' sounded dirty coming from his mouth, and Kara's mind drifted to places it shouldn't have. Her face warmed, and he smirked, knowing he affected her.

'What brings you here tonight?' she asked, trying to take the focus off herself.

'Apparently, you do,' was all he said.

'How is that so if we're only meeting for the first time?'

'Well, my plans fell through. Turned to crap, actually. So here I am, and here you are.' They sat in silence after his admission, never breaking eye contact. She wanted to delve deeper. Why had Valerio Kavalenko come to the bar? What was he hiding? He had wanted to know who she was meeting, perhaps she should have asked him more. She wanted to believe he would tell her, and the questions were on the tip of her tongue, but she didn't say a word. She worried about how she would react if she knew his truth. These thoughts were foreign to Kara. She wanted to deny all of them. She didn't want to be that person, finding romance when she least expected it. Romance she secretly yearned for. Romance where someone came to find her when she wasn't looking.

Kara knew she had a warped notion of love and wanted to replace it with compassion and lust. She wanted to truly let her guard down and let someone in close to her heart. But she felt her heart no longer recognised kindness or compassion. It had become brittle and filled with deceit, and she never allowed anyone to get close. She always believed she should deny her heart access to any form of love or affection. She often wondered whether anyone could make that change.

'Where are you going after here?' he asked, breaking her out of her reverie.

'Home,' she said, honestly. 'I only come for Frankie's martinis, then I go home.'

'Perhaps you've found a new reason to come back here and stay a little longer.'

She didn't have a chance to answer before his chair unexpectedly scraped back and he stood, towering over her. Val opened his wallet and pulled out a card. He flipped it over a few times as if contemplating its weight. When he looked back, his stare suggested he had made up his mind about Kara.

'Something tells me if I asked for your number, you would either give me the wrong one or nothing at all.'

Kara answered him with silence. But her reserve was fleeting. She tried to reach over and grab the card, but he was quicker. Taking it away, he looked at the card again, flipping it over in contemplation. Kara laughed awkwardly at their little game but quietly seethed at her failure to take the card from him.

'I'd like you to call me, Kara Collins, but I have a feeling you won't.'

He left the card next to his empty glass and turned around to walk away. She didn't reach out to grab it or try and remember the number on it. She stared after him. Just before he got to the door, he turned back, and walked towards where she sat.

'If you don't call, I know where you go on a Saturday night. I'll keep coming back till I see you again. Maybe then you'll give me your number.'

'What makes you think I'll come back?' she challenged.

'Because like me, Kara Collins,' he paused, measuring his words, 'you came here with no intentions. It's wonderful when you find something that leaves an unexpected impression, don't you think?' He leaned in to take his card away and walked out without a second glance. She wondered if she had finally met her match. Was the man who walked away someone destined to be in her life?

A loneliness she hadn't experienced before crept in. She shivered with emptiness. His aftermath had her chastising herself for not looking closely enough at the card. An unexpected stranger left her contemplating more than the martini she needed that night.

Michael once told her that you can't allow love in unless you've learnt to love yourself. Those words seemed insignificant up until now. A chance encounter had her thinking about the need for more within herself. The person that she was wasn't someone that Valerio Kavalenko would like to know. And he was correct when he said that she wouldn't call him. He was also right in knowing she would be back and not just for Frankie's martini's. Val was already lurking in the back of her mind like a troublemaker.

3

SADNESS

Kara underwent a gradual change. She experienced sadness with a subtlety that unsettled her. It was a hairline fracture in porcelain and, as time weighed on it, the cracks deepened. However the change occurred, the certainty of change for Kara was inevitable.

Sadness draped itself like black silk around her soul and blocked out everything. It was a challenge for Kara to shake off sadness, as it gripped her soul with a formidable strength. It threatened her ability to experience love, erasing any happiness she found and leaving her incapable of feeling any emotions.

The night before her sixth birthday, Kara begged her mother to try on the outfit she was supposed to wear for the party the next day. There was an air of excitement as she wondered how she would feel the next morning. Noah and Eli told her a few days before that, when she woke on the day, everything would be different. Secretly, Kara worried that somehow, when she looked in the mirror, she would not recognise the person staring back. The boys laughed at the distressed look on her face. And while she knew they were teasing her, apprehension sat heavy in the pit of her belly.

Feelings of excitement burst through the house at the

prospect of having all the family over. They didn't come over often, but her mother would regularly mention their names as if to imprint them in her mind. Kara's father told her that his parents died when he was a teenager, so she never had a chance to meet them. When he spoke of them, his face drew lines of sadness. These changes made Kara's belly flutter with a feeling she couldn't recognise.

But Pappi, or 'Pi' as Kara called him, was coming, and so was Nonna. Nonna was a kind lady who would pinch Kara's cheeks and then hug her until she felt like she could no longer breathe. Often Nonna would whisper words in a strange language that Kara didn't understand. Whenever they stopped hugging, Nonna would stare. There would always be a twinkle of sadness in her eyes.

Pi and Nonna were also bringing Kara's Zio Antonio. He rarely came to anything and, when he was there, his presence unsettled everyone, especially Kara's father. Kara was shy around him, but she didn't know why. She would hide behind her mother when they spoke, and Zio would ignore Kara. Her mother would tell everyone they needed to be kind to him because he was all alone. It was strange to think that Zio was alone when he had a family. Kara wondered why his family didn't keep him company.

'Are the boys coming with Uncle Antonio?' Kara asked.

'No, they're not,' her mother said.

'Why not?'

'Because Aunty Hannah has taken them on a long holiday and Zio doesn't know when they are coming back.'

Kara wanted to know why her Aunty Hannah had chosen to go away when it was her birthday, but her mother was quick to change the subject. When Antonio did come, he would sit quietly next to Pi, whispering things in his ear. Antonio's moods were as dark as the hair on his head. His eyes strayed around the room, taking stock of who was coming and going. He always seemed to be thinking before he did anything. Kara was relieved that he hardly ever came over.

Pi and Nonna's visits were also infrequent, and Kara struggled to remember what they looked like. She had vague memories of Pi's gravelly voice because it scared her. Like Aunty Lou, Pi smelled of cigarettes. But his scent was different. His was a deep tobacco smell, like darkness and secrets rolled in one. He spoke in the strange language using his hands, grunting with disappointment when Kara couldn't respond. He settled on addressing Kara's mother and didn't engage with her father at all. His voice carried an air of authority, which made Kara wonder why he was angry all the time.

'He's not angry he's just passionate about telling stories,' her mother said one time.

'Come, principessa' her mother called, bringing her back to the present. 'Let's go and try on your dress before your father sees us.'

The dress twirled around like the material was weightless. The pink silk was soft against her skin, and Kara relished the prettiness of it. Her shoes sparkled, and Kara laughed at the way they reflected light onto the wall. Her mother let her enjoy the moment until it was time to take everything off, securing it safely on a coat hanger ready for the party.

'Sleep well, my little Principessa. Tomorrow is a big day,' she whispered, and kissed her on the cheek.

But sleep came in waves of terror that night - frightening dreams of a man with dark hair and darker eyes. He followed her everywhere she went. When she tried to run, her feet felt as if they were cemented to the ground. When he caught up to her, he was covered in something red. His hands were like tree trunks and they reached, trying to grab her. Kara yelled, but no sound came out of her mouth, the tendrils from the trunk sealing it shut. Fear had her immobilised and, before she knew it, he was falling on top of her.

'*Karina, help,*' he gurgled.

Kara woke up screaming. Her father ran in and began frantically looking around the room as if he was looking for someone.

He then sat on the edge of the bed and hugged her. When she calmed, her father's eyes drifted to hers. She noticed he was holding a baseball bat, which he put on the ground before hushing her and telling her there was nothing to worry about.

'It was all a bad dream,' he said. Kara thought he sounded like he was trying to convince himself.

But the unsettling feeling from the nightmare didn't go away. Nor did it change when the sunlight streamed in, peeking through the curtains as if trying to tickle her with happiness.

Ready for her sixth year of being alive, Kara ran down the stairs with the weight of her new age. Excitement simmered at the prospect of seeing the house decorated. There had been a promise of balloons and streamers for the party.

Running into the kitchen, she found it empty. The lounge room was also the same, and she couldn't see anything at all that said it was her birthday. The house was eerily silent. She called for her parents. When they didn't answer, she walked back up the stairs, thinking that perhaps her surprise was waiting in their room. Pushing the door open, she found her mother sitting in her favourite chair, her face wet and her stare vacant.

'Mumma,' Kara called.

She stirred, smiling like she was seeing Kara for the first time.

'Come here, principessa,' she sobbed.

She rocked back and forth, stroking Kara's hair and telling her how much she loved her. Wanting to cry with her, Kara felt her sadness and wanted to take it away. It was her special day, and her mother was crying. She couldn't understand why, so she sat there in her lap, not saying anything.

Her father came into the room. He told her mother to let go, but she just held Kara tighter. It worried Kara that her mother was crying on her birthday. She wanted to believe they were happy tears because Kara was finally six. But she knew that the sadness that dripped down her mother's face was meant for someone else.

'Isabella,' her father tried again.

When she finally let Kara go, she smiled at her with an apology. Sorrow settled in the creases of her eyes. Her father reached down and took Kara in his arms, holding her tight while they walked out of the room. They left her mother in her green chair. Kara wanted to go back, to sit with her and make her better. But her father kept walking towards the kitchen, carrying Kara as if she weighed nothing.

'It's someone's birthday today,' he said, sitting her down on the island bench.

'It's mine!' Kara shouted, feeling like she needed to overcome the sadness.

'Karina.' It was the voice he used for disappointing news. 'We need to talk about today.'

'Where are my balloons and streamers?' she asked.

'We've had to make the party another day.'

She wondered why the party would be on another day when today was her birthday. Something in his eyes told her there was no other way.

'I'm sorry, Karina,' was all he said.

'But what about all the people that were coming? Pappi and Nonna were going to come today,' she told him. 'So was Zio Antonio.'

Her father shuddered at the mention of Antonio's name as if the devil whispered it in his ear. He went to say something but stopped himself. Kara saw something flicker in his eyes. He didn't say anything else, only that there would be no party. He told her that she could open her gifts, but not to bother her mother for the rest of the day.

In the days that followed, quiet grief settled like dust in the house. Kara's mother came downstairs a few times. When she saw Kara, she would stroke her hair and smile. She never said anything, and her tears continued to fall. She would scurry back to the bedroom and sit in her chair. Kara asked her father if something had happened. He told her that her mother had lost something that could never be replaced. Kara offered to give her mother one of her necklaces in the hope it would make her feel better.

'There are some things in life you just can't replace, Karina,' was all he said.

A few weeks after Kara's birthday, Uncle Nick and Aunty Lou went over with the boys. Uncle Nick greeted her father with a tight hug. He whispered something to Uncle Nick, then the two of them disappeared to where Kara's mother sat unmoving in her chair. It felt like everyone she knew had changed since her birthday.

Even Aunty Lou had an edginess about her. She kept looking over her shoulder, as if she was waiting for someone to come through the door. She smoked cigarette after cigarette outside, pacing in the backyard. She didn't come near Kara or smile at her like she normally would. There were no gifts for Kara's birthday because she had forgotten.

Meanwhile, the boys continued to wreak havoc while no one was watching. They circled like vultures, laughing and poking their fingers in her sides. At one point, Noah asked, 'How does it feel to be STINKS years old now?'

'Ha! Ha!' Eli chimed in. 'Princi-PISSA! Karina stinks.' He laughed with Noah by his side.

Anger bubbled up inside her. She wanted to explode and yell at them, only she knew better.

The boys continued to surround her, taunting her. When they'd had enough, they went in search of food in the kitchen. Kara knew there was no point trying to call Aunty Lou to tell her what they had been doing. She wanted to tell Uncle Nick, but her father didn't want them disturbed. She hoped Uncle Nick could help her mother with her sadness.

It wouldn't be hard to get the boys in trouble. They were always so sweet around her parents, but something told her that Aunty Lou and Uncle Nick knew exactly how much trouble they could be. Kara wanted them gone, but she also knew that would be impossible. So, she thought she would teach the boys a lesson that would make them leave her alone.

Locking herself in the bathroom, Kara took her top off. Grabbing the side of her arm, she pinched it as hard as she could and counted to twenty. When she let go, she noticed a big red welt come to the surface. She grabbed the same spot again and didn't stop until the red welt turned purple. The other arm received similar treatment. When she was satisfied that they looked horrible enough, she put her top back on.

But Kara knew that she needed more. She remembered when she accidentally made her nose bleed by picking it. She carefully put her finger up her nose and began to scrape the inside. At first, nothing happened. Then, her eyes began to water. Digging a little deeper, she picked the sides until a trickle of blood slowly slid down. She took her finger out and pushed it into the other nostril. She scraped so hard, that she sneezed, expelling blood from her nose.

She swung the door open, relieved that no one was there. When she saw that Aunty Lou was still outside, she ran past her, screaming at the top of her lungs. Her father and Uncle Nick came running down the stairs, paling when they saw her face covered in blood.

'What happened?' her father asked.

'The boys,' she heaved between sobs. 'They pinched me and then slapped me across the face.'

'What!' Noah yelled back.

'We did not!' Eli screamed.

Not waiting for them to finish, she pulled up the sleeves of her top. When Uncle Nick saw the bruises on her arms, he grabbed both the boys and pulled them into the other room. For a second, Kara was worried that they would tell the real truth and convince Uncle Nick it wasn't them. While they were gone, she pleaded her case to her father.

'They were calling me princi-PISSA,' she said. 'They didn't want to stop and when I asked them to, they started to pinch me.

They pinched me so hard and told me to be quiet. And when I started to cry, they slapped me.'

Fury crossed her father's face. Grabbing a tissue from the bench, he held it against her nose. Uncle Nick returned with the boys not long after, and he looked at Kara as if he could smell her lies.

'Karina, are you sure the boys did this to you?' he asked.

She nodded her head. She feared opening her mouth in case the real truth came out.

'Because I know that the boys have done some things before, but they've never done anything like this. You know the difference between the truth and a lie, right?'

'The boys pinched me then they slapped me. They've been picking on me since they got here. They always pick on me. They're always pinching me!' she yelled, looking at everyone.

'Nick,' her father cut in. 'I know the boys have picked on Karina before. But this is too far.'

'I just asked them about what happened,' Uncle Nick told him. 'They said they were in the kitchen the whole time and didn't touch her.'

'So you're calling her a liar?' her father challenged.

'No. What I'm saying is that something happened, and Karina is the only person who knows the truth.'

'We didn't do it, Dad,' Noah said. 'She's crazy - she did this to herself.'

'Be careful what you say about Karina, Noah,' her father warned.

'That's enough!' Aunty Lou, who had been silent the whole time, had her bag in her hand. She glared at Uncle Nick, leaving no room for guessing what she wanted him to do.

'Lou, stay. Isabella would love to see you,' her father said, trying to calm the situation.

'It's not worth it, Joshua,' she told him. 'Too much has happened, and nothing will ever be the same.'

'She needs you,' he said, desperation in his voice.

'She needs to decide if this life is what she really wants. And, if she does, what happens to any of you, knowing what happened to Antonio?' she asked both men. 'Who is next? Do we all sit around and wait? I don't want to be looking over my shoulder everywhere I go. This is no way to live.'

'Lou,' Uncle Nick said, lowering his voice.

'What, Nick? Are you worried I'll tell the truth?'

'The children are here. Don't you think this is something we should discuss in private?'

'Why? The children will find out one day. They need to know what they should be afraid of.'

'What do we need to be afraid of?' Noah asked, sounding unsure that he wanted to know that answer.

'Nothing. Your mum is just worried about Aunty Isabella is all,' Uncle Nick said.

'We should all be worried. We should all be looking over our shoulder, wondering if they'll come back to finish what they started with Antonio. He may have got what he deserved, but none of us are to blame for that. And I don't want to sit around and wait to find out.'

'What happened to Zio Antonio?' Kara asked.

'Nothing for you to worry about,' her father said, smiling strangely.

Aunty Lou shook her head in disbelief. 'She has a right to know. One day it might be too late to tell her. Isabella's family is her family. They will always be there, lingering, and we all know how situations like that turn out.'

Kara watched on, wondering what they all meant. She had so many questions. What family were they talking about? Was Zio Antonio hurt? What was the secret Aunty Lou wanted her to know? When no one said anything else, Aunty Lou smiled with a sadness that Kara had never seen before as she placed a hand on her shoulder.

'I'm sorry if the boys hurt you, Karina,' she said. 'No one deserves to be hurt.'

Kara was unsure what she meant by that. Then Aunty Lou grabbed the boys by their arms and left, Uncle Nick following closely behind.

After they left, her father stood at the door for what felt like an eternity. His head hung low. The house felt still in the aftermath, and her father released a heavy sigh. He closed the door, not saying anything else for a while. They walked back into the kitchen, and he replaced the tissue Kara was holding with a fresh one. The bleeding had stopped, but her nose ached from where the lining had been deliberately scraped out. He looked at her bruises and apologised on the boys' behalf.

'Don't let anyone ever lay a finger on you, Karina. Not now, not ever,' he said and then walked away.

After he left, Kara wondered if they would see Uncle Nick and Aunty Lou again. She wondered whether the boys would be punished or whether their parents knew the truth.

When she walked back up the stairs, she stood outside the door to her parent's room. Her father was asking her mother if everything had been cleared up.

'Yes, like nothing ever happened.' Her voice was soft, almost a whisper. 'Dad said everything was taken care of.'

'Business as usual?'

'Always.' She started crying.

Kara knew that if they found her lingering there, she would be in trouble. They didn't like it when she interrupted their quiet time. She went back to her room and played with the dolls she received for her birthday. It was where she often found herself in the months that passed.

Over time, her mother slowly came out of her room and smiled a little more again. But Kara knew that the spark she once carried was dimmed forever. She wanted her mother to call her principessa, but she never did again. She waited for the party her father told her would happen, but it never came. Sadness lingered in places that were once filled with happiness. Uncle Nick and Aunty Lou never came back, nor did Pi, Nonna or Antonio. No one ever spoke of the extra family that Aunty Lou mentioned ever again.

Kara noticed things being whittled away, especially the family and friends who never returned. But, more importantly, no one spoke of the subtlety behind the change in the syllables of her name. She thought it began as a test to measure how well she tolerated the slight variation. Once everyone pretended that the name Kara had always been hers, her reality became frayed, tethering itself away. Soon enough, Karina was lost, and the name Kara danced along.

4

TRUTH

Kara believed truth was a tessellation. It made versions of Kara to fit the shape of what she believed. Different shapes allowed different expressions and versions of the truth. This allowed her to move between her truths and judge herself accordingly.

Kara's truth did not rely solely on the words that she spoke. It was in actions and reactions, in causes and consequences, and, most importantly, in things that were far greater than she could take credit for.

Kara's truth was fragile and stretched when challenged. This stretching would only go so far, before everything unravelled. Deciding to unravel her truth was challenging. Allowing someone else to pick it apart was terrifying.

Kara found herself sitting in a single frontage house with ornate fittings. It looked like any other house in the suburb of Carlton. She took note of the orange shagpile carpet on her way in. There was a musty smell that seeped from the walls, as if lies were trapped within. The house felt eerie and sterile as if it whispered people's pasts.

While Kara sat and waited, she thought about her conversation with Michael.

'What do you think would happen if you don't go?'

'I'm pretty sure there was the threat of police if I don't turn up.'

'Never pictured you as someone who would be afraid to push boundaries.'

'This isn't about pushing boundaries - this about having no choice but to go. You were there. You heard what he said. Besides, this is something I think I really need to do.'

'Why?'

'Because perhaps I need a little help figuring stuff out. Is that so hard for you to understand?'

'What I don't understand is your incessant need to look for something irrelevant.'

'Do you think my life is irrelevant? Thanks!' She had huffed into the phone, annoyed that Michael wasn't supportive.

'I'm sorry.' She knew that he meant it. 'Will it change who you are, Kara? Will looking for the truth change how you live your life?'

'It's not that. I have to go. And it's just that...'

'It's what? You're looking for answers? What is it that you're missing? You have said that the past is irrelevant. Why would you try and lose that advantage?'

'Because suddenly it feels like a disadvantage.' She already knew what she was missing, but she didn't dare tell him. Her feelings towards her family were not something she wanted to share with anyone just yet, not even Michael.

'Expiscate,' he said.

'Do I even want to know? I hate that you throw me with words. Put it in a sentence.'

'Kara was about to be skilful in her investigation, which will be persistent.'

She laughed, hoping that he could hear her amusement. Michael always tried to derail her with words that made her think.

'One of these days, I'll find something you've never heard of, and then you'll ask me to use it in a sentence.'

'What can I say? I am a self-professed logophile, but I look forward to that day,' he said, laughing back.

'How much do you remember of your childhood?' she asked, not giving up on her questions.

'Only as much as I need to.'

'Why do you have to be so cagey with everything you tell me?'

'I'd rather you used the word "disclose",' he said. 'Because when we "disclose", we only share some of our secrets.'

If disclosure was connected directly to secrets, then Michael's truth was an encrypted relic of his past. Michael always insisted that he never told anyone any more than was necessary because he wanted to remain a private man. She considered herself lucky and grateful for the moments when he would share some of his life with her. It wasn't much, and she had to try and fill in the gaps with her own version of who he was, but it was something.

She recalled a night when they shared a bottle of wine, and she knew that his guard would be ever so slightly down. It was an opportunity to ask him questions knowing full well he would only answer because he wanted to and not because she was asking.

'So, I know you don't have any other brothers and sisters.'

'Correct. It's just me.'

'What about your parents?'

'Only my father.'

'Are they divorced?'

'No. My mother died when I was born.'

'I'm sorry.'

'Why? It wasn't your fault. Why do we always feel the need to apologise for something that we had no part in?'

'I think it's something we do.'

'Why? Does it validate your feelings? Make you feel better when you find answers to questions you have no right to ask?'

'Why can't I ask them? We're friends, aren't we?'

'Are we?'

She ignored him.

'Where did you grow up?' she asked.

'South Australia.'
'What made you move here?'
'Why so many questions?'
'Because I want to know more about my friend.'
'Looking for more validation?'
'Why move to Melbourne and not Sydney?'
'Because it's where I'm supposed to be.'
'That simple?'
'It's never that simple.'
'Do you have any other relatives here?'
'Yes.'
'Do you see them?'
'Yes.'
'What do you do during the day for work?'
'I work for my father's business.'
'Doing what?'
'Things.'
'Such as?'
'Running his business. Marketing, promotions, those sorts of things.'
'What do you promote?'
'Wine.'
'Your dad makes wine?'
'Why do you sound so surprised? We all have history. Some of us share what we need to. Even then it's more than we should.'
'What's the name of the wine company? I can't believe you've never told me before.'
'What would it change?'
'Nothing, I suppose. Just nice to know a little more about you.'
'And now you know.'
'What's the label called.'
'Augusti Wines.'
'Can't say I've heard of it.'
'It's a family name.'
'So you're here to promote your wine.'

'Among other things.'

'Among other things you won't tell me?'

'Yes, because I'm ending this conversation.'

'I'm pissed you didn't bring wine, and you make me pay for it.'

'I know you can afford it.'

And that was how he had abruptly ended their conversation.

'And if people knew more about you,' she asked him, 'what would they know?'

He remained silent. In moments like this, Kara wished he wasn't on the phone but sitting across from her. She wondered about Michael's past, but people were entitled to their privacy, even if she found that irritating.

'Why do you want to know about your past?'

'Why don't you ever answer any questions?' Kara challenged him. When he didn't respond, she added, 'And I want to know because I can't remember.'

'I still don't understand what you want to know.'

'There are some things that I think I remember, then I wonder if I've made them up. They're foggy ... I don't know if they're true or not,' she said.

'Memories are overrated.' He laughed. 'We all know that.'

'I don't know. I feel like part of me is missing and I don't know how to find it.'

'I worry about what will happen once you do find it. Are you prepared? What happens if you find something you don't like? Once something has been heard, it can't be unheard. Maybe, deep down, you already know that it's facinorous, and you're not equipped to handle it.'

'Far-what?' she was all but yelling at him. 'I swear you say stuff to make me feel dumb. Just talk to me like a normal person.'

'It means extremely wicked. Imagine that, Kara. You, the queen of wicked finding something even more wicked. That would be amazing.'

'I just need to know ... or...' She stopped herself.

'Or what? Does the sudden need to know have anything to do with the mystery in the bar?'

Val invaded her thoughts like he had done ever since she met him. She hadn't been back to the bar because she wasn't ready to face the reality of what she wanted. She couldn't help but wonder if sitting in the waiting room was a bad idea as well. Perhaps she should get up and leave with her secrets intact, like Michael suggested.

'Verisimilitude,' Michael said. 'We all have similar truths.'

'I have no idea what you're talking about.' Kara told him again. 'You annoy me more than anyone else I know.'

'I am anyone else, Kara.' He paused so his words sunk in. 'Look up the word. Let me know if you find what you're looking for.' With that, he hung up.

Kara wondered why she couldn't remember anything before the age of eight. Her knee skipped up and down restlessly while she waited.

Someone called her name. She stood and walked over to where he waited.

'I'm Ray.' He smiled at her almost apologetically. The window of opportunity to run closed. Even if she wanted to, the thought of fronting the police department made her sit tight. Obediently, she followed him into the safety and sanctuary of his office.

The sparseness of the room was immediate. There were very few personal items on display. It was vacant and sterile.

Two leather chairs faced each other. They were far apart - perhaps that was deliberate. A heavy wooden coffee table sat in the middle, with a box of tissues on one side. Ray had already defined where everyone was supposed to sit. Feeling as though she should challenge him already, Kara deliberately nudged the box to his side while his back was still turned. He fussed with something on his desk, then walked back with a folder.

Kara's folder.

He stared at it as if it already contained her most intimate thoughts. He didn't say anything for a while, and the silence made her even more uncomfortable.

He held her gaze, his face unreadable. It unsettled her because she wanted to believe she was very good at picking up traits in people who gave few hints. She thought about Val and the instant connection she felt they shared, the way his eyes bored into hers. But she couldn't deduce anything from Ray. He was giving nothing away, which made Kara fear nothing would get past him either.

Wondering if she should take charge and ask questions, she thought of asking something inane like why there was nothing personal in the room. But she also knew it was likely to maintain the impression of neutrality. It was a clever tactic. But she still didn't like it.

The silence between them stretched like gum. The ticking of the clock on the wall was a steady rhythm. Kara moved in her chair, unsure of what to do. If he wasn't going to say anything then neither would she. She reflected on how strange moments like these were, where everything felt amplified. She was sure he could hear her heartbeat, her breathing. But what she found most unsettling was that she felt as though he could read her thoughts. And while she tried to shut them down, they were broadcast through everything she was doing. She had come voluntarily, so it made sense that she should explain why she was there. But she didn't. Kara wanted to be defiant because she hadn't really come here of her own free will. But, at the same time, she could no longer ignore the larger issue at hand, namely her behaviour.

'Kara, I want you to know, no matter what you tell me, this is a safe space,' he said.

He spoke to her as if she was an old friend, but Kara wasn't sure she wanted to let him in. This man had done nothing so far to justify her trust. Her anxiety had her feeling reckless, so she leaned over the coffee table and took a tissue from the box she nudged earlier. He watched her intently as she folded the tissue over and over, never saying a word.

Michael popped into her head. She could almost imagine him sitting there, telling Kara to hold steady and to let Ray do all the work. What Ray didn't know was that Kara had been sitting in her silence for a very long time and wore it like a comfortable hug. Her silence protected her from people who wanted to destroy her reality.

The tissue continued to bear the brunt of her anxiety. Ray watched, as if she was a child throwing a tantrum. When she had nothing left of the tissue to destroy, he smiled, almost asking if there was anything else she would like to do before they started.

'Would you like to tell me why you came here, Kara?'

He was measured and composed like he had years of practice asking the same questions. He didn't ask anything else, just waited for an answer, steady and unfazed. He didn't seem to care that time passed and nothing had been said.

Feeling smug, Kara wondered if she could push this further. She decided to play a little game: for every question he asked, she would rip up another tissue. Leaning over, she pulled another one out of the box. He watched her intently, giving her space as the strips fell onto her lap, one mess sitting with another.

'I can see in your report that you have been ordered to come here. It sounded like an unfortunate incident. Do you want to tell me what happened before that?'

His eyes didn't leave Kara's as she leaned over and took another tissue. The strips fell into a pile on her lap. She must have appeared either deluded or compulsive at this point, and Ray might have thought she was a complete psychopath who had a tissue fetish. If she asked him anything, the little game was over, so instead she sat and continued to stare at him.

As if he sensed she was playing games, he politely pushed the box closer, smiling at her as if she didn't appear half-deranged.

'Take as many as you need.'

Kara didn't take a tissue because Ray hadn't asked her a question. If he was growing impatient with her, he didn't show it. The lines around his eyes did not crinkle. He didn't fidget or take any other notes. He waited for her to answer, or at least say something.

His eyes didn't leave her face until she broke contact, shifting in her chair. Kara looked around the room trying to find something that would give her insight into this man. Without it, there was no way that they could build a relationship. Trusting someone didn't come easy, even if Kara was the one who sought Ray out.

Val appeared vividly again in her mind. He had done nothing to warrant her trust but, after only a simple encounter, she was sitting in a stranger's room, trying to simplify her complex issues. Looking around the room, she stalled with every tactic she knew.

On the wall to her left were framed degrees. A bookcase near the window cast an ominous shadow. She took note of some of the titles: *The Five Archetypes, Dark Psychology and Understanding Other People.* In among the mix, she noticed a copy of *Black Books* and smiled. He must have a sense of humour - maybe this would be the missing key to their relationship.

She wanted to know how old he was. He didn't wear a wedding ring, but that could be deliberate. There were no pictures of family or friends. His desk had a large figurine of an owl that was looking directly at Kara. It was unnerving, and she felt the need to turn it around. To the right was a black-and-white line drawing of a young woman. When she looked again, she realised it was one of those old pictures with a hidden old woman in it too. She wasn't sure which woman she was supposed to see first. He noticed her looking at it, but he didn't question her curiosity. It was as if Ray knew she was looking for clues about him.

'Have you been to see anyone before me? Spoken to someone professionally about what happened?'

Rip went another tissue, floating into her lap.

'Kara, I can't make you talk to me, nor can I force you to tell me things you're not ready to share. I'm willing to sit here and wait if that's what you need. But I want you to try and trust me.

Am I correct in assuming that trust might be stopping you from talking?'

She leaned in and took another tissue, sat back in her chair and proceeded to tear it up as well. He didn't stop her or ask why she did it. After letting her have her moment, he continued as if nothing happened.

'I've noticed you looking around my office. Is there anything in particular you're looking for? Is there anything you would like to know more about?'

Kara took the tissues with flair, making sure he noticed. She put them on top of each other and ripped them down the middle. There was smugness in her actions. It was childish and she knew she should feel some shame, but she didn't. She didn't care what he thought of her, because at any point she could get up and leave, even though she hadn't.

He waited, not asking her anything else. Then, he looked at the watch on his wrist and scribbled something on the piece of paper in her folder. When he stopped writing, he closed the folder, put it on the coffee table and rested the pen on top.

'Trust is important,' he started. 'I'd imagine it took a long time for you to decide to reach out to someone.' He looked at her, then at the tissue box. She felt a little deflated that he wouldn't play her game.

'I'd like to help you establish that trust. I want to make you feel comfortable here. This, as I said before, is a safe space. Your safe space. But, I can't help you unless you want me to.'

His words sat in the air. Ray waited for her to say something. When she didn't, he leaned forward, took his own tissue and sat back in his chair. He didn't rip it to shreds the way Kara had but let it rest on top of his knee, complete and not ruined.

The hour ticked away. When her time was up, he took his tissue, stood up and headed over to his desk. He placed the tissue inside the folder, put the whole thing under the sacred storage of the owl, then walked to the door and rested his hand on the handle.

'Thanks for coming in today, Kara. I think we've made progress.' Ray opened the door and stood there, letting her know that her hour had come to an end. Kara reached over, grabbed her bag then walked out. She was at the door standing next to him when he smiled and said, 'Don't you?'

He looked over at the tissue box. She realised that he had asked her a question, and wondered in that moment if all the people who came into her life conspired to challenge her. Michael, Val and now Ray seemed to figure out who she was pretty quickly. That seemed both funny and daunting at the same time. Perhaps she wasn't as adept at shifting her truth as she thought. As she left, Kara knew Ray had found a little of her real truth. She had to come back so he could help her find the rest of it.

5

WAITING

Kara waited for attention like it was a game. When she found herself in that place, rules did not apply and the consequences for her actions seemed irrelevant. It was here that Kara understood that people could get hurt.

Time made waiting muddy. Her mother's silence left one single, long memory. She dimmed by the day. Kara wasn't sure who she waited for; maybe it was Pi and Nonna? Maybe it was her Zio Antonio. At times, she wondered if it was Uncle Nick and Aunty Lou that she expected, or the sound of the boys' laughter. Kara wouldn't have complained if they returned to bother her. Secretly she missed them all. While the boys always tormented her, she couldn't deny that they filled the house with a certain mood: fulfilling, joyous and largely contagious. But they never showed again.

Every attempt Kara made to try and get her mother out of herself was met with an excuse. She overheard her father on the phone one day saying her mother had sunk into a deep depression. She wasn't sure who he was talking to, only that he was concerned. He said she wasn't leaving her room and that she wasn't eating. She recalled him saying perhaps she needed to be medicated.

Kara didn't understand what 'depression' meant, and she didn't want to bother her father with her questions. She wondered if the depression was linked to what Aunty Lou said ... maybe depression meant her mother was now looking over her shoulder all the time. If this was the case, Kara knew she had to help. She wanted to try and help her mother so she could stop looking over her shoulder.

'Let's go to the park,' Kara tried.

'Not today,' her mother replied.

'Do you want to watch a movie with me?'

'I have a headache today. Maybe another time,' she would tell her.

'Can we go get ice-cream?'

'It's not the weather for it.' She would sigh and look through the curtains staring into the street.

Kara's dad noticed her attempts. He called her into the lounge room one day and asked her to sit down.

'You've been very nice to your mumma lately.'

'She's sad all the time. I want to cheer her up.'

'I know you do,' he told her, tenderness in his voice. 'But your mumma needs some time.'

'Is that because of the depression?' She wanted him to know she could help.

'How do you know such a big word?'

'I overheard you on the phone. Did something happen to make Mumma sick? You said she needs medicine.'

'Yes. Something did happen,' he said, collecting his thoughts. 'Do you remember your Zio Antonio?'

'Yes. He was the scary one.'

He laughed a little, but it didn't reach his eyes. 'I suppose he was a little scary. You see, your mumma is sad because something happened to your Zio Antonio.'

'Did he get hurt?'

'Antonio got into a little bit of trouble.'

'Did the police take him?'

'No, the police didn't take him.'

'Then what did he do?'

'Well, I don't know the whole story, but unfortunately your Zio Antonio is no longer with us.'

'Where did he go? Is he with Aunty Hannah?'

'No. He's not with her either.'

Kara could tell her father was struggling with how to tell her what he wanted to say. He took a deep breath and said, 'Unfortunately your Zio Antonio died.'

Kara knew death was final and it made people incredibly sad. That would explain why her mother was so sad.

'So Mumma misses Zio Antonio because he's dead and not coming back?'

'Yes, something like that.'

'How did he die?'

She noticed her father shifted in his seat.

'He died in his sleep.'

She wanted to feel something about the news her father had given her. She felt sad for her Aunty Hannah, and for Angelo and Carlo. She wondered if this news made them sad with depression as well. She wasn't sure if she should be feeling sad like her mother or whether she was supposed to cry, but Kara didn't really feel anything at all.

So, with news of her Zio Antonio's death, Kara waited through her hours, growing despondent and restless. She began destroying things she knew had little or no value. Toys lay scattered with missing limbs, dolls had jagged-cut hair, and trucks that once belonged to Noah and Eli lay tyre-less on the floor. Lego was strategically strewn all over the carpet in the hope that her father would step on it. Some nights he would scream in agony, cursing the toys that weren't picked up, yelling he was sure they grew horns in the middle of the night. Somewhere in the back of Kara's mind, she knew she should feel bad, but it never lingered long enough to worry her.

Around the time Kara turned eight years old, she began to feel like the little attention she got was allotted. The days of spontaneity were gone, and it felt like all the parties along with the music that once created happy memories had stopped. Trips away were a thing of a very distant past – she missed the smell of burnt petrol from the rusty old car.

Thinking about those moments made her incredibly sad. And she felt like she couldn't tell anyone, especially her parents, which made her wonder if they even cared anymore. But more than anything, she wanted to believe that, no matter how long she waited, and regardless of what happened, they loved her. Love wasn't perfect, but she was beginning to understand that it hummed quietly within people's hearts. She knew her mother would protect her like a lioness protecting her cub, and she knew her father would throw himself in front of a bus if he needed to. That type of love was ingrained within the soul. That type of love was forever.

But Kara also noticed her mother finding the effort to smile at her, or even touch her, often walking away with tears in her eyes. Kara wanted to believe those tears were her love pouring out, but she knew better. It was something more. Zio Antonio's death shifted something within her mother, and it was dominating everything she did.

It also made Kara feel restless in the house, especially when her mother and father would whisper to make sure Kara couldn't catch what they were saying. Her father would follow her mother around firing questions, '*Have you spoken to them? Are they still in Adelaide? Did they say where they were going? Why is he flying there? Do you know when they will be back? Did your mother tell you anything more? Is she coming here? Is your father going to speak to them? Has Hannah been in contact? Does she need to leave?*'

Her mother never answered, only shaking her head. He would walk away looking defeated by her refusal to answer the questions. Kara wasn't sure if her mother was saying no, or if the head shaking meant something else.

Sometimes, he would see Kara standing there, knowing she had seen their interaction, and he would smile apologetically.

'What are you doing?' he would ask her, like she hadn't been caught standing there.

'Is Mumma coming out of her room today?' she would ask.

'Maybe a little later. I think we should keep quiet today so we don't wake your mother.'

'Fine.' That was the only thing she could say before walking off knowing that everything was not alright. When her father was despondent like that, he didn't reach out to touch or comfort her. He would just say something banal like 'The rain has stopped' or 'Are you playing with your dolls today?' and then he would change the topic.

Months passed since Kara found out about Zio Antonio's death, and all she wanted was to have her life back to normal. Her mother began to surface a little more from her bedroom. She would join them for breakfast and dinner and make polite conversation, before retreating to her room. Her father would try and engage her mother's interest, 'Did you know that Kara got second place in her athletics race today?' he would say.

'Well done,' she would reply automatically, then, after a moment, add something strange like, 'Make sure you stay away from the fence line.'

She never asked why she wasn't allowed near the fence line, because all she could think about was how she wished her mother would say more. When her father would continue to talk about the things Kara had done at school, Kara saw it as an opening to tell her about the friends she made, about the projects they were doing, about the teacher who made her laugh. Her mother would smile and ask simple questions, making everything feel normal again, but Kara knew her mother was already thinking about other things even while she was sitting there.

And that was how they slipped back into a quiet rhythm. Conversation slowly bloomed and Kara waited, believing that everything was going to return to the way it once was.

Then, one day, she overheard her mother and father talking.

'For her own safety, we should take her out of school,' her mother said.

'Why? Have you heard more?'

'No.'

'Then why?'

'You know why?'

'Actually I don't!' he yelled. 'You don't give me much anymore.'

'The less you know, the better.'

'So you're making decisions for me now?'

'No, I'm making sure you and Kara are safe.'

'So you do know more?' he pressed.

'I only know that we should look at home schooling.'

'Lock her in the room?' he asked.

'No one needs to be locked up.'

'Then how would you describe it? What do we do with an eight-year-old who needs to be out with her friends? Will they be allowed come over and see her? Or do we isolate her even more?'

'It's for her own safety,' she said.

'If her safety is an issue, then you need to tell me why.' Kara could imagine him running his hand through his hair like he did when he got frustrated.

'You should see it from my point of view.' She was all but whispering, as if she knew Kara could hear.

'How can I do that when you only tell me what you think I need to know?'

'That's why I'm telling you now.'

'I don't know what you're trying to tell me, to be honest. I get the feeling you've heard more and you don't want to tell me. If that's the case, it's very unfair. You have always been honest with me about everything, up until now. Don't shut me out because you feel the need to protect me.'

'I'm not shutting you out. I'm keeping you in.'

'Kara belongs in school. She belongs with people her own age. Perhaps then she'll ...'

'She'll what?'

'I'm worried about her. I've noticed some things lately, especially in her room.'

'What sort of things?'

'Have you seen her dolls? They all look disfigured.'

'She is an eight-year-old girl. That's what children do,' she deflected.

'I think there's more to it. It feels deliberate. I can't explain it,' he said.

'I think you should think about what I've said.'

When he left the room, Kara's father looked unconvinced.

After that conversation, Kara kept to herself. She didn't want to stay home because she liked school. She didn't want to get in trouble, so she stayed away from the fence line. And she made sure to pay extra attention in class so she could bring home grades that her parents would be proud of. She did, however, notice her father seemed to walk around with a sense of unease, almost as if his sense of waiting became more profound.

But Kara also found that waiting quietly still wasn't enough - she wanted more from her parents. She wanted to feel like they had during hot summer days, where they laughed with reckless abandon, when death was not their sole focus and Kara was the centre of their universe, the child who they truly loved and would do anything for.

Waiting for them to give her some of their time kept her occupied. She wanted to see how far the depths of their love could be pushed, whether their fear of loss could initiate something other than the sadness that enveloped both of them. She wondered if she could see how much they loved her by their reaction. Would her mother be scared or would she be dismissive, ignoring her and continuing to whisper her secrets to her father? And what of her father? Would he be fearful of losing her, or would he continue with the same sad smile?

Sometimes Kara wished she had known her father's parents. Had they been similar to Pi and Nonna? Sometimes she thought her mother and Pi were very similar. When her mother hugged her and called her principessa, she thought she was more like Nonna. But Kara was her child, her only child, and curiosity had her pushing those limits. It was her mother's reaction she wanted to see the most.

Kara's house was not very big, but it was functional. Kara's father once said that they only needed enough space to hold them. He argued they only needed enough bedrooms for the people that lived in the house, and that if anyone wanted to stay, he would direct them to the nearest hotel.

The house had its intricacies. The slightest pressure of a step made the floorboards creak. They bowed and buckled over the years, and often alerted Kara's mother to her presence.

One morning, Kara decided that she needed to do something because she hadn't heard laughter in the house for a very long time. She wanted to make them both laugh and panic, so they would have something to talk about again. '*Kara, that really wasn't funny this morning,*' they would say, then they would laugh at the absurdity of it in hindsight. She hoped it would give them a chance to speak about it, to spend time with her while they waited for Kara to retell the story. '*What detective movie did you copy that from?*' her father would ask, and she would tell him about how the bodies lay unmoving when they were discovered.

Her intention set, Kara was in the kitchen making herself a snack when she decided that she would lie down on the floor and pretend she was dead, just like in the movies. She lay there waiting, knowing her mother would eventually come because of the smell of burning cheese.

Soon enough, she heard the washing basket drop to the ground. Kara knew her mother would quickly approach her, she could feel her panic before she opened her mouth. She lay there, her eyes closed, motionless like a ragdoll as her mother picked her up, shaking her and shouting.

'*Kara*,' she yelled. Principessa!'

It was the first time in a long time she had called her anything other than Kara. She missed that. But, most of all, she missed her voice and the way it held so much love for her. She yelled for Kara's father, who came quickly when the smoke alarm started to blare. It would have been a sight to behold, smoke billowing from the sandwich maker while Kara lay on the floor, the toast charred beyond redemption. She thought about how funny it would be when her father would recall scraping the burnt cheese from the sandwich maker later.

She let her mother linger in the moment. The people in the movies were often very still, and she was careful not to give herself away. Her father's breath was on her face while he checked for a pulse.

'Did she pass out?' he asked.

'I found her here!' Her mother yelled loud enough so the outside world could hear.

'*Kara!*' They were both yelling as if she lay somewhere in the distance and not in her mother's arms. Kara inwardly smiled thinking of how successful she had been. Something as simple as lying on the floor with her eyes closed could cause such chaos; the movies had been right.

'Do we call the ambulance?' her father asked.

'Call someone. Anyone!' her mother yelled back at him, as if he should have already been out looking for help.

Kara could hear him rushing for the phone, dialling numbers she had learnt were for emergencies only. She wondered whether now was a good time to open her eyes and let them know she was unharmed.

'Kara, open your eyes,' her mother yelled, as if she sensed what she was thinking.

Her father's panicked voice said, 'They want to know if she's breathing.'

He relayed the messages from the call centre. Kara wanted to lay there a little longer before the charade was over.

'They said to check her pulse then roll her on her side,' he said before he moved back to where her mother was.

It was weird to hear how panicked her parents sounded, yet a small part of her felt thrilled to know they could be pushed this far. The fear her parents were experiencing was catastrophic. She wondered whether this was how scared her mother was when she found out about her Zio Antonio. But, if so, then she didn't want her mother to fall into the same deep depression as before.

It was then that she knew she was done with her charade. Kara knew she had instilled fear in her parents, and, for a brief moment, she wasn't a small, insignificant child.

She stripped away all their facades of strength. It was an indescribable power to have. Her father sat there, holding her hands and repeating, 'Hold on, Kara,' as if he couldn't do anything to help her. It was the most contact she'd had with him for a while, and she savoured the way his hands felt in hers.

When at last she opened her eyes to look at her mother, her face was contorted in pain. Kara was momentarily crippled by panic. Her mother was wild, looking around the kitchen, clutching onto Kara while desperately waiting for help. Her father was pale; terror replaced all the colour on his face. Lights were flashing in the background like a party over his shoulders, and Kara knew that the ambulance was near.

Her mother's neck was red and splotchy all over and big streams of tears were falling down her cheeks. She called Kara's name again, to make sure she was alive.

'*Kara!*' she yelled, as a guttural sound came from her mouth.

'She's awake,' she heard her father say before he stood up.

No doubt he would be running to the door to let the paramedics in or tell them that Kara had woken up. Kara figured now would be a good time to end her little charade, so she stood up and looked at her mother as if nothing happened. She saw a frazzled woman staring back in shock, as if the child standing before her was not her own. Her face changed to one of disbelief.

'*Kara!*' she screamed at her again. '*I thought you were dead.*'

She was breathless, and her voice shrank with the prospect of death. Death terrified people. Her mother's crying slowly stopped, then only disbelief remained between them.

'She's fine.' She could hear her father apologising to someone at the front door. 'I'm sorry that you had to come out.'

Before she knew it, she was lying on the sofa and the paramedics continued to prod her

'Can you tell us what happened?' they asked her, shining a light in her eyes.

'I don't know,' she lied. She didn't want to tell them the truth. She only wanted to laugh with her parents later.

'Did your tummy feel funny at all?'

'No.'

'Did you bump your head?'

'No,' she repeated.

When they were satisfied there was no cause for alarm and that Kara didn't need to go to the hospital, they suggested that she spend the day resting on the couch. They packed up their bags to leave but not before they spoke to her father again.

'Yes, we'll call the doctor if we think she needs to go,' he told the paramedics. He closed the door with an exhaled goodbye.

The bedlam Kara created was over for now. She knew she should have felt something other than satisfaction. And maybe, after the ambulance officers left, she should have told her father that it was all a joke, that she thought it would be funny to see the ambulance coming into the street with their flashing lights. Maybe she should have said sorry to her mother for putting that fear in her eyes. Maybe she should have sat with her mother and told her not to cry, that it was an accident, and she didn't mean it. But she didn't, because they never had the laughing moment like she thought they would. They never asked what movie she pretended to recreate. They never told her how funny they thought it was. They all sat there in the silence that she was very accustomed to, thinking that no one was ever going to speak again. They had found sadness rather than laughter.

She stared at both of them as if she was looking at them for the first time. The shock of what happened was still evident on their faces. Her mother's anguish was turning to anger, and Kara relished that small victory because she had shown an emotion other than sadness. Her father stood there motionless as the chaos settled around him.

She knew that if she waited, something might happen. Her mother was waiting for her sadness to disappear. Her father was waiting for her mother to resurface and be who she once was. And Kara wanted to wait so she could show them she was more than they thought she was.

6

DISRUPTION

Change is like a storm that whispers seductively. Knowing this allowed Kara to understand how to navigate life and the disruptions that came her way. When Kara felt unsettled, it permeated every part of her life but also allowed her to believe that transformation was possible.

She questioned how and when things happened, whether there was any rhyme or reason for the encounters that came her way. Perhaps the people Kara met were there to persuade her off the comfortable path that safely cocooned her from the turbulence within her life. Her notion of change and the acceptability of that change were significant for things she accepted. She began to understand disruption as a kind of new adaptability. Her resistance to change shifted with her enthusiasm for it. It was as if there had been a clearance in her inner storm the unpleasant fog lifted, and the appearance of a new relevance became clear.

It had been a long, tedious month since Kara's encounter with Val, and she couldn't stop thinking about him. He was the new disruption that she suddenly wanted to entertain. Val's presence left little room for argument, and she was reluctant to admit how much that appealed to her. An admission like that was an acknowledgement that she had relinquished control of her emotions.

A fantasy of seducing Val ran constantly in her thoughts. She thought about what would happen to her after she got what she wanted with him, whether she would be able to walk away. She wondered whether she could keep him secured in her memories, detached and distant, in the aftermath. She didn't know why, but she knew it wouldn't be easy to walk away from a man like Val. She wanted to believe he was the type of man who believed in love. That single encounter made her crave him with magnitude that shook her core. He oozed sensuality. Worse than that, he gave her hope that she could do better.

She didn't want to acknowledge the fluttering butterfly feelings that hope gave her, but she eventually accepted them both when she walked into the familiar bar on Thursday night. Frankie's smile reminded Kara how much she missed the place. Her martini appeared instantly.

'Scared to come in on a Saturday?' they asked.

'No,' Kara replied, flustered. 'Maybe.' She smiled then took a sip of her martini. 'Maybe I just wanted gossip.' She didn't sound convincing, not even to herself.

'Maybe you should come in this Saturday. He'll be here. And he doesn't leave until we close ... he orders his wine and stays for hours. It's cute,' Frankie said, winking at Kara.

Sensing Kara was interested, Frankie started to give her all the details of Val's visits.

Frankie tried to reassure him. 'She hasn't come in tonight,' Frankie would tell him. 'Maybe she'll be in a little later. Sometimes she comes in before we close.'

'I'll just sit and wait over there.'

'Of course. Wine?'

'Please,' he told them. 'And if she comes in, make whatever she likes to drink.' And, according to Frankie, he would sit and wait till they were almost closed, pay his bill then leave.

Michael, however, had his own opinion of Val. Having never

met him, he told Kara that men like Val were always up to no good. Perhaps his stumbling into the bar that first night was no accident, and his intentions were not as honourable as she wanted to believe.

'He is no lummox,' he told her.

'Sentence?'

'Val was not a clumsy nor stupid man,' he said.

'How would you know? You haven't met him,' she challenged.

'Because Kara, dear friend, he's seen you. I too have seen how men look at you. This Val that you speak of has intentions, and believe me, they are less than honourable. I'm worried we don't really know anything about him. He's been showing up every weekend according to Frankie. Stalker properties, if you ask me.'

'You think everyone is less than honourable.' She laughed. 'And I doubt he's a stalker. Frankie thinks it cute and, to be honest, so do I. There's something about him, something I can't put my finger on. Maybe it's because he left me sitting there that first night.'

'Val didn't leave. He found someone worthy of returning for. Just like you will keep going back to that little bar and return for him.'

She quickly hung up on her friend after hearing his version of the truth.

After a month of denying herself a potential encounter with Val, Kara walked up the rickety stairs of New Gold Mountain and found him sitting in the booth exactly where Frankie said he would be: a glass of wine nestled between his hands, and his eyes focused firmly on the entrance. His smile was electric when he saw her, especially when she sat down in the booth next to him.

There was no awkwardness in their exchange, even though Kara tried to be selective with how much she shared. Curiosity gently brushed between them through the night. Val shared warm words and Kara held on to surreptitiously.

She was mesmerised by his intellect and charm. She made a

mental note of all the things he said, filing everything away to dissect later. There was no judgement in his brown eyes. She felt like she could completely forget who she was and be the person he wanted her to be. She wanted to believe that their meeting was serendipitous, but she also knew enough to know he would walk away. That felt like reason enough to never let him completely in.

And so, in that cosy little booth, between their varying worlds, hers like hard water, his soft like a snowflake, she found their connection comforting and terrifying. Val realised this, giving her the space she needed, listening with attention, never asking for anything more than she was willing to give.

As the dwindling embers of evening faded in time, Frankie began to clear tables around them and Kara reluctantly handed over her number. For a fleeting second, she wanted to write down the wrong one. It was the perfect opportunity to have no further contact. Instead, she handed it over willingly, knowing his intent was always clear. And after that night, she sat and waited like a pariah by the phone.

He messaged the next day, asking if he could see her again. She read the message over and over, thinking about how to respond. She wanted to see him again. She already fantasised about him, even craved him. But she walked away from her phone without responding.

She was terrified of what her feelings could mean for her, terrified that she had never felt like this with anyone. Throughout the years, Kara believed it would be unfair if she found happiness, when her mother spent her whole life grieving the man she once loved. She leaned on guilt as a tactic so she would never allow anyone to get close. But Val made her want to push aside the guilt and say yes, so that was exactly what Kara did. It was also how she found herself sitting again in what Val called 'their little booth' at New Gold Mountain.

Michael kept telling her that, whatever this was, was destined to fail. When she laughed, he defended himself, telling her his view wasn't pessimistic so much as realistic. He told her to protect her heart at all costs, because all relationships were disruptions.

Sitting and clutching her bag, Kara stared at her martini. Now and then, Frankie would give her a knowing smile, easing her anxiety. It didn't take long before Val showed up. His presence dominated like it did every other time. He walked towards Kara with a comforting smile, and part of her evaporated on the inside. This man would be perfect for anyone who would allow him in, she just didn't know if she was that person.

Val leaned in, kissing Kara on the cheek.

'You look beautiful,' he whispered in her ear.

Kara smiled. 'Thanks.'

'I'm so glad you came tonight,' he said. 'I didn't think you would show up.'

'Why is that? We've been here before.'

'Showing up and being present are two different things.'

'Maybe I wanted to see if you were bored yet.'

'I showed up again because there's something about you. I wanted to trust that you'd come back on your own, that you felt that same connection I did. Maybe I'm wrong.'

His statement lingered between them. He smiled with a knowing recognition, and it was enough to make her want to get up and leave. Except she didn't. She sat with a steely excitement and a fluttering possibility.

'You're right. I don't trust people.' It wasn't a lie.

'I get that. If you ask me, people trust too easily.'

'And you trust me?'

'Can I get you another drink?' he said, deflecting.

Kara noticed her glass was empty, so she raised it in the air to let Frankie know she needed another. Frankie looked over to Val.

'Frankie wants to know if you want a drink.'

'I'll have whatever your friend is making you,' he told her. Kara held two fingers up, and Frankie nodded.

'You do come here often, don't you?'

'If I didn't know any better, I'd think that was a cheesy pickup line,' she said, laughing.

'I don't do cheesy lines. I tell the truth.'

They sat and stared at each other as the word 'truth' rolled off his tongue. Kara had always thought of truth as something maligned. You could buy gratitude with counterfeit honesty, and honesty could be deceptive. But his version of 'truth' appeared more like a challenge to prove him wrong, although she knew she had no obligation to prove anything.

As she contemplated her truth, she saw images of her mother sitting in silence. She felt there was no difference between them: both overthinking everything with toxic rumination. Val appeared confused by her discomfort, but he didn't push her to elaborate. He sat, hoping for some kind of response, while Kara was caught in the crossfire in her mind. It was shouting, 'Run, he knows who you are, he knows about your past,' and, at the same time whispering, 'Screw it, and screw him.'

Making her excuses, Kara headed to the bathroom. When she locked the cubicle, she noticed how badly her hands were shaking. There was something unnerving about Val's presence. Unlike the other night, tonight he had come to challenge her, as if he knew more about her than he wanted to let on. But there was no way for him to know about her.

She was private. No social media. No Facebook. No Instagram. No TikTok. She had no current employer, and there were no photos online.

Michael however would be sure to tell her if he knew anything about Val. He also never shared any photos of himself or posted anything on social media. But he used them, telling her it was the only way to stay up to date with what was happening in the world. He would say he, 'needed to know who was out there.' If Michael knew anything about Val, he would be sure to use fancy words like, 'corrigible' or 'recalcitrant' to describe him.

Kara took a few deep breaths to settle her mind before she returned. She felt destabilised by his presence. But what if he was genuine? Could Val want to be with her because he saw something worthwhile in her? But he didn't know her, not really. Kara spent her whole life nurturing her malintent. She kept those sentiments with her as she sat back down and picked up her cocktail. Val smiled at her as she took a drink, and she couldn't help but smile back.

'I have to say, I don't know how you drink this crap!' His face scrunched in disgust as he took another sip.

'Sorry, but you did say you'd have what I was drinking. Frankie makes my martinis extra filthy.'

'Then you have weird taste. This stuff is rancid.' He got up and walked over to the bar, and she was thrilled to watch. This guy was perfect on so many levels. A part of Kara sweetened with the thought he could be genuine, that maybe there was a possibility she could find love. But she shut that thought down as quickly as it surfaced. Kara could not love. How do you love when you've never been shown it was possible? When you have no memory that it ever existed?

He came back with a glass of red wine, raising it to her. 'Cheers. To milder, more intoxicating things.'

He brought the glass to his lips, and her gaze desperately followed them. She wondered what it would be like to taste them. He licked them seductively. She leaned in closer, holding her glass, wanting to inhale his power and make it hers alone. She suddenly realised how much she missed that heady feeling.

'Cheers,' she said, holding the glass to her lips. 'To things that burn with purpose.'

It was at that exact moment Kara knew she was ensnared by him and her guard was completely down. She didn't care about his past, where he had been or who he had done anything with. She didn't care that the ring she saw on his finger that first night was not on tonight. She didn't care that he didn't tell her why he showed up at the bar when he did. He didn't ask anything of her, but everything about him screamed that he wanted her to relinquish control, for her to allow him in because it could be wonderful to share.

'Where do you go when you do that?' He didn't miss anything.

'What do you mean?' she played coy, even though he could sense things in her that others couldn't.

'Just then, you went somewhere. You did it the other night too.'

'Sorry, I didn't realise I was doing anything,' she lied.

'I don't expect you to tell me everything, Kara. But I think there's something about you. It's the reason I keep coming back. And I'd like to keep coming back. I find you intriguing.'

He sipped his red wine letting his tongue linger on his lips longer than was necessary. Kara inadvertently licked her own at the same time, and he winked.

A blush crept up her neck at getting caught staring.

'Can I ask you something?' he said.

'You can ask me anything, but you may not like what you hear.'

'Why did you come tonight? It's like you're here, but you're uncertain. And I don't know if that uncertainty is because of me or you. It's like you're challenging me, but you don't like to be challenged. I can't quite figure it out.'

'Maybe I don't want you to figure anything out,' she said challenging him.

'What would happen if I asked you?'

'Asked me what?'

He leaned in again to speak to her as if they were the only two people in the room.

'I don't think you understand, Kara. I won't stop until I figure you out. Because, deep down, I believe you want me to figure you out. You wouldn't have come back here if you didn't. I see you thinking about possibilities, like how you were trying to figure out what my lips tasted like after I drank my wine.'

He sat back in his chair savouring another slow sip. It was

almost indecent how his tongue slipped across his lips. At that moment, Kara was lost. He wanted brutal honesty, but she wasn't sure he was ready for it. He wanted Kara to give him something he could hold on to. But while he waited, all she could think of was the lies she had fed others throughout her life.

'And what do they taste like?' she asked him, her gaze never leaving his lips.

'They're yours, if you want to try them.'

Kara swore the whole room heard her swallowing. She had never met anyone like Val before, and she knew he would keep trying to uncover her truth. Her heart hammered in her chest because she was about to give him a little. That was dangerous. Being vulnerable was not something that came naturally to Kara. Michael would be swearing eloquently right now if he thought that she was entertaining the idea of sharing what he deemed to be more than necessary.

'I came out tonight because I like having honest nights. I can't remember the last time I had one of those. And I enjoyed your company.'

'I like honest nights too. More than you could possibly believe.'

'It sounds like you've come across some dishonest times,' she said, extending the invitation of truth. When he didn't say anything, she kept going. 'It's rare to find someone and sit with them for a whole night and just talk. I didn't feel any expectations from you. It was nice.'

'Expectations are little disruptions,' he told her. 'But the good kind, if you let them be.'

Exhaling a breath she didn't realise she was holding, Kara sat back and realised she had no idea who she was. That was the most honest she had ever been with anyone.

'I have to admit, I wasn't out looking for anything when I first saw you. The opposite, really,' he said. There was a hint of sadness in his voice, but it disappeared as quickly as it appeared. 'But you've intrigued me, Kara Collins, and I like it.'

'To be honest, I'm not looking for anything and I'm not very good at stuff like this. But there's something about you.'

He stood from his chair and moved over to sit closer to her in the booth. She looked over to Frankie and a smile appeared with a cheeky waggling of their eyebrows. Val's closeness upended her thoughts and all rationality left her. He draped his arm over the booth, leaning in closer. She could smell the red wine on his breath.

He whispered in her ear. 'I think your friend over there wants me to leave.'

'Who, Frankie?'

'Yes, Frankie. They keep looking at you.'

'Thank you for your flattery,' she told him politely. 'But what Frankie and I have isn't like that.' She winked back at Frankie, who watched them like a soap opera.

Val didn't laugh or make any attempt to sit back. He looked at Kara with a scorching intensity, and she knew she was about to be ruined.

But he didn't give her a moment longer to react, leaning in and kissing her gently. When he finished, he pulled back and looked at her, waiting for her response. Kara did nothing but look at his lips, thinking of the blistering effect they'd had on hers. When she didn't stop him, he leaned in again kissing her, taking his time. The kiss stirred things in her she had never experienced before, and a part of her hated herself for it. When he pulled back this time, he reached for his glass of wine, sitting next to her as if he always belonged there.

The need to berate him dissipated. Instead, she sat in her chair, wanting desperately to touch her lips ... no one had ever kissed her like that before.

He took another sip of his wine and said, 'I've wanted to do that since I met you.'

'Why didn't you?'

'Because I was worried you'd slap me,' he said, laughing.

He had been thinking about her. How was it that someone

could be thinking of her? Val didn't seem like someone who would let an opportunity pass him by, yet that night he let her be.

'I should leave,' she told him.

'Why? Is it because I kissed you?'

'Yes. And no.'

'I can kiss you again to make you stay, if you like.' He was smug.

'I liked you kissing me. But it's too much, too soon.'

'Kara.' He breathed her name. 'I want to do more than kiss you.'

'I don't know you,' she said, defending herself.

'I'm not a one-night stand. Don't treat me like one.'

'How should I treat you, then?'

'Come with me, and I'll show you,' he said, challenging her.

'I'm not sure that's a good idea, Val.'

'Just so you know, I'll keep calling you until you come out again. I like you. That's not easy to say, especially to someone you hardly know. But I feel like there's a fire in you that I'd like to challenge.'

'What if you don't like what you see?' she asked him.

'I can't see it if you don't let me in.' Val's eyes flashed with heat she knew she wanted. 'Come with me.'

He had no idea who she was. There was a possibility that Val was genuine. But she worried she would push him too far and, when he saw who she was, he would leave and break her.

And she desperately wanted him to kiss her again, wanted him to follow through with his words from earlier. She wanted to follow him home. Instead, she stayed in her seat and reached for her glass again. He smiled at her, knowing she had relinquished some of her control.

'I'll try not to slap you,' she told him. 'So don't give me a reason to.'

He raised his hands in the air. 'I come in peace.'

With confidence she didn't know she possessed, she took charge and leaned towards him, kissing him long and hard. His hands found her face, and he cradled it, holding her steady. When they broke apart, he ran his thumb along her swollen lips, and he smirked. She wanted those lips all over her body, where they would hum to the beat of Val's.

The night drifted slowly, floating unencumbered. When it was time to leave, he offered his hand, and she took it, linking only her pinkie finger. He didn't push for any more, as if he knew that taking the rest of his hand would be too much for her. As they left for his place, she knew peace would not find her. She was unsettled, and it wasn't because of her apprehension of Val, but what she was rapidly feeling for him. She was terrified by the thought of him breaking her, because fear was like a marble – solid with the potential to shatter. She walked with him knowing there was no turning back. She had shed a part of herself with him that night. Val was reaching corners that she never allowed anyone to see.

7

DESPERATION

Kara found desperation could cling like a bothered butterfly; its wings beat hard out of necessity, manifesting what it needed with urgency. At some point in her life, she realised everyone would experience a form of desperation that was raw and palpable.

Desperation confused her beliefs and rendered everything and everyone around her irrelevant in her attempts to tame it. She lost details in a sea of desperate emotional blandness. Rationality left her like a dying ember, feverish and erratic, skewing her notion of reality. In the throes of desperation, Kara's emotions grew. They moulded the person she became and, soon enough, all her energy turned inward. All that mattered was making her outward self something she could control perfectly.

That was how Kara felt when grief's pointy talons embedded themselves in her heart one rainy morning. She was eleven years old when her father decided to leave her and her mother forever, banishing them from his life. It was no mistake on his behalf, and there were no warning signs.

At some point, he decided that this family wasn't worth his time. Their relationship crumbled. It was now a fragmented memory with a packed suitcase and no backwards glance. He didn't stay to explain himself, as if she was listless reason of nothing. Kara had so many questions for him, all of which went unanswered. He walked out the door and out on his family. It was a memory that bled within Kara's soul.

On that morning, Kara had woken up to find her mother sitting in the kitchen nursing a cup of coffee. She clutched it with both hands as if salvation lingered within. Kara wanted to take the mug out of her hands, to break the trance she was in. But what if, when she woke from wherever she was, she was completely different?

It was the first time Kara felt fear for someone other than herself. She knew this uneasiness would always be there. Terror tickled under her skin. She wanted to the comfortable embrace only her mother knew to give, not the terror of possible abandonment. Her mother was naked and floated in the breeze, distanced further by the silence in which she sat.

Frank Sinatra sang softly in the background, something about *doing it his way*. Her mother's gaze lingered on a spot on the wall, unmoving even when Kara approached her. Her eyes were glazed with unshed tears. Only when the song ended did she look up and notice Kara standing there. Her mouth curved slightly in recognition. As quickly as it appeared, it misted over.

'Karina.' She breathed her name like a memory Kara wasn't privy to. 'Kara,' she corrected.

It was all she managed to say as she closed her eyes. With a sigh, she dropped her head, releasing a tidal wave of emotion and tortured tears. Kara held her breath, not moving, watching it all unfold. Her mother kept repeating, *'He's gone.'*

Kara stood frozen in the kitchen, her mother would break a little more. Not understanding what was happening, Kara walked over to where her mother sat and asked, 'Who's gone? Tell me, Mumma, who is gone?'

Like a sinking anchor, desperation lodged in Kara's stomach.

She knew it was her father, but she didn't want to believe it. How could he be gone? Where did he go? Why didn't he say goodbye? When would he be back?

'Where is Daddy?' Kara asked.

'He's gone.'

'Where has he gone? Will he be back soon?' She was answered by her mother's sobs all over again.

Her mother was broken into a million little pieces. She had surrendered herself to her newfound loss. Kara stood there watching her, wishing she could change how she felt. But she knew in her heart that the grief her mother was experiencing would isolate her from happiness forever. She was a dying wind disappearing with her husband's vanishing shadow.

'Do you want to go outside so we can sit and wait for him together?' Kara asked.

'No darling girl,' her mother told her. 'There's no point waiting outside. No one is coming.'

'Are you mad at Dad?'

'I'm not mad, Kara.'

'I am. I'm mad because he didn't say goodbye. I want him to come back. It's his fault we're sad,' she said, tears streaming down her face.

'It's no one's fault.' Her mother tried to soothe her. 'Your dad did what he had to do. I don't blame him. We all make choices. Please don't be mad at him.'

Kara remembered that day because her mother was never the same again. After that day, she stopped trying. She would stay in the house, sitting in her chair and looking out the window. Kara knew her mother was waiting for him. She was holding onto a little ribbon of hope, in that it would repair the tear in her heart. Kara often wondered whether her mother ever stopped loving him. But it didn't matter if she did - her father never came back.

Not long after, divorce papers shattered what should have been an eternal togetherness. The ink should have been dry, but her mother's tears smeared her father's signature. The letter's finality extinguished all traces of hope which, until then, lingered like a thief. Now it stole her mother's remaining breath. It left her clutching her chest, gasping. Kara's father severed himself completely from their lives. It broke her mother completely.

The paperwork remained on the desk in the spare room, untouched and unsigned. It was as though there was no hurry to make things final. During that time, Kara thought that her mother waited with hopeful patience: a fickle feeling, like desperation. Both promised the possibility of more and, when more was no longer possible, they turned to longing, and longing turned to despair. And despair was a cruel bitch.

Days turned into weeks, weeks into months, and suddenly two years passed. By the time the final papers arrived, her mother's light dimmed to a dying glow.

'It is done,' she told Kara. 'He is finally free.'

After the papers were signed, Kara's mother was a shell of a person. She would smile, but it would never reach her eyes. Kara would try and make polite conversation, knowing her mother was always sad. Her father's memory had been completely removed. Frames that held photos of happier times were now filled with pictures of Kara smiling awkwardly.

Kara tried desperately to give her mother the happiness she lacked, but it was getting increasingly difficult each day. Her mother had once taken pride in the way she dressed. Now all she wore was a robe over her night dress. She had lost all respect for herself. Where her hair was once styled and perfect, it had grown long and unkempt. It was heavy, like the loss her heart bore. Her eyes were lifeless, joyless. Once she sang and danced with laughter, now she remained silent, tormented in her thoughts.

She was lost, Kara knew this, but she tried every day to give Kara something, anything of herself because she knew Kara desperately needed it.

Sometimes it was a soft kiss on the cheek, other times there would be gentle fingers running through Kara's hair. But no matter how hard she tried to find that glimmer of hope, Kara knew that her mother's happiness was lost.

She was incapable of real affection, struggling through the days, letting emptiness settle. She would sit by the window, pulling the curtains back, peering up and down the street. She always flinched at noises Kara couldn't hear or understand, but it became worse after her father left.

Maybe it was in those reflective moments that she decided she would never love, never sacrifice her heart and let it beat for another. She wanted it to be imprisoned, caged and beating against impenetrable walls she put up. She wanted it safe. She knew little of love, but she knew it hurt those who let it.

She would make sure she never got hurt.

Kara was often desperate to try and change the course of her mother's behaviour. She often begged her to go out so they could do things together. Kara even stood on a chair behind the couch to brush her hair. It was greasy and would slide between Kara's fingers, but she would brush it in the hope of resurrecting her.

'Let's make it pretty and smooth today, Mumma,' Kara would say.

'Thank you, Kara,' a half smile lifting the corners of her lips.

And that was all Kara would get.

By the age of thirteen, she longed to see people suffer ... she wanted them to feel how she felt. She was angry, and it viciously bubbled inside her. Kara wanted to hurt people, not physically, but emotionally.

She also knew she could lie to get what she wanted.

'I don't think I can go to school today, I have a headache,' she would tell her mother. 'I think I have a temperature, I was sweating all night,' she tried to lie to her. 'My period came this morning, and my cramps are really bad.' She would hold onto her mid-section and pray her mother would believe her.

'It's a pupil-free day. The teachers are planning their classes.' She hoped that if she stayed home with her mother more, she would be able to remember who she was and would come back to her and be present the way that Kara saw other mothers being.

Kara would see her friends with their mothers and long for that sort of connection. When they saw Kara, there was pity in their eyes. Poor Kara and her sorry excuse for a mother. Kara was a representation of a broken family. She avoided mirrors wherever she went. Her reflection showed her tattered like the clothes she wore, unwashed and dirty. And the kids at school saw her desperate truths for the lies they were.

The reality was that her mother didn't wash her clothes anymore, and she barely washed herself. The only time she went out was to get food at the grocery store, and that became less and less frequent. So, Kara started to take the money she knew she kept in her wallet to go and buy things by herself. The harshness of these lessons didn't go unnoticed by Kara. It was fuel to add to the growing fire in her belly.

Kara's father faded into a raised scar. Now, the only means of connection they had with him came in the form of his monthly donations. Her mother's slurred vodka nights spewed her hatred for him, shunning his money saying they didn't need it. She would often yell and throw things around.

'Screw him and his pity money!' she yelled, throwing the envelope it came in one night. 'Screw all of them!'

It was ironic because it was the only time her mother showed any real emotion, and ashamedly, Kara always felt relieved when she saw it.

It was hard not to feel like the one to blame when her mother was like that. Kara was the link to the rusty chain of a broken marriage. But each month the money would appear in the mail with no return address. Kara would retrieve the thrown envelopes, and open them to take the money. It was always bittersweet because she wondered how they would have survived without it.

Kara questioned everything after her father left. She wondered how love could strengthen a person only to break them at the same time. How words written on paper could be tattooed permanently on someone's heart. Did this mean that everyone was the same? Was it her father's decision, or was her mother responsible as well? What could she have possibly done to make her father walk away? Or, in his case, into the arms of another woman.

A letter came one day saying her father had met someone, and he was going to marry again. The letter didn't have any real finality to it. It was as if it carried a hidden meaning that Kara couldn't decipher. It messed with her in ways that she couldn't comprehend. She wondered if he would have another child. And, if he did, would he one day turn his back on them the way he had her?

'When Dad sends those letters to you, does he ever send anything to me?' she asked one day.

'Perhaps he's too busy,' was all her mother said before quickly changing the subject.

Kara played every scenario of his new life over and over. Happiness was her father with the new family swinging in the park, laughter radiating from happy bike rides and warm nights swathed in bed with favourite stories. The lulled sound of his new child's sleep followed by sweet kisses and goodnight. She hated that he could do that with someone else.

Desperation mingled with hate. Kara wanted to grow up knowing that one man in her life could love her unconditionally. But when feelings come with conditions, love is shaped, forced. Love should not be fenced by square confines. Its shape should shift and change with the shape of your heart. It should bend with strength rather than be snapped by weakness.

'Why did he leave?' Kara asked again, hoping for a new answer.

'Because he needed to.'

But her father ruined everything for her. He drained the well of love and sealed its entrance so no one could ever get in. No matter what her mother told her, he moved on while Kara and her mother lay in love's destructive path. Kara felt like she lost more than her father. He didn't take her with him. He didn't even ask if she wanted to go. He gave up. He let go of the rope that tethered him and let it slip away.

Her mother barricaded her heart with desperation. Kara was ignited by fury. She wanted to burn everyone else in her path. She resolved that no one would ever come close. She would never let anyone unravel her, no matter how hard they tried.

8

UNFAMILIAR

Any new relationship thrives on unfamiliarity. It lives on those unfettered moments, where awkwardness sheds its skin, and comfort fills within cracks to spur on something thrilling and exciting. For Kara, every moment felt new smiles, laughs, stories, hands, touches, stares, hellos and goodbyes, quiet little vacancies where she felt at ease. The unfamiliar became a new comfort. Kara found being with Val effortless. The two of them connected like satin and freshly bathed skin. Soon enough, the unfamiliar which Kara once found so foreign, was soft and pliable, and the two of them were ready to be moulded together.

Moments of potential discomfort were replaced by familiarity within the crooks of possibilities. The air around them felt charged and palpable. Electricity simmered with their newness. Their conversations flowed with ease. Each smile, a first. Each laugh came from a different story. The touch of skin came with moments of bliss followed by subtle exploration. There were no hellos and no goodbyes, only the existence that expanded with the time they created for each other.

With every moment, the unfamiliar became familiar. It was worthy of honesty, something Kara still struggled to believe in. They lived separate lives but somehow managed to find each other in the dwindling minutes of every day. And while Kara relished the newness of everything Val had to offer, Michael still implored her to have a different view. He reminded her how trust should be earned. She wondered if Michael was deliberately growing distant as Kara grew closer to Val, and more than anything she didn't want the quaintness of their friendship to be thin and fragile.

Michael was a staple in her life. She needed to find a way to convince him that he too mattered. She would forever be grateful to him, and that would never change. He called Kara while she walked with Val, sounding terse and full of judgement. It was very unlike Michael, and for once, Kara didn't know where she stood with her friend. Kara let go of Val's hand and walked far enough that he couldn't overhear her conversation.

'Did the brown-eyed devil keep you up all night again?' he asked her.

'Is there a problem here?' She was quick to question. 'Because if you have a problem with him, please tell me so we can get it over with. You are important to me, and that will never change.'

'But?'

'No buts, Michael. What would your fancy word for importance be?'

'Paramount,' he said after a few seconds. 'Although that does sound more like the title of a movie. Would you like it in a sentence?' He was trying to make light.

'No.'

'Then by all means go ahead.'

'Michael,' Kara began. 'It is paramount that, after everything we have been through, you remain my friend.' She tried to laugh, but she knew it was useless. Michael was very uncomfortable with the unfamiliar.

'I'll always be your friend, baby girl,' he told her. 'It's not you I don't trust.'

They were silent on the phone for a while, and she knew he was waiting for her to say something before they hung up. He always waited for her to have the last word.

'Odious,' she blurted out.

'Put it in a sentence,' he threw back at her.

'Michael is being extremely unpleasant towards Val, who he has never met.'

She laughed, but there was no laughter from the other end. Kara waited, for something, anything. When he didn't say anything, she knew she had the last word and hung up. She looked at the phone, willing him to call back, but he didn't. Instead, she heard her message notification ping on her mobile. It simply read:

Odious towards Val 'whom' he has never met.

We are solid.

Be careful.

That was what Kara needed to know, everything had been restored to the familiar with Michael.

She hadn't noticed Val standing behind her when she tucked her phone back in her bag. He didn't question who she had been speaking to. Now and then, he would glance back letting her know he was there.

Val reached out and held Kara's pinkie as they walked back to his apartment. They settled into an unspoken rhythm when they walked. He would reach for her hand, and she only ever offered her little finger. Now and then, he would run his thumb along her pinkie to remind her that there was more if she needed it. But Kara never asked for more, content with what they had.

Laughing at some crazy story Val was telling her about his shift at the hospital, she found herself stopping mid-conversation. They were almost at the end of the road near Val's place when Kara swore she heard her name being called. Turning in the direction of the sound, she shielded her eyes from the sun. Squinting, she tried to make her eyes focus. But Kara couldn't see anything or anyone on the other side of the road. Her skin crawled with a familiar feeling, like it had the night at New Gold Mountain, and she scanned the streets again to see if she could find the source of her discomfort.

Noticing that she stopped, Val asked if everything was alright. Kara shivered in the sunlight. She shook her head. She couldn't see anyone standing on the other side of the road, so they walked off, Val draping his arm around her and pulling her in close.

'Sorry,' she said, shrugging off the uncomfortable feeling. 'I thought someone called out to me.'

'Hearing things now, are we?' he joked.

'Something like that.' Kara laughed, but an uneasiness settled inside her.

Val's apartment was set in a quiet little alley in the middle of Melbourne's CBD. It always felt like it was welcoming Kara home.

'You look amazing today,' he said, leaning in and kissing her on the cheek.

'Thank you,' Kara replied, still feeling shy and unsure around Val, especially when he complimented her for things she thought were mundane.

'Don't thank me yet. My mind has us in all sorts of positions and all of them end with you screaming my name,' he told her, walking straight into the foyer as if he hadn't just made her insides implode.

In the lift on the way up, Kara took a deep breath, thinking about the possibilities that awaited her. She smiled at Val and his dimple puckered. He pushed her into the corner and attacked her lips and mouth, making her a puddle of unfamiliar lust, not stopping until the bell let them know they reached the right level.

Val's apartment was neat and organised. There was a sparseness to it that suggested he hadn't been there long. There were a few photos in frames, which he told Kara were of his parents and his brother. Apart from that, the apartment looked like it only was somewhere to store his shoes and rest his eyes.

Kara sat on the sofa and waited for Val to come back with the glass of wine he promised. Her mind reminded her to stay guarded. He knew almost nothing about her. He often asked questions, but she never gave him straightforward answers. When he returned, he sat down next to her, glass in hand, and she knew something was amiss.

'Have you been with him?' He took a sip of his wine and raised his eyebrows, letting Kara know he would be able to tell if she was lying. Val was always forward when he wanted to ask questions, but this one caught Kara off-guard.

'Who?' she asked, even though she knew.

'Your mystery caller, who you told I was *odious*.'

The wine spilled from Kara's mouth, and she caught it in her hand so she didn't stain the sofa. A laugh slipped from her lips but, when she looked over to Val, the dimple that appeared earlier with amusement was gone. He was serious. Her laughter died down when she realised he wasn't going to smile back. Placing the glass on the table, she turned to Val, who was looking intently at his wine.

'No,' she told him honestly. 'I've never been with him. And I never will. He and I are friends. Just friends. Nothing more.' She said it as if it would describe everything Michael was to her. 'We've been through a lot together.'

Val nodded, but it was more acceptance than an indication he believed her.

'Are you going to have a problem with that? Because he will always be in my life.'

'I don't know him,' he said. 'And he calls you all the time. When he's not calling, he's messaging you. How would you feel if I had a female friend who did the same with me?'

She understood what Val was trying to tell her, but Kara knew Michael would always be a part of her life, regardless of what Val thought of him. She realised Val wanted her to recognise his suspicion.

'Wait,' she said. 'Are you jealous of my relationship with Michael?'

'Do I have reason to be?'

'I didn't peg you as the jealous type.'

'Maybe I too, am cautious about who I choose to spend my time with.'

His remark stung. He had followed her, not the other way around. He had chosen to turn up at the bar every weekend, hoping she would be there. And since she decided to go back, she hadn't given him any reason to be jealous. But the way he spoke to her, questioning her integrity, had her thinking something happened to Val that he didn't want to share. He looked determined to extract some sort of truth from her, like he wanted to blame her for something that wasn't her fault. He wanted to catch her out in a lie.

'It's not pleasant, is it?' Val asked.

'It's not that.'

'Then what is it?'

'I've never had to worry about someone else being in the picture or being in my picture. I've never had someone stay this long.'

'So, you'd be unperturbed if I started to call women I've known in the past? You would be comfortable with me being familiar with them day and night?' He waited for her to answer. When she didn't, he got up and left her sitting alone on the sofa. 'I thought so,' was all he said as he walked off.

Confused by what happened, Kara let out a breath she hadn't realised she was holding. The comfort she felt earlier was long gone, and she was trying to silence the confusion in her head. The evening had been tainted.

Val was standing in front of the window, gulping the wine in his glass. Unsure of what to do or say, Kara sat there. The silence between them was uncomfortably familiar: two people lost in a moment of translation. How quickly it could move from feeling secure to sitting empty, thinking unspoken thoughts?

When he didn't return to where she was sitting, Kara wondered how she could turn the night around. Her relationship with Michael was complex, not many people understood it. They shared a history that would take a while to explain. Dredging up her past was not something she wanted to do right now. Val wanted something too personal and raw. She wasn't prepared to say more about her friendship, even if it meant Val was making his own conclusions.

So, she reverted to the only thing she felt comfortable with: her old self. She hoped her actions would help evade his questions.

Kara stood up and walked cautiously towards Val. He could see her in the reflection of the window. Without hesitation, she took off her blouse and unbuttoned her bra, and she knew she had his attention. He turned, as predicted, taking her all in. For a moment, Kara felt powerful knowing she was not lost inside herself, that she could do this without hesitation.

She reached for the button on her jeans, but Val lowered his eyes, looking at the floor instead. It wasn't the reaction she was expecting. When he looked up again, he reached out to touch her nakedness but second-guessed himself. Regret had him stopping and pulling away. He shook his head again, denying himself permission to go any further. When he sighed, it was a lament.

Frozen with embarrassment, Kara covered her exposed self, bending awkwardly down to the floor to retrieve her clothes.

'Kara.'

But she was too far gone to even think about what he was trying to say. The sudden rejection whispered around her like she was naked in the wind, and she was desperate to put her clothes back on.

'Kara, stop,' he said, but she already had her top on inside out and was rushing for her bag. When she found it, she threw it over her shoulder, no doubt looking like a dishevelled mad woman, and walked with purpose towards the door.

'Kara!' he called again, not moving.

'We met when I was unwell,' she said with her back to him. 'He has saved me in more ways than one. He is my friend. My only true friend. I don't expect you to trust him.' She wondered if she should explain further.

When she turned around, she looked directly at Val, who looked wounded. His rejection of the offer of her body should have been her only concern, but a part of her had broken because he was the only person to have ever told her no. She wanted him to be there for her, to try and understand more about her.

'I just thought, for once,' she said, wiping at the tears she hadn't realised were falling down her cheeks, 'perhaps someone could trust me.'

'I'm sorry.'

'It's okay,' she said with more conviction than she believed she had.

When he didn't offer her anything else, she gave him a little more of her truth.

'The truth is, whatever this is between us is very unfamiliar to me. I don't know what I'm doing, and I need my friend. Michael is my only friend. And while you don't understand what he does or doesn't mean to me, he is the only person I can turn to when you do shit like this. If you had someone who you called or messaged that you considered a friend, I would trust you. Especially if you told me they were your friend and nothing more. But,' she wiped at her face and drew in a deep breath, 'don't put your insecurities on me. If you want whatever this is between us, then you have to trust me, like I trusted you.'

She walked out the door, not waiting for him to respond. Perhaps there was nothing she needed from him in that moment. But somewhere in the fragmented familiarity that Kara recognised, she wondered if they could find a different version of reality where the unfamiliar between them would be banished once and for all.

9

EMOTIONS

Emotions are like balls of tangled ribbons. Kara found emotions held an air which naturally lifted with emotive buoyancy when she thought she was light with love. It was why she kept hers wrapped tight and close to her chest.

But it wouldn't be long before Kara found out her walls stopped anyone from seeing the depths of her inner thoughts. It was here she felt most desperate, where she created a shadow like existence by burying her feelings. She was loathe to let anyone in to see how she truly felt. She stored these emotions like poison, and she managed them the only way she knew how, self-sabotage.

Kara accepted her emotions, and they settled within her with a quiet tranquillity. She found it hard to believe everyone in her family felt differently, especially her father. She often wondered if she was the way she was because of him, as if some broken chain of his DNA linked them in a way that allowed hate to be transmitted between them. He had been selfish with his love and disregarded her mother and her feelings with significance.

Kara wanted to believe her father's love was toxic. It fuelled what little belief Kara had in love. She felt as though her love was a burden and it would bury her with its weight. It sat heavy, not only on her shoulders but deep within her soul, and she tried to with everything she had to tamp those emotions down. She wanted them to stay hidden for when she needed them most; only then would Kara allow herself to harness the blackness that flowed through her veins.

Kara hid behind her emotions. Hatred had taken over the last remaining intact blister of love, and its skin had burst open with it. She felt possessed by the way she felt about her father. When she looked back and tried to remember him, the memories felt strained and unreal. It was getting harder to remember him kissing her on the cheek before he would go to work.

There were so many questions she wanted to ask him. But, as time passed, she realised the impossibility of this. Kara would look at the envelopes with his handwriting, hoping one day she would see a return address on the back. She had written letters to him that she wanted him to read. She told him things in those letters that mattered to her. She wondered if he would have any interest in knowing about them. But when nothing more appeared on the envelope, just her mother's name and address, she stopped looking and, eventually, stopped writing. The letters remained, folded and boxed, the lid sealing in her thoughts and feelings.

So, Kara kept all the things she wanted to ask him hidden, especially from her mother. She wanted to shelter her from her questions because she knew she was beyond fragile.

Her mother barely existed, and Kara found herself trying to understand how her mother could be so broken. She wondered about love's destructive capacity and, felt like her existence was a burden to her mother.

Kara was a reminder of the things her mother had lost. Although she never said it, she knew her mother saw in Kara her failed marriage. Kara carried constant memories, the type that couldn't be buried, a reminder of everything that was broken.

And then, as if the emptiness of divorce wasn't enough, they had to move out of their home.

'I don't want to go,' Kara told her mother.

'It will be a new adventure.'

'I don't want anything new. What about you? You loved this house.'

'A house has walls and a roof to shelter us. We attach ourselves to things because we find comfort in them. They are security. But when that changes, we change. And this is our time for that change.' She continued packing.

The choice to stay had been taken away from Kara. She and her mother moved.

Selling the house left her mother enough money to buy something decent and a fresh coat of paint, a place that would hold new memories for Kara and her mother. And the newly painted walls would soak up the new feelings, sealing in the sadness her mother thought Kara didn't notice she carried.

'What do you think?' her mother asked her when she was done.

'I miss our old house,' Kara told her.

'Things change, and we need to change with them.'

'Do you think he's changed?' Kara asked.

She wanted to ask more so she could try and piece together the puzzle. She was always wary of asking about him because while she wanted to know, the thought of what she would learn threatened to tear her apart.

Her mother hesitated, cautious, not wanting to reveal the true extent of the hurt she harboured. She became adept at masking everything she felt, or at least everything she didn't want Kara to see.

'It doesn't matter what I think anymore.' She sighed, and then said nothing more.

They moved from Carlton to the northern suburb of Epping because her mother was adamant they make a new start. Here, monotony stretched the length of each street. All the houses had the same façade, the colour of the bricks the only distinguishing feature. They were stark, emotionless and empty. Row upon row, they were nestled in suburbia with concrete driveways as far as the eye could see.

There was nothing complex in the street, nor any warmth in the view. The suburb was as bland as the colour beige. It felt like a graveyard where divorcees went to die. This was noticeable in the dying trees that swayed in front yards, desperate for water, hoping for revitalisation. The houses provided security from dusk till the fall of the night. In the morning the embers of filtered light would come through, promising a false warmth.

The first morning in their new house, she found her mother sitting among the unpacked boxes, staring into a steaming cup of coffee. She smiled at Kara, half in sympathy, half in apology, acknowledging that was all there was.

'Did you sleep well?' she asked.

'I slept on and off all night. How about you?'

'I swear I heard every little crack throughout the night. It's amazing how you let your imagination get the better of you,' she said, trying to make light.

'Maybe,' was all Kara said.

'It will get easier.' She half-smiled at Kara.

This was where Kara's life would continue. Her mother didn't care about maintaining anything around the house. The overgrown lawns added another layer of isolation. There were no flowering plants in the garden like in their old house. Flowers were something to look forward to ... hope. And hope was something that belonged to other people, not Kara or her mother. Kara had left hope sealed it in the boxes she took with her.

Kara wanted to feel something for the new place they lived in. She wanted to have an emotional connection to it to see it as something other than consistently sad.

Some nights, her imagination ran wild. It would happen when dusk settled and the streetlights twinkled with a hum of repetition. She would look out of her window and pray that friends she made would come over, like they did for other kids. They could sit in her room for hours listening to music, exchanging songs and talking about bands they loved. Her mother could knock on her door and bring in sweet drinks and popcorn, and she would laugh at their fascination with bands she never heard of.

When they wanted to escape, they would all go outside and practice flips and gymnastics moves for their sporting sessions for school. They would blush and talk about the boys in class and jump to different conversations like comparing fashion trends or counting the money they saved from their part-time jobs. Laughter would follow them like butterflies that skimmed their skin.

Kara imagined that, when it was time to come in, her father would put his fingers in his mouth to whistle. The sound was so loud, it would bounce like a warning. And Kara and her friends would laugh, knowing there was no room for argument. Then they would hug and say their goodbyes with promises of seeing each other tomorrow. It would be wonderful and fun.

Once inside, Kara's parents would tuck her into bed, showering her with kisses. They would tell her how proud they were of her, whispering words of encouragement so she could do her best in life. This was all they could ask of her and, no matter what, their love would be enough to get her through. Kara was strong because they believed in her. She would be someone because they made sure she followed the right path, and she could do anything because their love allowed it.

Kara would then close her eyes and wait for dreams to come and tickle her with happiness. Sleep would drift through the night like a fairy floss smile. The night would whisk away any worries, revealing a better next day. And, while she slept, the hushed stillness of the neighbourhood would relax through the night, exhaling into the innocent similarity of the following day. She would imagine her mother and father pouring a glass of wine and unwinding after a hard day while she slept.

'What did you do today?' her father would ask her mother.

'Nothing exciting,' she would reply, downplaying her day.

'Don't think what you do isn't important,' he would tell her.

'Enough about me,' she would laugh. 'How was your day?'

'Long and exhausting. I think it's time for a holiday.'

'Sounds wonderful,' her mother would tell him, excitement in her voice.

A trip for the three of them. He would look into it tomorrow.

Then they would sit on their sofa and turn the television on. Laughter would erupt while watching something crass. Her mother would rest her head on her father's shoulder, and he would kiss her softly, knowing she would soon fall asleep.

Emotions would swirl heavily around them. They would talk about making their family bigger, giving Kara a brother or sister. They had spoken about it before. They would be proud of the way Kara would help, and she would embrace the role with loving honour. Kara always wanted a sibling.

Then her mother's breathing would slowly taper off as she fell asleep. Her father would gently tell her it was time for bed. They would lie there together for a while and, just before they would both fall asleep, he would whisper, '*I love you.*'

Together they would dream of loving moments filled with sweetness and forever. Love would surround them through the night, cocooning them in their happy place. They would be the perfect family with the perfect life.

Except imagination is a fiend that ruins minds. This was not Kara's reality. Her home was a house, her mother existed and Kara lived between the two. And she wanted nothing more than to settle in to her life, knowing her mother tried. It was the reason that emotions mixed with nostalgia often threatened to leak from Kara's eyes.

10

HONESTY

Honesty was the anchor that kept Kara tethered to the reality she shared with those around her. This was at the very core of how she saw herself balancing the fineness in her life. And Kara wanted acceptance because it validated the structures that protected her and her heart. Without honesty, Kara's beliefs became truths. When Kara's truths became skewed, so did her reality. And when reality no longer served its purpose, she abandoned it. But her truth was that love was something to be denounced, avoided at all costs, yet here she was embracing it.

Everything Kara sought in life became a dishonest portion of the truth. Love was a terrifying prospect because it left her vulnerable.

Kara chose to be vulnerable and wanted to weather her storm. She wanted to stand proud in her defiance and accept all her flaws, all her cracks and all her vulnerabilities. She wanted to abandon her constructed realities. She tried to explain this to Michael on the phone before she arrived, but he was curt, swearing something about being ill-advised, preposterous and flagrant.

'By later, I'm hoping you mean you'll call when your quasi-bullshit session ends,' he said, his voice slightly raised.

'I'll call you. I just need you to not be an arse right now and support me.'

'Like brown eyes would?' he questioned, his voice terse and full of judgement.

'Michael,' she breathed. 'I'm not in therapy.'

'Then what do you call this relentless pursuit of bullshit, Kara? You're in the office of someone whom you hardly know and you're giving them intimate details about your life. Meanwhile, the man who you have been intimate with, extremely intimate may I add, has zero idea where you are and what you're doing. I call bullshit.'

She could hear his chest heaving on the other end.

'You're the one who always tells me to only be a little honest.'

'This is also true.' He laughed.

'Then I don't understand what the problem here is. One minute you're telling me to guard myself at all costs, and the next you're challenging me, wondering why I haven't told Val anything. Maybe I'm not ready to throw all my crazy at Val. I need a little time to figure some things out. I really don't want to mess this up, Michael.'

'I'm just looking out for my friend,' he said, wanting to make light of her situation. Michael was her friend. They had been through a lot together.

'Why is it lately all our conversations seem to be about me, and all civility seems to be out the window?' she asked him.

'Always deflecting,' he retorted.

'Not deflecting. I feel like we only have heated discussions lately. I miss my friend.'

He was quiet for a while. Kara wanted Michael to recognise that some things had changed in her life, but their relationship was the one thing she needed to remain the same. While Val was a constant beat in her life, she was also navigating changes with him. It was her commitment to Michael that was important, and she desperately needed him to recognise that.

'I'm here,' he told her.

'Really? Because it feels like you're nowhere near where I am,' she said, surprising herself with her honesty. And, judging by the silence on the other end, it had done the same to Michael.

'Martini later. I'll buy. Frankie misses you too.'

'I'll let you know when I'm done,' she told him.

'Twire,' he said. And, when she didn't respond because he knew she would have no idea, he added, 'To look, Kara, peep and peer covertly, if you need to,' and hung up.

It was the first time he didn't wait for her to end their conversation.

Shaking her head in disbelief, Kara dismissed Michael's cryptic words and thought about Ray. She knew she had come back because she wanted to make a difference within herself. So, she found herself sitting in the waiting room again, leaning over and pulling out a tissue in preparation.

The door swung open, and Ray walked out, immediately noticing what was in her hand. He only nodded at Kara, then walked over to the woman behind the desk, whispering something in her ear. The woman stood up and walked into Ray's office. She was gone a few minutes then returned to her desk without acknowledging Kara at all. The smell of coffee suddenly permeated the air, and Ray walked towards her with two cups.

'Ready?' he asked before turning to go into his room with the expectation that Kara would follow.

When they settled into their seats, his eyes travelled to the tissue Kara had scrunched up. Kara stood up and walked over to the bin, dropped the ball of tissue in and sat back down. Ray watched without saying a word. When she sat back down, he nodded to the cup of coffee.

'I didn't know if you drink coffee or how you have it. I've left it black. Would you like sugar or milk?'

Kara was like a petulant child in a staring competition. Ray didn't move, and now Kara was the one who felt uncomfortable. Perhaps it was the way he was staring at her. She caved.

'No sugar, thanks. I like my coffee black. Most psychopaths do.'

'I don't think a person's taste in coffee defines who they are. After all, what would someone say about me? I have three sugars.' He laughed at his own joke.

He allowed his words to sit in the air while he sipped his sweet coffee. Sitting in his office, Kara wanted to feel comfortable with this man. She had learnt over the years to trust her instincts, and she doubted that Ray had any hidden agenda. He appeared tolerant, especially with Kara. But his silence was fleeting.

'The last time you were here, you didn't want to talk. May I ask why you came back?'

His questions left no room for a yes or no answer. He knew what to ask so Kara had to explain herself. She also knew there would be no turning back. She exhaled as she began.

'My whole life, I have pushed people to see what sort of reactions I could get from them.'

'What sort of reactions did you try and get?'

'I don't know how much time we have for that conversation,' she said, trying to break the tension. She knew Ray had heard worse than what she was about to tell him ... at least, that's what she told herself. 'I've always managed to try and manipulate people. Or circumstances.'

'When you were here the other day, did you think by not speaking to me you were manipulating the situation?'

She thought back to the tissues she had torn to shreds. The fact he knew what she was doing made her feel more uncomfortable and embarrassed. For the first time in a long time, her face flushed, and she knew Ray noticed her discomfort. Rather than mock her, he gently steered her in another direction.

'So, people and circumstances ... is this reciprocal behaviour, a tit for tat?'

'No. It's more because I'm completely screwed in the head. And I'm sorry for the language you may hear from me.'

'Kara, please don't apologise. I want you to feel comfortable in this room. If you don't feel the need to share something, I want you to think about why that is.'

Kara melted a little into the chair wondering if that was true. Could a person reduce their burdens by speaking? What did this say of real honesty? Ray was offering to listen to her honest truth.

Sensing her apprehension, he said, 'Can I ask you what you're thinking about?'

'I'm wondering how I try and unpack everything that goes on in my head.'

Honesty. The notion was foreign to Kara, and it sat bitter on her tongue. She had nothing to be honest about, yet the thought of lying to this man terrified her. She was fluent in her deceit and couldn't fathom someone catching her, but there was something gentle about Ray and a part of her didn't want to disappoint him. The reality was she had come back. She wanted to try and turn things around for herself.

But can a stain be completely removed, or will it remain noticeable forever?

'Why don't you tell me why you thought now was the time to come and see someone? Am I right to assume you thought you needed some help?'

How did she get here? She wanted to tell him she woke up one morning with an empty bottle of vodka and a bunch of pills scattered around the floor. It sounded desperately poetic and probably something he wanted to hear, but it would be a lie. She thought of another story: she could tell him that she sat in her car listening to Fleetwood Mac. The lyrics tell her to go her own way and, while the music played, the fumes from the exhaust counted down the seconds to eternal sleep. But that too would be a lie.

Kara knew she could sit there and think of all the things she could tell Ray because she wanted his sympathy. She would thrive off it. It would be like fertiliser for a brand-new reality for herself. But she didn't tell him any of this.

'Do you want to start by telling me about your family?'

She shook her head. Part of her wanted to run at the prospect of talking about her family. The other half wanted to spill like a waterlogged dam. Her family secrets were buried too deep within and unearthing them would mean reopening raised scars in her heart. She didn't want to bleed her family yet. She looked at the coffee table, desperately wishing she had something to shred.

She suddenly felt shy, as if she had disappointed someone she cared about. This feeling was foreign to her. She genuinely didn't know how to deal with it, so she pretended like it didn't exist. She wasn't supposed to care about Ray; he was there to care about her. She wanted to lie until that horrid clock ticked long enough for the session to be over. But she didn't, because she didn't want to run anymore. The exhaustion she carried weighed heavily upon her. She was tired, especially of herself.

'Let's not talk about family or friends. Maybe you can tell me a little about what you do. Do you have a job?'

'That's easy. I'm a flight attendant,' she said, the lie slipping easily from her mouth.

He continued to stare at her, waiting for her to unravel. For a split second, she allowed the thrill of that feeling to permeate. Once that second was gone, she knew without a doubt he also knew she was lying. It wasn't because he said nothing at all, but because he waited in his chair, comfortable in his cleverness. Ray knew she could not maintain this charade with him much longer.

Kara opened her mouth to continue with her lie, but he stood and walked over to his desk. In an instant, he was holding the manila folder, Kara's manila folder. She knew he saw who she really was. When he sat back down, he extended the folder out to her, like a peace offering.

'I'm not here for either of us to waste our time. This is not a game or a way to see if you can manipulate me into believing whatever it is that you think you can tell me. When you came to my office, you had to fill in this questionnaire. I'd like you to take a look at it.'

'Honesty is a two-way street,' he continued. 'If you're not honest with me, then you're not honest with yourself. We all have choices in life, Kara, and if you want these sessions to continue, then you have to be honest with me.'

His words began to filter through the cracks that were forming. It was like seedlings desperate for sun, waiting for the rays of light that will wake them from slumber. He was offering sunshine to nourish something within her. She shook her head in acknowledgement of his words and reached for the folder.

'I know what I wrote,' she told him.

'Why did you tell me you were something other than who you are?'

'Because, sometimes, hiding behind lies is easier than telling the truth.'

That was the most honest answer she had ever given anyone. Kara's whole life had revolved around deviousness and deception, and she didn't want to be that person anymore, especially not with Ray.

'Sometimes I lie so much it becomes my truth.'

Honesty. It was the identity she created to blanket her twisted reality.

'I'd like you to take the two sheets that are sitting inside the folder. Think of it as some homework for you to do between now and our next session. And I want you to be honest with me, Kara. This will only work because you allow it to.'

Kara reached for the folder and took the two sheets out. There were questions on there she knew would need complete honesty.

'When you're done, email them to me so I can have a look before our session next week.'

He then said nothing. Kara felt her old life dying in each second that went by.

'I'll fill them out as best I can.'

Kara left Ray's room with the sheets folded in her purse. She smiled to herself, feeling a little better than when she left home in the morning. The sun shone on her face, and she shielded her eyes from it. Some cracks in her life weren't yet ready for so much light.

She reached for her phone, which had been buzzing in her bag the whole time she was with Ray. Four unread messages appeared, all from Michael:

Why are you looking for answers?
Talking to a stranger will get you nowhere. Come to the bar!
I'll buy you a drink (or two)
Call me when you're done.

Except Kara didn't call Michael. She deleted the messages, feeling guilty for only a second. She scrolled through her contacts until the name she wanted appeared.

Val was the honesty she wanted. When he answered her call with a 'You coming over?' she welcomed it with a knowing smile. She decided next week she would bring her own box of tissues to Ray's office.

'I'll be there as soon as I can.'

11

FRACTURES

Kara felt like her ability to remember was fractured. Her memories were hidden in her mind. She tried to exhume them when she needed them to hold on, but they fell apart. The memories she cherished the most stayed, because she allowed them to. Other memories were stored in the recesses of her mind, too painful for her to recall.

She felt as though her pain was measured within those memories. So, Kara tamped everything down, trying to repress these memories, until tiny little cracks appeared like segments in her mind.

When Kara was sixteen years old, she believed her life was like a tethered feather, caught in a relentless wind rendering her unable to fly. Her memories were fractured, and she couldn't remember anything of her childhood years. She believed the memories she had were lies to replace the truth. When Kara looked back on her life, she viewed it through a false lens. She only saw glimpses into the cracks that never healed. It gave her reason to never look back and gave her the strength to tolerate the intolerable.

Because of this, Kara had the foresight to use the word 'no' with its full power. It was powerful and complete with its simplicity. It could punctuate her life with the commas they deserved, rendering explanations useless. As such, she treated everything with little regard, viewing her life through opaque dreams. Memories sometimes descended while she slept, as lightly as a feather, pulling apart as easily as spider webs.

The fractures allowed Kara to maintain a distance from the people in her life. This extended to her life at school, where she hid in the breaks of her mind because she knew she was different. Kara never wanted to be like the other girls. Life taught her she didn't belong. 'Her kind' would never be a part of close-knit circles. The world existed around her and her mother, and Kara felt like she watched it through a dusty window.

But fortune brought her a friend. Her name was Larn Warrick, and Larn didn't suffer fools lightly. She never showed pity, and showed little regard for what she called the *'inconsequential necessities of playtime trivia'*. Her loathing of schoolyard politics matched Kara's loathing of everything in life. Larn hated the girls in the school as much as Kara did. They shared a common animosity even though they were different.

Larn had a stability in her life that Kara desperately craved. Her family welcomed Kara with an openness she knew she had no right to be part of. But, even though Kara knew this, she allowed a small part of that life to nestle in the corners of her heart. She knew she should not accept their kindness. She should have disregarded her feelings and given them the distance she knew they deserved. It would only be a matter of time before they too realised Kara didn't belong.

Kara never understood why Larn wanted her as her friend, but she welcomed Kara on the first day as if she had waited for Kara her whole life. She didn't ask questions or dig into Kara's family life. They existed on quiet conversations and knowing glances. Larn was tall and lean, a portrait of perfection. Her body, like her personality, attracted stares from everyone, while Kara was happy to hide in her shadow. This never bothered her: she found solace hiding in fractures where no one could see her. Larn's hair shimmered with chestnut beauty, framing her face and high-lighting her captivating eyes. She had a smile that was infectious and, no matter what, she always wanted Kara by her side.

It wasn't long before Larn started to glance back at the blatant stares from the boys. Kara noticed the way she would try and sneak a look, not wanting anyone to notice. And when Ethan Hughes smiled back at Larn one day, something in Kara erupted. She knew her friendship with Larn was over. Kara was walking the corridors of school one day when she caught Larn and Ethan talking, their moment together intimate.

Ethan leaned in and smiled at Larn, whispering something in her ear. Before he left, he gently touched her cheek like she was the most precious gift on earth. Larn smiled back at him, dropping her head, suddenly sweet and shy. When Ethan walked off, Kara managed to make eye contact with him. His smile was smug, as if he knew what girls like Kara were and where he wanted them beneath him.

Kara hated Ethan in that moment, and she wanted to destroy him for taking away the one person who had never left her side. She knew that if Larn started a relationship with Ethan, Kara would be all alone.

The weeks that followed fortified Kara's feelings regarding Ethan. The gentle touches turned into hands meshed together and kisses that lasted longer than she wanted to acknowledge. She tried to look away each time she saw them, but found herself drawn to what they were doing. One night, when they were laying on Larn's bed, Larn told her she didn't want their friendship to change and that Ethan, or 'E' as she called him, was there for fun.

But Kara saw the way Larn searched him out whenever he was around, the way her heart openly fluttered and her whole demeanour changed when they were together. Kara smiled for a while, pretending she was accepting their relationship. Kara also knew she was cunning. She wanted to break them both.

One morning, Kara waited by the lockers knowing Ethan would be there soon. She wanted to see his face when he found the note she left. Ethan walked in not long after, surrounded by his friends, conveniently without Larn. The enormity of what Kara was about to do didn't weigh her down. It was revitalising. The person she truly was, was about to flourish.

As he opened his locker, Kara noticed Larn walking towards Ethan. Larn was smiling, radiating as love's tender hands swept along her glowing skin. But Kara's focus stayed on Ethan. In that split second, she knew Ethan was making a decision, one that would most likely shatter Larn.

He opened the note, quickly read it, then folded it and put it in his pocket. Kara knew what it asked: '*Have you fucked her yet?*' She contemplated what her response would be if he had been intimate with Larn. But she knew, without doubt, regardless of what Ethan and Larn had done, she would follow through with her plan.

Ethan looked over in Kara's direction as if he knew she had written the note. And she didn't dare look away, challenging him. She already knew what his answer was. He kept looking Kara's way even when Larn walked up to him and, when he slung his arm around Larn, he gently swayed his head back and forth, admitting to Kara he hadn't.

No one else noticed the subtle movement, especially not Larn, who waved to Kara as she walked by. The innocence of it all felt toxic to Kara. At that moment, she didn't need to know anything else. She knew Larn wouldn't put herself out there for Ethan. She told Kara not too long ago she was waiting for a sign that Ethan was the one. Kara delivered him a different sign.

The next morning, Kara waited by her locker again. Ethan showed up alone like a child waiting for candy. He opened his locker and found the second note. He looked up at Kara and she returned his gaze, waiting for his response. He was agitated, running his hand through his already messy hair. Kara knew she had no right to focus on his looks; this was never about what he looked like. This was about destruction, that familiar feeling of hatred simmering through her veins. To have the knowledge she was about to ruin something. Ethan opened the note again, reading as if he wasn't sure what to make of its contents.

'*You don't have to wait for me.*'

He closed his locker and started to walk Kara's way. She knew one of two things was about to happen. He would either expose her, or he would succumb to her offering.

Kara waited unperturbed. People like Ethan didn't frighten her. She relished the fact his morals were as deplorable as he was fake. His strides pounded into the hard floor matching the rhythmic beat of her heart. As he walked past, he stopped long enough to whisper, 'What about Larn?'

Ethan kept walking, not waiting for Kara to answer. Kara knew Ethan was fickle; in that split second, before he walked off, Ethan's pupils dilated at the prospect of getting what he wanted.

Kara wasn't stupid, she knew what boys wanted. Larn's beauty was exceptional, and Kara knew hers was not. But she knew she could make herself noticeable when it mattered.

Kara never told Larn she'd had sex before. Last winter, Kara invited someone over. She didn't tell him her name, and she never asked for his. When they got to her house, she opened the door, the sound drowned out by her mother's television. They quickly snuck to her bedroom and stripped out of their clothes. Putting her finger to her mouth to silence him, she pounced on him like a hungry tiger, like she had seen in the movies.

His arms and mouth were all over Kara, and she let him do whatever he wanted. Kara detached herself completely; she didn't want her first time to be anything other than something to get over.

When he was done, he noticed the blood stains on the sheets. His face matched the crimson red he saw. He apologised profusely as he dressed with the speed of light. Kara should have cared, but she didn't. She was grateful to him because she now knew she could use men for sex. It paved the way for her to use whoever she wanted.

So when she spotted Ethan hovering near her locker the

following morning, she knew everything she was planning was about to fall into place. She saw him slip a note through the tiny grill and walk off before anyone could see what he had done.

When he went around the corner, she opened her locker to find a note inside. '*When?*' A sinister smile spread over Kara's face. She quickly scrawled her address on the back of the same note and dropped it in his locker. Then she walked through the corridor to meet Larn as if she wasn't about to ruin her life. She felt alive and was buoyant with the thought of destruction.

That night, she sat up watching television. Her mother had gone to bed when she heard a gentle knock at her door. Ethan stood there, smirking like a cocky little fucker. She didn't even say hello to him, letting him in, then walking up to her room. Ethan followed like an obedient puppy dog.

'Why do you want to fuck me?' was all he asked.

But he never got an explanation as Kara started to undress. 'Shit!' was the only response she heard as she walked over to him naked, grabbing his face and kissing him as if it was the last thing she was ever going to do. He moaned into her mouth, forgetting Larn and devouring Kara in an instant. She had officially crossed a line that would never be forgiven.

They continued to meet like that for a few months. Ethan would show up at her house, and primal instinct would turn them into wild animals. They would reach orgasmic peaks before tumbling back down. Larn was never mentioned, and she knew nothing of what was happening. Kara maintained their friend-ship, pretending Ethan didn't exist when they saw each other at school. It was as if Kara never led a double life.

But Kara eventually grew bored with Ethan. He was becoming needy and speaking of leaving Larn so he could be with Kara all the time. He wanted more, and all Kara wanted was less. She didn't want emotion, just physicality. When she told him she thought they should stop seeing each other, Ethan asked, 'Why?'

Kara simply replied, 'Because.'

He laughed on his way out, saying he would ruin her, but he

had no concept of who Kara was. She knew people like Ethan, but Ethan had no idea that someone like Kara existed.

It took a week before the rumours started to surface. She was walking to her locker one morning when she found Larn standing there with bloodshot eyes.

'Is it true?'

Rather than feeling the shame she knew she should feel, Kara smiled at Larn with pity in her eyes and replied. 'Yep.'

Larn stormed off sobbing down the corridor. Kara only shrugged. She should have felt bad that she had ruined her friendship and shame for seducing Ethan. Kara should have run after Larn, begging her for forgiveness. But instead she did nothing.

Kara waited until her plan fell into place. It had been eight weeks since she had broken Larn. Eight weeks since she and Ethan stopped sleeping together, and eight weeks before another cycle of her period meticulously came again. A knowing smile broke on her face. Enough time had passed for the rumours to simmer down, but Kara was about to bring them up all over again.

That morning, she didn't use a tampon or a sanitary pad when she dressed. Sitting in the classroom, she knew it would take about half an hour for everything to unfold. Kara could feel the wetness between her legs. Within minutes, it would be all over her uniform. She looked over to Ethan and winked, then bent over, pretending to be in pain. Their English teacher, Mrs Travis, looked up from the lecture she was giving, stopping mid-sentence when she saw Kara grimace.

'Are you alright, Kara?' she asked, concerned.

Kara continued to stay down pretending to be in pain while holding onto her mid-section. All eyes were on her. Kara continued to groan. Mrs Travis rushed over to her table, concerned something was seriously wrong, panicked, telling everyone to remain in their seats.

'What's the matter, Kara?' she asked again.

'It's ...' she pretended to stammer, contorting her face with fake pain.

'It's what, Kara? Are you not feeling well?' Mrs Travis wiped Kara's hair off her forehead like a loving parent. The gesture alone should have made Kara stop what she was doing, but she had come too far now to relent. For a split second, she felt sorry for Mrs Travis, and the lie she was about to tell, but she shelved those feelings as quickly as they surfaced.

It was then that Kara screamed as if the agony she was experiencing was real. It sounded convincing. She wanted everyone to hear her horrific pain. She stood up, and there was a communal gasp from behind her because she knew that everyone could see the blood stain on her dress. Kara looked over to Ethan, who was concerned. Larn kept her head down, not wanting to make eye contact. Kara had shattered Larn, but what was about to come next would be cataclysmic.

She turned back to look at the stain on her dress. The fake tears rolled down Kara's cheeks as she looked at her English teacher, who was still fretting with concern.

'Mr Travis ... I think I'm losing Ethan's baby.'

12

DREAMS

ara knew that dreams did not only come to her in the middle of the night. They also appeared during the day, taking her away from her present, allowing her to vacate sections of her life with disparity. Her dreams were at times attainable. When she reached those goals, her life felt fulfilled because she could define who she was.

Kara's dreams also encapsulated more than a second of her time. When she slept, she allowed herself the ability to glide through her mind, creating a show of inexplicable definition. Here, seconds ticked by like shadows behind her eyes, but not always in a way that left her fulfilled. When her dreams haunted her night, it was as if a mystery beckoned her to delve deeper into what she saw.

She asked for a type of recognition only she could explain. Her dreams manifested themselves, like a backwash of unwanted excess. The dreams slid through every night taking her to a different temporality. And, when they appeared to repeat themselves, she questioned what she saw and what it all meant.

In the light of day, Kara's dreams appeared innocuous and fleeting, but at night, when her mind surrendered to the heaviness of sleep, her dreams called to her in a way that demanded recognition.

Kara knew these feelings well. Dreams had often been a tumultuous pathway in the embers of her night. And the recognition she felt that night was instant because there was a sadness which multiplied into a million separate currents. It crawled along her flesh reminding her where she was: walking a familiar path to the iron gates that closed heavily behind her. They allowed entry only to the chosen few.

Today, the chant she heard was different, and she knew there was someone new. She followed the path crossing over the bridge, the gravel crunching under her toes, the sound echoing in the ever-expanding silence. Turning, Kara looked for the familiar track that led her from the bridge. The chant stopped, and she knew she was extremely close. A peacefulness settled within her, taking her fear. Familiarity lingered like a stale scent: childhood laughter mixed with smothered hugs. As she walked further, she saw the kind woman behind the door who always greeted her with recognition.

'Hello,' the woman said.

'Hi Piper,' Kara replied with familiarity.

'I'm glad you made it back.'

Kara could hear her, but her voice felt smothered, almost like she had covered her ears with her hands.

'I noticed you stopped on the bridge. Did you want to stay a little longer today?' Piper asked.

Kara's mouth felt like it was stuck with gum. But if Piper noticed anything, she didn't say a word. She was comfortable and unhurried waiting for Kara's reply. Thoughts raced through Kara's head at a dizzying speed, and she tried to shake them to say no. Everything slowed, and she was running to catch up to her body.

There was a sudden shift in the air, and Kara noticed Piper's devil-wicked smile. Piper knew she had Kara trapped. As she struggled to move, the air felt thick. With each breath, Piper got closer and closer.

'You want to know, don't you?' Piper's voice circled Kara. Kara tried to turn to see where Piper had gone, but each time she tried, Piper vanished. Unruly laughter surrounded Kara, mocking her.

'You want to know if he's here? All you have to do is ask ... I'll give you all the answers you need.'

Piper's laugh was now maniacal, and her head seemed larger somehow. Kara tried to run, but tar stuck her feet to the now-compacted gravel. Piper was behind her, grabbing her, pulling her forward, telling Kara she would take her to him. Kara's legs wouldn't keep up. She didn't want to go because she wasn't ready to see him. She tried to tell Piper no, but Piper had a hold of her, suffocating her with her grip.

They struggled back and forth, and Kara knew she needed to make it to the other side of the bridge. If she made it there, she knew she could get to the gate and go home. Freeing herself from Piper, Kara ran, but her feet felt useless. She fell, smashing her body into the ground, the *thump* winding her of what little breath she had. Looking up, Piper stood over her with a saccharine-sweet smile. She looked angelic, but Kara knew she was anything but.

'Tell me,' Piper demanded. 'Tell me, and I'll let you go,' she heckled over and over. Her voice terrified Kara, whose tears were running down her cheeks.

'You know I need a name, or you'll never find him.'

Kara shook her head, not wanting to say anything. But she also knew Piper wouldn't let her go until she did.

Joshua,' Kara whispered to the wind.

Kara woke. The remnant of the dream rattling her like a haunting wind pushing through a billowing curtain. She could smell Piper: like a stale perfume, dewy and unwelcome. Kara's breath caught, her lungs tight and her legs tingling, numb with fear. The nightmare had consumed her whole body. Its rancidness settled in her mouth, its sourness churning her stomach, threatening to spill the contents of last night's dinner. It toyed with her heartbeat; she could feel the syncopation in her toes.

She was immobilised from the waist down, and Val's leg draping over her didn't help. He slept through her restlessness. Her eyes were closed, trying to clear the last of the nightmare, inhaling slowly so as not to wake Val.

It took effort to exhale without making too much noise. If she moved, he would wake and ask questions Kara wasn't ready to answer. And Val noticed everything, especially when Kara withdrew. He saw her when she would shut down and deny him access. Yet no matter how many times she tried, he managed to get the answers Kara thought she could hide from him.

It had been more than six months since Kara walked away with Val from New Gold Mountain, and Val was becoming Kara's constant. He was the ever-present beat, pulsating new life into her broken one, making her forget who she was and what she had done. She allowed her heart to open a little so Val could settle in, and it terrified her. It was new and unknown, but she knew she liked it.

As he slept, Kara questioned everything. What if everything she believed about love was wrong? What if Val proved that his love was all she ever needed? Her heart was beating faster, but this time for a different reason.

Val shifted, slowly pulling her closer to his already warm body. His arms were like a steel vice around her. He kissed the side of her neck and, for a moment, she was lost to his sweetness. His fingers ran up and down her arms, leaving goosebumps. It allowed her to momentarily forget about her nightmare.

Kara and Val had only recently started staying the whole night at each other's places. Rather than sneaking out before dusk, they found it easier to lay in bed until they needed to face the world. They were in a blissful bubble of newness, and neither of them wanted to leave it. But Kara knew if she didn't try and leave now, her past would resurface and haunt her and Val, like it had in her dreams.

'Are you going to tell me what had you shivering this morning? And don't tell me it's because of my wonderful mouth.'

She kept her answer short. 'I had a nightmare.'

'I know you have nightmares. I've noticed them before. You seemed pretty scared this time. Your legs were thrashing around.'

'I don't want to talk about it,' she told him as she tried to get up.

He pulled her back down, and she was lost to the concern in his beautiful eyes. He was frowning, and Kara desperately wanted to run her fingers along the little creases to smooth them out. There was beauty in the depth of his worry, and Kara hated that she had put it there.

'I'll tell you about it one day, I promise, but I don't feel like I can right now.'

'Is it because you don't trust me? Because, Kara, we've done some things in this bedroom you needed to trust me for. Don't shut me out. I don't want to be an outsider looking in. I don't belong out there. I want to be in here,' he said, pointing to her heart.

He waited for her answer. She knew if she didn't open up, it could fracture their relationship, and rebuilding it would be hard. He continued to stare, probing her eyes for answers.

'It's a dream I have all the time,' she explained. 'More like a nightmare, actually.' She laughed because she found the nightmare absurd, especially now that she was talking about it. 'It's a cemetery I've never been to, but I could give you exact details of everything there.'

'So you've never been there, but you know it exists?'

'Yes.'

'So what happens when you get there? Are you looking for someone?'

'I'm always looking for someone.' She tried to make light of the heavy conversation. But it was laughter that no one joins in with because nothing is funny.

Clearing her throat, she continued to tell him all about Piper, her familiarity even though she had never met her, and how Piper knew she was looking for someone. When she finished, she shrugged like it was no big deal.

'So, who is Joshua?'

She blinked a few times hoping to erase his question. Val must have heard her calling out the name. Hearing it coming from Val made her curl her toes, her secrets threatening to unravel her. Shaking her head, she freed herself from Val and quickly got dressed. The whole time he lay there, waiting for a reply. When she was fully dressed, telling him nothing more, she headed for his front door.

She didn't look back even as she moved through his apartment. She didn't want to give him an explanation. Val was too close to her truth, and she needed to leave. She always needed to leave. She had said too much, and Val looked at her with pity instead of lust. She would give anything to go back and erase it.

Perhaps she should have stayed home ... that way she could have wallowed in the aftermath of the nightmare on her own. The name still lingered, echoing in her head, *'Joshua, Joshua, Joshua.'*

Kara pulled at her hair like a lunatic, pacing in Val's small lounge room, willing the name to go away. She could hear Val moving about in his bedroom, but Kara didn't want to wait to give him anything else. It felt too raw.

When she got to the door, a gentle knock startled her out of her self-loathing. There was no choice but to open it if she was going leave. And, when she opened the door, her heart stopped at what she saw.

A dishevelled woman appeared on Val's doorstep like an angry ant. As if someone had taken away a crumb she was trying to carry. She looked at Kara as if she was that person and Val was her possession. Kara squeezed her eyes shut and willed the woman to disappear. But part of her relished the woman's agony. She had seen that look before, and it was one of pure defeat.

Her shoulders slumped under the emotions weighing her down. Her dull eyes were an insipid green. She was hurting like an exposed tooth, and Kara had put that pain there. For the first time in what felt like ages, smugness settled in Kara's psyche.

'Alexis.' Val's concerned voice snapped Kara out of her thoughts.

The woman's head shot up, and her hand covered her mouth. A ring sparkled, blinding Kara, and she knew then who she was. Crocodile tears fell from the woman's face and splashed onto her patent black shoes. She sobbed on his doorstep and crumpled to the floor. Val moved towards her and, in his haste, he accidentally pushed Kara out of the way. He didn't even look at her as he knelt beside the woman. Alexis.

'What are you doing here?' he asked her.

He gently pushed her hair back out of her face so he could see her eyes. The gesture was an intimate one, one Kara loathed straight away. She hated Alexis with everything she had, and she knew this woman would be a blight.

Val helped her up, and together they walked over to the couch. He didn't say anything to Kara. Alexis' sobs continued, and Kara knew it was time to leave. She was now the audience to a private exchange. One she has no right to be a part of. Walking over to the door, she looked back at where Alexis sat. Her glare towards Kara was venomous. Standing her ground, Kara found herself staring back, not wanting to give away what she was feeling.

Alexis appeared broken, and Kara felt like the mistress leaving the jaded couple alone. She wondered how she had missed all of it. But she knew people like Alexis, and Alexis looked like she had practised this scene many times before. She was comfortable with her performance, and she wanted Kara to know she was now in charge.

Kara had lost because she was standing at the door, unwelcome, while Val fussed over Alexis. Kara wondered how night-time terrors escaped into daytime because this nightmare was new.

Alexis was now a protraction. Excitement built in Kara, and hatred whispered with passion. Alexis would crumble, and Val would be an afterthought. Turning to leave, Kara looked at Alexis one more time. She nodded her head in recognition, not backing down from Kara's stare.

'I wouldn't kiss him, if I was you,' Kara told her. 'You'll taste me, and it will ruin every dream you've ever had about the two of you.'

Kara walked out, leaving her dreams behind.

1 3

———

FAVOURS

Kara recognised favours were futile if the cost was too high. They could sink her life with the amount of purpose they required. But she knew favours could allow her the freedom of exchange, a tit-for-tat situation that appeared to be mutually beneficial. This allowed her to believe in mutual benefits, which helped her make others believe the favours were fair, even if they weren't.

Kara knew one thing for sure - she needed the power of belief so her favours could be effective. But Kara's belief in everything had been shattered by one man. Her father ignored her vulnerability, throwing her to the ground as if she didn't exist. She stewed in her denial, thinking she never wanted her father to return, that she never wanted him to show up on her doorstep and tell her everything was going to be fine. The bitterness Kara stored because of this threatened to overwhelm her. She tamped it down, defining future relationships.

She caught glimpses of herself and wondered if her reflection was real, whether this was the person she was meant to be. But Kara felt like she was a commodity. She was the tale that tore apart real-life stories, especially her own life. With this in mind, she continued to empty her heart of emotion, love included, steadily taking control of herself.

Kara's mother relinquished whatever control she once had. Her life no longer mattered. She now only existed for Kara, and the stark reality of her mother's life was reflected in Kara's. As her mother withered, Kara needed to enable herself. She needed to fashion her reality and future. Knowing she had the power to do that, meant she could make her lies be her truth.

She wanted to secure her own means. She knew there was money from her father which remained untouched, but it would stay that way for a very long time. She wanted her money to be her own, and not to owe anyone for it. Thinking about the money from her father made her wonder about him. Was it possible he had more children she didn't know about? Could Kara have a brother or a sister? If so, was he giving them all his love while withholding it from her? The inequality of the situation spoiled thoughts of tender moments. Those memories of father's love remained fractional. And Kara needed her acceptance to extend beyond those feelings so she mattered, regardless of what her father had done.

Despite her father, she knew her mother loved her. Still, Kara was surprised when her mother spoke of introducing her to a kind-hearted man who would give her a job.

'So, I just go down and ask him for a job?' Kara asked her mother.

'Yes.'

'How do you know he will give me a job?'

'He's an old friend of your grandf—' She stopped.

'My grandfather?' Kara asked suspiciously. 'You never even talk about him, let alone who he knew. Why now?' She tried to push, desperate for answers.

'Kara,' her mother exhaled, knowing Kara wasn't going to leave it alone. 'Gio is an old friend of the family. He's a good man, and he's willing to give you a job if you want it.'

'Like that? No questions asked? No resumé? No interview?'

'Like I said, he's an old friend.' That was all she said.

It should have bothered Kara her mother had 'a friend of the family' she knew nothing about. It should have bothered Kara her mother mentioned her grandfather so fleetingly, but she knew better than to ask questions she would get no answers to.

So that was how eighteen-year-old Kara approached a larger-than-life man called Giovanni 'Gio' Ricci. He owned the local fruit store, Ricci's Fruits, not far from where they lived.

When Kara asked him for work, he said, 'I try you for a week. But listen, what-you-name?' He lengthened the vowels in her name, adding an Italian flair that sounded like it never left his local village. 'Kara,' he said extending the '*a*' and the '*r*' so they rolled around the room. 'No funny business, or I no give you the job. I do a favour for your mum because she a good lady and your grandpappy, Pi, he was a good man.' He walked off without looking back. She thought about asking him more questions about her grandfather, but she didn't want to push her luck when he was giving her a chance. Maybe one day she would ask Gio about her grandfather, perhaps when she had earned some of his trust.

Settling into a routine, Kara would wake up every morning and get ready for work. The fruit shop was always packed with customers, most of whom Gio knew by their first names. He would greet them with a casual smile, gently steering them around the store, always making sure they never left empty-handed. And everyone who came in loved him. He sang songs in his native Italian, and Kara could picture him singing to his children and grandchildren and telling them stories about the old country.

Kara would often find herself smiling when Gio was singing, but she mostly left him alone. He was a shrewd businessman, but he also had an easy acceptance about him. And Gio's acceptance was something she didn't want to challenge. After all, he had believed in her enough to give her the job.

Desperation propelled Kara to please Gio. He didn't ask any questions as long as Kara was doing the work. And if he didn't ask, then she didn't have to answer. She saved money over the few months she worked there. Now and then, she would buy something special for her mother, if only to try and see a little light in her dimming eyes. Money was a new greediness that meant security, some version of happiness. And it was the happiest they had been in a long time. But happiness, like everything else in her life, was not a guarantee.

One Sunday afternoon, Gio called Kara to tell her he wouldn't be in. He asked if she could open the shop and wait until help arrived.

'Sorry *Kaa-r-aa*,' he strained down the phone. 'Something come up. Is just for while. Can you open shop? My friend's son, he come to help.'

'Of course,' Kara told him, pride settling in her chest at the responsibility Gio was giving her. 'Is there anything else you want me to do?'

'Ah, no,' he answered hurriedly. 'Jus make sure, the truck, they deliver on time. If not, call Salvatore. He is the one who help extra with the truck. The number, you find in the office, and he fix up the driver.'

'Umm, sure,' she told him. She quickly asked, 'Do you need anything?' She wanted Gio to know she cared, especially since he had given her the job, no questions asked.

'Imma alright,' he told her. 'I just need the day off. The boy, he come to help,' he reiterated.

'Get better,' she told him. After she hung up, she realised she didn't know whether he wasn't going to work because he was sick or because of something else.

It was still dark out, and winter's chill wrapped itself around her, threatening her with the bitter cold. The roller door to the shop was halfway up. Snippets of light broke through on the ground, highlighting footsteps. Kara knew someone else was there, but what she saw on the other side of the roller door stopped her in her tracks. Tattooed and all lean muscle, a man who she had never seen before was lifting boxes, readying them to be emptied and stacked. Kara stood motionless, gawking at him, her mouth slightly open.

Sensing her, he looked up and sneered, as if Kara revolted him. He carried on with his boxes like she didn't exist. Standing there, uncomfortable, waiting for instructions, she watched him walk off into the back room. Making her way to her locker, Kara got her apron and walked back into the shop.

'Would you like me to start unpacking the boxes at the front?'

'They won't unpack themselves,' was all he replied.

Nervousness rattled her. His hostility was unwarranted, and she had no idea who this man was. She didn't think he wanted her to know.

'I'm Kara,' she told him.

'I know who you are.'

And with that, he walked off into the back room. Kara busied herself with the work that was ahead and, before long, customers trickled in, propelling her through the day. Without another word spoken to her, the tattooed man went about moving the boxes, never making eye contact and never saying a word.

When the last stream of daylight surrendered itself, the emptiness of the shop echoed in the quiet. Closing the till at the end of the day, Kara took the earnings to the back where they could be secured in the safe.

It was the scent of smoke drifting from the door outside that caught her attention. Curious to see who was smoking, she peered outside to see the tattooed man expertly blowing smoke rings. Entranced by what he was doing, she didn't notice him looking at her when he asked, 'Is everything closed up?'

She nodded her head as if her voice was elsewhere.

'You worked hard today. You should go home.'

It was a forceful dismissal, one Kara knew left no room for conversation. But she was Kara, and if he was presenting her with a challenge, then she was more than willing to let him know she could play.

Shoving the door open, she walked up to him and grabbed the

cigarette out of his hand. He didn't stop her, just stared with his bloodshot grey eyes and watched Kara as she took a long drag, boldly exhaling even though her lungs were screaming. She blew the smoke directly in his face, and he didn't flinch as she dropped the cigarette on the floor. Turning to leave, Kara reached for the door and casually looked back, winking.

'See you tomorrow,' she said, then closed the door.

The next morning, there was an uneasiness in the street. The quiet street stared back with emptiness, but she still felt she was being watched. She looked around again, checking to see if anyone was there. When she was satisfied no one was, she walked back into the shop. The creepiness lingered even as she noticed the shop's door ajar and the familiar shadow crawling along the concrete floor. Kara stood in the doorway, staring at the piles of boxes already out and waiting to be stacked.

'You're late,' was all he said as he walked off.

'I'm not late. Gio tells me to start at this time.'

'Well, I'm not Gio, and I'm telling you you're late. Work starts at six, not seven. Understand?'

'I guess I understand,' she said, cocking her head to the side.

Kara wanted to know where this aggression was coming from. She still didn't know who the tattooed man was. He walked directly towards her. 'You guess? Let's get something straight. First, you start when I tell you. Second, you don't guess, you listen. Understand?'

'So, are you my boss now? I don't even know your name.'

'Yes. Dom.' And with that, he turned around and walked to the back of the shop.

He left Kara there, his name on repeat in her head. *Dom, Dom, Dom....*

He was sexy and angry and everything Kara knew she should stay away from. But she knew she wouldn't.

Three weeks later, Gio had still not returned. She tried to call him several times to see how he was feeling, but the phone went to his voice mail.

'That's weird,' she told her mother one night. 'I've tried to call Gio, but he's not answering. Do you know how to reach him?'

'Why do you need to call Gio?'

'He's not been in the shop for three weeks now.'

'What do you mean?' her mother asked, concern etched in her face.

'He called a few weeks ago and told me to open up. Said he needed the day off. He hasn't come back since, and I can't get hold of him. Not that it matters. Dom's helping.'

'Dom? Who is Dom?' Her voice sounded almost panicked.

'Some son of Gio's friend.'

'And his name's Dom?' she asked again.

'Yes. He's been there since Gio called.'

'How come you didn't say anything earlier?'

'Because I didn't think it mattered.'

'It matters, Kara!' she yelled. 'Who else is in the shop with you?'

'The usual people. All the other staff. Why?'

'Just ...' she stopped herself, reining her panic in and not finishing her sentence. 'Just be careful.' Then she smiled, her behaviour a complete reversal of only moments ago. Kara knew, when she went back into the shop, she was going to be far from careful. It didn't matter if Gio came back or not. Dom was a hedonistic adventure she needed to make a reality, and she would make sure no one would ever find out. Kara understood everything she needed to do. Dom would be a name she would exhale with the breath of his next cigarette.

At the day's end, Kara found Dom alone, smoking at the back. The ember was like a beacon. He watched as she approached and took the cigarette from his hand. He didn't say anything to her, only watched as she inhaled. As if knowing her intention, she was pinned to the wall behind her. He didn't say anything else as his mouth found hers, devouring Kara with forceful expectation. She could easily have said no and cried playing the victim, but she was far from one. Kara allowed Dom to find the path that would satisfy her lust. When they were both finished with each other, he lit two cigarettes and handed one to Kara.

'I don't want a clingy woman,' he said. Kara knew that was non-negotiable. 'And don't think you can ask for favours after this.'

Dom didn't need women like Kara. But what Dom didn't realise was she didn't need men like him either.

'Who said I wanted a clingy man? And don't worry, I don't need any favours.'

'You'll rethink that one day.'

'Why would I do that?' she challenged.

'Be careful *Kaa-r-aa,*' he drawled. 'Men like me know things that haunt little girls like you.'

'Oh please.' She laughed at him. 'You don't know anything about me.'

He shook his head. 'It's cute you have no idea,' his tone mocking.

'No idea about what?'

'Any of it?' he said, trailing his finger over her cheek. She felt caged; she had no idea what he was referring to. For a moment, she was scared. Dom had a glint in his eye that Kara wanted to ignore. His pupils darkened, and his smile promised pain. But just as quickly as it appeared, he stepped back, smiling instead like a lusty teenager, like they shared a private joke and she knew exactly what was happening. She smiled back, pretending to be unfazed, as if she knew what he meant. Only she didn't. They silently finished their cigarettes before walking back into the shop.

'I'll see you in the morning,' he said as she left.

Dom and Kara continued to see each other after work then leave as if nothing had happened. It was a relationship that came with a welcome detachment. Kara didn't want anything more from Dom, and he understood that. Dom wasn't the type of man who stole casual glances at you as he walked past. He was the type of man who had a past she didn't want to know about. Whispers of his outside life filtered through from the other employees, they used words like 'notorious' and 'gangs', but Kara didn't bother with their conversations.

And while the business continued to exist, Gio's absence was noticed by Kara. She wanted to ask Dom, but thought better of it. Something was off, but she didn't want to seem like she was prying into the business. It was hard enough to feel like she wasn't being watched daily. The feeling she got when she walked into the alley in the mornings didn't change. Some days she would run to the shop expecting to find someone when she turned. But she never looked back and never asked anyone else if they felt the same.

Towards the middle of summer, Dom told Kara to close the shop early. The other two employees had gone home early as the day's sun rendered them exhausted. Dom pulled the roller door down, waiting for her to walk out. He didn't move to share a cigarette but stood there, staring at Kara as if she knew what was going to happen. Kara walked up to the roller door while Dom waited. Just before she ducked under to leave, he called her.

'Kara,' he smiled, sizing her up and down like she was an inside joke. 'You don't need to come back anymore.' The news was matter of fact, as if he wasn't tearing her livelihood away.

'Why? What have I done?' she asked as she headed back into the shop, not wanting to leave without an explanation.

'I owe you no favours. The shop's closed till further notice. So I'm giving you notice.'

Dom turned to walk off, and she grabbed him by his arm. He looked down. She should have been ashamed of how he looked at her, but she wasn't. Kara knew exactly what she was doing, and lust didn't stick around to form attachments. He shrugged Kara's arms away and kept walking. Kara followed him because she knew she hadn't done anything wrong and she needed answers. Dom had no right to walk away, only she did.

'Why is the shop shut? You didn't say anything about it last night. You can't just tell me not to come back. What the fuck is wrong?' She looked at him, trying to see what he was hiding, but he was a stone wall with guarded eyes and gave nothing away.

'Poor little Kara,' he mocked.

She swallowed the lump in her throat, an uneasiness creeping up her spine. She looked around, even though she knew the two of them were alone in the store. Dom didn't take his eyes off her, the smirk fixed on his face.

'What the hell is that supposed to mean?' she asked him.

'It means whatever you want it to mean.'

'I have no idea what the hell is happening here. One minute I have a job, then you come in throwing your weight around like you own the place.'

He stepped forward, his face suddenly so close she could feel his breath. He leaned over and rubbed his nose against her cheek. 'I'll miss your hot little body,' he whispered in her ear. 'It's a shame it's going to go to waste.'

She stepped back, desperate for some distance from Dom. She realised she knew nothing about Dom. Gone was the man she had been intimate with. Forgotten were the moments they shared together. This man who stood before her had promise and purpose. This Dom was intimidating. She knew she should leave, run to the safety of her home, but she didn't. She worried he would catch her if she tried to run. She waited, part of her wanting him to tell her more. But Dom didn't and instead walked off, stopping only once, to look back at her with a sneer of pity.

Kara knew this sudden change in personality had nothing to do with whatever happened between them. Whatever connection they'd had was now a severed. She should have felt used and dirty, but she didn't.

Swallowing the lump in her throat, she nodded as she watched him walk away. Kara understood this was a battle she didn't have the power to win. There were no favours to be won, and there never had been.

'I'll go,' she told his shadow in the office. 'But I'll call Gio tomorrow to find out why.'

'There's no need to call Gio,' he told her as he walked to the back door. 'Gio died four months ago.' He smirked. 'Oh, and by the way, *Kaa-raa,*' she could hear him mocking her from where she stood, 'tell your mother when you get home my father, Aldo Cartelli, sends his regards. He might be able to sway some favours for her again if she needs them.'

HURT

Hurt had a rhythm and logic, and Kara could not comprehend either. It brought new, unfathomable feelings she was reluctant to share. She found that hurt clawed its way out of her heart, showing her everything that she once had, everything that had been and everything she was trying to hide.

Kara's inability to distance herself from hurt was something she struggled with. Logic had no place in her rattled comprehension as she found herself pacing up and down in Ray's room. She felt nervous, like she had made a mistake in calling him. She found herself chewing her nails to stall everything, including talking. And Ray sat there patiently, watching her go back and forth, never saying anything.

Her mind replayed going back to Val's door with cinematic excellence. When that episode finished, she thought about her recurring nightmare. A fresh round of hurt would circulate through her thoughts, making her want to pull at her hair so they would stop. Everything flooded back with clarity and tears she didn't want, leaving wet tracks down her face. Kara heaved with unspent emotion and all the while, Ray watched her unravelling without moving.

Her bag, however, continued to rattle in the corner as if overtaken by a swarm of bees. It stopped, then it would begin vibrating all over again. Kara knew it would be Val calling her. When she failed to answer, the text messages began. She could only imagine what they said:

Where are you?

Come back so we can talk.

It's not what you think.

Call me.

I want to talk to you. Please call me.

I'm sorry.

His persistence was an attempt to calm her, but she wouldn't let him in. He didn't deserve any of her time. He had chosen Alexis over her in a split second, and Kara refused to be an afterthought.

Ray noticed Kara staring at the vibrating bag. While she wanted to mute it completely, Kara was also curious to see how many times he called. She walked over to her bag and picked it up, ignoring the constant buzzing, and dropped it outside Ray's office door. If the bag was not in view, then Val couldn't intrude on her thoughts. And her thoughts were currently a collection of fragments hurtling in a million directions.

'Kara,' Ray gently commanded. She stopped chewing her nails and looked his way. 'Are you ready to tell me what happened?'

Kara nodded as if, somehow, Ray knew exactly what she needed to tell him. She had learnt Ray wouldn't say anything else unless she did.

'I had a nightmare at Val's - it's one I have regularly. He started asking questions, which isn't unusual, then I freaked out which, again, isn't unusual, and then his ex-girlfriend or someone, maybe fiancée, showed up, and I freaked the fuck out, like ... really fucking freaked.' She exhaled all of it in one breath as if everything she told him would explain how she felt.

'Why don't we start with one thing at a time.' He placed the folder on the table and sat back in his chair. Ray had her undivided attention. He was genuinely listening to her, waiting for Kara to exhale her madness.

'Tell me more about the dream, this nightmare you keep having. Why do you think it keeps happening?'

'Because I'm always fucking looking for him!' He didn't flinch or look offended. He sat in his chair and waited for Kara. 'I'm always looking for him because I think he's dead.'

'Who is the "he" you speak of? Is it someone close to you?'

'My deadbeat father. The one person in the world who should have been there for me, and wasn't. He took off and never came back.'

Her chest felt like it was at breaking point with her admission. Kara hadn't spoken of her father for years, even though she thought of him all the time. He haunted her during the day when she thought she had seen him. And, when night came around, she looked for him among the dead. Whether he was there or not was no longer relevant. He was a ghost of her past that had burrowed mercilessly into her psyche.

'Kara, before we go any further, I'd like to ask you something. During one of our sessions, you said you weren't ready to talk about your father.'

She nodded incapable of speaking.

'Why are you ready to talk about him now? This is a huge part of your life. I need to know, that once we start, you will be truly comfortable with what we talk about.'

Ray waited while she gathered her thoughts. Kara had never spoken about her father to anyone. Her mother couldn't even mention his name without a torrent of tears following. He became an enigma and he haunted Kara more in her adult years than he had in her youth.

'I'm not comfortable with any of it, Ray. But a big part of me wants to know. I knew when I was a kid that he left. He packed up one day and took off. Left me with my mum, who tried so hard to be everything, even when she knew she was failing. I had to grow up quickly, and no one was there to help me. No one!'

Kara reached over for a tissue to wipe away the tears she no longer felt ashamed to let fall. It felt cathartic to let out some of what she had been harbouring for so long. Her father was like a crematorium; when he left, he burnt every possibility and reduced her life to nothing but ash.

'How did you feel when he left?'

'I was devastated,' she whispered. 'I couldn't believe my father, the very person that was supposed to be there for me, just up and left. He didn't even say goodbye. I didn't even get an explanation as to why. No one told me anything. We moved houses, we moved suburbs, and he was nowhere to be seen. The only thing he left behind were cheques with no return address. I didn't know where he went, how to find him or, if there was anyone he left with. I know my mother was there to pick up the pieces of our lives.' She found herself standing up and pacing back and forth all over again.

Her head shook as she tried to rid herself of feelings she had denied since she was small, feelings she hadn't allowed to surface or questioned. Existence didn't stop because she decided it should. Existence was like a plague, penetrating her hollow memories and festering there without the ability to savage anything.

'Do you blame yourself?'

'What do you mean?'

'From what you've said, your father decided to leave you and your mother behind. I want to know, whether at any point, you thought any of it was your fault?'

It was then Kara completely shattered in front of Ray. She thought of all the nights she spent longing for her father. All the nights she stayed awake and waited, wishing he would come back and take her. Hoping he would change his mind, and he would reappear to rescue her. Thinking about how she wished it was all a mistake and that, if he saw her again, he would say sorry and change his mind.

'I blamed myself for a very long time. I was just a kid. I was so worried it was all my fault, that I had done something wrong.' She took a deep breath. Her lungs didn't feel like they could function anymore. For a moment, she was that frightened little girl all over again, sitting in the kitchen being the grown-up to comfort her mother. Right then, Kara hated her father even more.

'Tell me what you're thinking.'

'I hate him. I hate him for everything he ever did in his miserable life. I hate him because I blamed myself. I thought I was the reason he decided to leave, that I was the reason our family wasn't good enough, so he had to go and find someone else. He's got another daughter. I don't get why he stopped being my father, but he's happy enough to be called dad by someone else. Explain what sort of sick twisted person does that.'

'How do you know he has another family? Or another daughter?'

'My mother told me.'

'Do you know if he ever re-married?'

'I never wanted to ask my mother. She would have known, but it hurt to ask her. I didn't want either of us to hurt more than we already did.'

'Did you ever want to look him up? Or find your sister?'

'I wanted to try once, but I also didn't want to look too hard. I wanted him to disappear off the face of the earth. And I don't know enough about my "sister". But I also didn't want to see what or who it was that made him happy.'

'Do you think this is the reason why you have this recurring nightmare? Perhaps looking for him in your dream is your subconscious telling you you'd like to find him. Our subconscious mind tends to delve into parts of our lives we try not to focus on consciously. And I think a few things have happened here. Firstly, you dream of wanting to find your dad, am I correct?'

Kara nodded, pulling a manic lifetime of thoughts and nightmares into a neat line.

'Second, when the possibility of finding your father becomes apparent, you choose to leave. Why do you think that is? You often find yourself running. What you need to ask is, why you feel the need to run or distance yourself from a situation, especially when you want to know the truth? You ran here,' he continued. 'You didn't wait for an explanation from Val. You assumed you knew the truth without waiting to hear what it really was.' He stared at her, and she knew he saw the true her, whoever that was. 'What you need to ask is why you find yourself running all the time.'

She thought about her father and his new family, and it crushed her with an immovable weight.

Kara's father fled. He woke one morning and left. He allowed love into his life, then took it with him and raised another daughter. What did she give him that Kara didn't? What did she have that allowed his heart to be possessed by her? How did he decide that her love outweighed what she felt for him?

Maybe Kara made her father question the very fabric of love causing him to give his heart away to someone else. To explore feelings that allowed ambivalence to be left without any control. Just maybe he relinquished the right to Kara's love, accepting the possibility of the pain. Kara desperately wanted it to not matter, but it did. And, with that admission, tears cascaded down her cheeks again.

'I've always believed he hated me. I don't know if that's true or not, but when you wake up one morning and your father is gone without explanation, you start to wonder.'

'What is it you wonder about most?'

'That it was all my fault.'

'Why would you think that?'

'Because I never behaved like a normal child should. I did things growing up, acted out, lashed out, destroyed things. I've often wondered if that's the real reason he left.'

'Did anyone ever tell you this was the case? Children act out all the time. What makes what you did any different?'

'Did you lie on the floor and pretend to be dead so you could get a reaction from your parents?' She didn't hang her head down at her admission; it was something she remembered doing vividly.

She told Ray something a little more personal. When he didn't answer, she told him more. 'I did worse than that. I faked a pregnancy to get back at a girl who did nothing to me except be my friend. I destroyed her reputation and her boyfriend's, and I didn't care about the consequences.'

'How did it make you feel? Hurting the people who cared about you?'

'Ethan didn't care about me, and he was insignificant as far as I was concerned. He put his own needs before everyone else. People like him deserve everything they get. And Larn, I'd like to say I was sorry, but at the time I didn't care. I do now. She didn't deserve what I did to her.'

'Do you think your behaviour at the time was you looking for some sort of validation?'

There was no doubt in her mind what she did to Larn and Ethan was abhorrent. She destroyed her friendship with Larn over her need to be reckless and out of control. And, in the process, she had been expelled from the school.

'Let me ask you this,' he continued, noticing she was struggling to reply. 'Who punished you for what you did to Larn?'

'They called my mother in and told her what happened.'

'Did she yell at you? Ask you why you did it?'

'I remember her sitting in the car, calling me something like foolish. She asked me if I was deliberately trying to ruin my life. And then she was silent. My mother's silence was scarier than her yelling. I remember she muttered something under her breath. I think she swore, but I can't be too sure.'

'What did you want to happen?'

'I don't follow,' she told him honestly.

'Did a part of you think your behaviour was bad enough that your mother would call your father as a part of your punishment?'

'He wouldn't have come even if she did.'

'Did you want her to call him?'

'A part of me always wanted her to call him. But he never gave her a chance.'

'So I ask you then, do you think the things you did as you got older were a cry for help? Every time you did something, lashed out, behaved badly, your mother was the only one there to come to your rescue. Is that right? It makes me wonder if everything you've done over the years was a deliberate attempt to try and get your father's attention ... to regain the security you felt when you were together as a family.' His face showed genuine sympathy. He understood that Kara lost a large portion of what her family life should have looked like.

'Kara, I don't think your parents leaving each other had anything to do with you. As a child, we find security in our family dynamic. Our parents' roles are defined and meant to be permanent, but when the dynamic somehow splinters, or tethers itself from what we know, it's quite normal for us to try and lay blame. It sounds like you place a lot of that blame on yourself when, in fact, your parents never explained how the parameters of their relationship came undone.'

Kara knew Ray had shown her a new truth. She had never been given an explanation. Her tears fell freely at the revelation. Ray leaned over to give Kara a tissue, and she smiled at his kind gesture.

But it was the commotion outside the door that suddenly had their attention. The door swung open, and her thoughts were momentarily suspended as the woman from the front desk appeared frazzled behind Val's brooding figure, his brown eyes laser-focused on Kara, his head turning between Ray and her. He was livid.

'I'm sorry,' the woman told everyone. 'I tried to stop him.'

'Call the police, Rose,' Ray said to his secretary.

'No,' Kara stood. 'There's no need to call the police, is there, Valerio?'

The room suddenly felt claustrophobic, and no one said

anything for a while. Val stared at Kara and Ray, while Ray sat there waiting for an explanation.

'Thank you, Rose,' Ray told his secretary. 'Apparently there is no need for the police.'

'How did you find me?' Kara asked Val. 'More importantly, why did you find me?'

She wanted to be furious with him, but he had run to find her. Feeling momentarily flustered by his chivalry, Kara remembered the broken woman on his doorstep and her sympathy waned. 'What about Alexis? Did you bring her along as well?'

'Kara.' Ray's voice pulled her out of her thoughts.

He stood and walked over, extending his hand to Val as if they were old friends who had recently reunited.

'Perhaps I should introduce myself,' he told him. 'I'm Ray, and you have intruded on our session. Val, is it?'

It was Val's turn to look humiliated. Whatever he had thought when he barged in, was clearly not correct. 'Shit, I'm sorry,' he said. 'I assumed when I saw the address and the house you were with someone else. I should have known better when the woman in the front room started after me.'

'Wait! How did you even know where I was? Are you stalking me?'

'Kara,' Ray said. 'Why don't you wait for Val to answer before you jump to conclusions.'

'The other night when you stayed over, I went through your phone. I noticed Ray's number and didn't know what to think. I never know what to think, actually. You never let me in, and I've been trying. So I went into your phone and added a 'find my phone' alert that linked your phone to mine. I wanted to know you were safe.'

'What you actually mean is you thought I was seeing someone else, and you wanted to know who it was.'

'Kara,' Ray interrupted them. 'This is an invasion of your privacy. We can call the police, if you want to.'

'Thank you, Ray. And you're right, I'm definitely pissed, but it won't be necessary to call the police. Perhaps someone needs his own session to sort his shit out. But not with you.'

She was furious someone invaded her privacy like that, as if she had no right to be herself without someone feeling the need to control her. She wanted to reach over and slap him, but something stopped her. The look of defeat in Val's eyes levelled her with something she had never felt before, the kind of sympathy that took the hurt away and made your heart flutter like it had been brushed with a feather.

'Kara.' Ray interrupted her reverie.

'I'm sorry,' Val said. The apology seemed genuine. 'I'll wait outside, if that's no bother to either of you, but I don't want to leave here without you, Kara.'

'I don't think you staying in our waiting room is a good idea. I'd appreciate it if you waited somewhere else. If Kara is ready to see you after her session, that's entirely up to her, but for now I'll have to ask you to leave,' Ray said undeterred by a wounded-looking Val.

Val left at Ray's request, leaving Kara momentarily stunned. Her thoughts ran rampant, and she found herself wanting to scream or pull her hair all over again.

'Kara, can you tell me what you're thinking right now? Do you feel safe?'

'I don't know what to think. I'm supposed to be pissed at him because he's invaded my privacy and made assumptions about me. But, at the same time, he cared enough to show up and fight for me.'

'There's a fine line between wanting to know about someone and stalking. I'd like you to think about that as well. What Val did today doesn't do him any favours in the trust department. Trust comes with honesty. It's something the two of you need to consider carefully. When you called me today, you made assumptions about him and who Alexis was. You have a lot to unpack, Kara. I believe the dream you had triggered a lot of the hurt.'

She smiled at Ray, a silent thank you for giving her the time to process things she didn't want to acknowledge.

'And stop running, Kara. The person you are running from holds the answers to your questions. Don't be afraid to ask.'

'What if I don't like what he has to say?'

'Then at least you'll have your answers, and you can work on closure. I believe you've been looking for that since your father left. You can't help yourself if you don't allow people to help you.'

She knew he was right. She thought of Val, who she hoped was waiting somewhere outside for her. Kara had never had someone go to those lengths to know who she was. She never allowed anyone to get that close. But Val was different, he wanted to know her, to be there for her, and a small part of Kara wanted to let him. Whatever this situation with Alexis was, she knew she should hear him out.

'Before you go today, Kara, I want you to do a few things for me. If you have another nightmare, I want you to think about what brought it on, and what would happen if you went looking for your father in it. Also, let Val explain what happened. It's only when we have all the answers we can objectively make the right decisions.'

'I know.' She laughed. 'Because you know what happens when people assume, right Ray?'

'Exactly.' He smiled back at her, proud of the progress she made.

Kara opened the door and walked out to the street only to find Val standing there tapping his foot. Relief settled in his deep brown eyes as he waited for Kara to acknowledge him.

'Come on, you stalking arse,' she told him and stuck her pinkie out.

But Val didn't take her pinkie. For the first time, he grabbed her hand and secured it firmly within his. The hurt she felt was momentarily suppressed in the comfort of his grip.

HAPPINESS

Happiness was a measured, complex emotion for Kara that changed depending on how she wanted it. Some days, when she felt carefree, her happiness danced around effortlessly like ribbons in the wind. Other times, when she was flailing, unable to answer herself, she would create false worlds to exist in where she could be happy, a least for a little while.

Kara created something that benefited only her because she needed it. She wanted to believe this place was one of honesty, but more importantly, Kara could blatantly ignore the expectations she placed on herself here.

She desperately wanted to find purpose in her life, especially as her twentieth birthday drew near. Her last real job had been with Gio and, when that ended with a dismissal courtesy of Dom, her mother insisted she not work again. She told her the money would always be available. Living in her own apartment courtesy of the funds that had been saved for her, her time was languid with no demands.

Just for fun, she would occasionally open her computer to look for a job, knowing she would never apply. Her lack of ambition to find work mirrored her lack of degree and lack of qualifications, and she would find herself shutting down the computer as quickly as she opened it. Knowing she was squandering her father's money gave Kara a sense of satisfaction.

But the happiness she felt knowing she didn't have to work was part of a constructed reality, a curious place where no one could reach her. A place where consequences belonged to other people, not her. In this world, no one had the ability to hurt her. In her blissful, hazy world, she shut the door on reality and burrowed into hedonistic self-destruction.

It was a self-imposed isolation that provided her own narrative, leaving her questioning everything her twenty-one years had challenged her with. She wondered if happiness was a construct people built to camouflage their true feelings, a mask people wore when their reality was shifting. Or was happiness transient? Could we bend it on a whim to change with our shifting personalities?

Happiness swelled somewhere within Kara wanting to shine through her ever-grey moods. Kara wanted it to break through her ominous clouds like warm sunshine and protect her with a comfort she desperately needed.

She didn't need to question the depth of her misery. It anchored her, weighing her down to the pits of despair. It renewed during the weekly phone call with her mother. She was still suffering, and it permeated Kara's life through osmosis. She stopped visiting her mother when the emptiness she felt in the house they shared clung to her even after she left. The phone calls didn't make her feel any better.

'What did you do today?'

'Just the same,' she would reply.

'Have you been out anywhere nice lately?' Kara would ask, making strangled small talk, hoping that one day she would surprise her and say yes. But her answers never changed.

'Nowhere. I have everything I need here.'

'You need to get out,' she would tell her. 'Maybe even a visit to the market. I could meet you there.'

'There's no need to trouble yourself. You have important things you need to do.'

'You're important too, Mum. Let's meet for coffee this week,' Kara would offer, hopeful, even though she already knew the answer.

There were never any coffee catch-ups or trips to the market. Kara was consumed with guilt over it. She worried she never tried hard enough with her mother, even though she had never known what to do or how to do it. Her mother didn't have any friends. And even when she passed on what Dom told her, the name Aldo Cartelli, nothing had come of it.

'*It's no one,*' she told her abruptly. '*If anyone ever mentions that name again, you need to tell me.*' She then mumbled something Kara thought sounded like '*no good was going to come from of any of it*'. She never elaborated on what she meant, and she never mentioned Aldo Cartelli ever again.

It felt like her mother had given up, as if the notion of happiness didn't exist for her, only for others. Kara knew she too could easily go down that path because of all the things she had done, and knew she would inevitably do. But Kara wanted to explore happiness and tether out the possibilities it had to give.

The apartment she lived in was small and cramped. The neighbourhood was rough, and she often wondered how she could live there without getting hurt or robbed. So, she kept to herself, knowing if she did that, people would generally leave her alone. She adopted a 'think lots, say little' motto, and it served her well.

The smells that filtered into her room from the street would often change with the progression of the day. And most days, the window to her bedroom relayed the undeniable stench of pot. She had never been tempted to take drugs before, and had only smoked the occasional cigarette with Dom. But after getting off the phone with her mother one day, her despondency grew, and she didn't care. She wanted to explore a new side of herself - a new type of happiness that she couldn't get on her own.

Taking the stairs to the next apartment, Kara knocked on the door and waited. The smell continued to shamelessly escape under the door, and she wondered if she should leave. But she wouldn't allow herself to do that. She always responded to challenges with determination, and now her mind was set. She knew she would be fixated on it until she tried what she wanted.

The door opened, and cursed judgement stood before her with eyes as red as devil's fire. His tattooed arms bulged under his black T-shirt, and his jeans sat perfectly on his hips, making Kara wonder for what he looked like underneath it all. While she admired the man standing at the door, he peered down at her, his eyes narrowed with questions. He seemed to be wondering whether it was a good idea for her to be standing there, but he didn't say a word.

Kara always gravitated to men like this. All it took was his crooked smile to pull her in. She wanted to show him she wasn't afraid, even though she should be. She wouldn't allow her fear to overwhelm her. She stood, like a petulant child, challenging the man for something she wasn't sure she needed. She was waiting for him to swat her away like an annoying insect, but he didn't. He stepped back, turned around and walked in, allowing Kara to follow.

Kara took stock of his meagre possessions, namely the big glass object sitting on the end of the coffee table. Smoke still swayed from the top like an erotic dancer. The once-clear glass was now a mottled brown, with grime on the bottom that had most likely accumulated over the years.

A woman lay passed out on the couch, not noticing Kara's intrusion, her left arm dangled from the end. She looked content, as if she had found her own happiness.

Something wriggled inside Kara, screaming that this was not what she had been looking for. As if he read her mind, he said, his voice husky, 'You should never look like that. She's fucked.'

When he looked at Kara, she felt obligated to explain why she was there. 'I'm Kara, I live one floor down.'

For some reason, Kara felt it was important to establish a relationship with him, even though this would be nothing more than a simple transaction.

'J,' he rasped, saying no more. She didn't need to know anything more either.

'I could smell weed from my window. I was wondering if you knew where I could get some.'

J studied her for a while. She sensed some judgement, but that thought was quickly dispelled when J exhaled.

He shook his head. People like J didn't care about who or what Kara was. At the end of the day, J ran a business, and Kara had the money to fund it. Reaching into his pocket, he pulled out a bag and handed it to Kara.

'How much?' she asked him.

'For you, darlin',' he grinned, 'this time, it's nothing. But let me know when that isn't what you're looking for.'

'What makes you think it's not?' she asked, feeling cocky with the challenge.

'Because lovely things like you don't need weed. Sweet things like you need to be happy, and that stuff will only take you so far. I've got some shit that will blow your mind, make you the happiest you've ever been.'

Part of Kara wanted to laugh at this stoner and his thoughts, but she didn't. Instead, she grabbed the sealed bag and turned around without saying another word.

'I'll pass on the other shit,' she told him before getting to the door. 'I'd hate to end up like Sleepy Sally over there.'

'You'll be back,' was all he said before closing the door.

Kara rolled the joint with perfect ease. She took a match, struck it against the rigid wall of the packet, and watched it ignite. The scent of phosphorus lingered in the air, and she watched the match dwindle towards her fingertips. She lit the joint and inhaled. Her lungs filled and she coughed uncontrollably, spluttering smoke between each breath. The burn was unlike anything she had experienced before. She tried again, this time slower, patient with herself, and breathed out a slow, steady stream.

It didn't take long before her body started to mellow, and her thoughts became slow. She felt relaxed, numb and completely oblivious to her surroundings. She found her favourite playlist on her phone. Sinking into the music, her mind wandered. She wondered if J was right … did she need more? Maybe feeling different was exactly what she needed. Feeling soft and calm was pleasant for now, but she was intrigued by the happiness J described. She contemplated an elevated happiness, even if it was brief something other than her version of normal.

Stoned and completely unfazed, Kara closed her eyes and settled into her numbness. No one could touch her here, and before she knew it, she was happily falling asleep with thoughts of 'Riders on the Storm'.

No dreams of cemeteries or hidden bridges haunted her. Nor were there any questions about her past. There was a parallel life that promised a true happiness that was tethered to her current state. But she knew it was not real and somewhere in the recesses of her mind, sober Kara called to her stoned self, reminding her this too was not real. Kara wanted and needed more, something that held a promise to be both wonderful and scary.

The following morning, Kara woke from sleep's gentle caress. Memories of her fleeting happiness twirled in monophonic scenes. J was right - the joint had taken her only so far, and perhaps it wasn't what she had been looking for. Kara wanted to know what 'more' felt like, and she wanted the happiness she was looking for to bounce with energy.

He smiled when he found her standing outside his door again.

'Knew you'd be back,' was all he said.

'How does no one complain about the smell of your apartment?' she asked as she followed him inside. Kara noticed Sleepy Sally was no longer on his couch. A half-lit joint sat in his ashtray. He followed her gaze, then nodded, giving her permission to smoke it if she wanted to. But Kara refused, knowing what she was about to ask for would be bigger and better.

'People know to mind their business,' he told her.

She shrugged and waited as he rifled through his draws.

'If anyone asks, you never got this from here. Don't bring shit back here. Hear me, darlin'?'

His face settled with a terrifying seriousness, and Kara wondered for a moment whether this was a big mistake. But it was too late, and she was leaving with something whether she wanted it or not.

'What is it?' she asked holding onto the little bag even though she had a good idea of what he was selling.

'Some of the best blow you'll ever have, darlin'.'

'My name's Kara,' she reminded him. 'And I'm not your darlin'. How much?'

'Four hundred for the gram. It should last you a few weeks. Slight little thing like you wouldn't need much, so be careful. And don't be taking anything else with it. Don't mix, not even a few drinks. Just enjoy it for what it is. I don't want cops around here.'

He stared at Kara with expectation, waiting to see if warning had sunk in. Kara barely noticed. She knew she had never had anything like this before, and the thought made her excited. She pulled her wallet out and handed over her money. His hand lingered on hers for a second too long, and she pulled it away, wiping it on her jeans. J was not her friend. Men like J knew people, and people like Kara didn't want to know anyone.

'I could give you your money back, if you want to earn this,' he told her. 'Blow for blow?'

'Take the money. Get Sleepy Sally back and ask her for a blowjob. I'm sure she'd be down for it.' She walked out, J laughing as she closed the door.

In her apartment, the innocuous white powder sat on her coffee table drawn up into two little lines. J told her to go slow, and she knew she needed to do exactly that. This wasn't something she had done before. The only times she had seen it was in *Scarface,* where Michelle Pfeiffer made everything look sexy.

Hesitation churned in her stomach. She wondered if what she was about to do was right, whether it was the right way to find her happiness. The need to escape, to find something other than what and who she was, was what she was looking for, right? And surely, if the weed made her mellow, this would be the perfect way to explore happiness. She found herself staring at the white powder for what seemed like forever.

J's warning about how much she should have remained in the back of her mind. She rolled up a ten-dollar note and brought it up to her nose, inhaling the happy white powder. She gagged with her first inhale. Rancid flavours trickled through the back of her nose, burning a path into her throat. She chugged the glass of water on the table next to her and leaned over for the second line. The taste was no better. The bitterness scraped down her throat like disinfectant. She swallowed hard, trying not to vomit.

Within seconds, her hands were clammy, then her vision started to blur. In the few lucid moments she remembered, her heart rate skyrocketed, leaving her gasping for air. She reached for her phone and managed to dial triple zero but had no idea what she told the operator on the other end.

Fear like she had never experienced gripped her, constricting her. With each beat of her heart, she prayed someone would come and find her. Everything became hazy, and the happiness she sought had never seemed farther away.

Shaking, sweating and barely breathing, Kara lay down on her sofa for what seemed an eternity. Someone pounded on the front door, but she couldn't get up, exhaustion overwhelming her. Her body felt like lead. She opened her mouth to speak, and it was dry. Muffled voices were nearby. She thought she heard someone call '*Miss*', but she couldn't be too sure.

Then they were in her apartment. She knew they had seen the white powder. She should have been mortified, but her heart galloped out of her chest, and it wouldn't stop. Desperation made her close her eyes for a second. Movement hurt her body. She felt something sting her arm and she worried about her reaction to it she needed medicine to make everything stop.

Perhaps it was '*canon you wear me?*' that she heard, the voices sounded like they were underwater. '*Itch-cal*' was the next word, but she wasn't sure if it was correct. '*Heap shoe*' were the words her foggy brain collected. It was a man, and she swore he kept repeating the same thing over and over, '*Itch.... Cal... Ike...All*" he said every word getting more insistent. Finally, she succumbed to the sounds of her beating heart. When that slowed, she wondered whether the quest for happiness would be her final undoing.

'Stay with me,' was the last thing she heard.

OPEN

As she grew older, Kara wondered if anyone was truly open. She believed openness came from honesty, because honesty was a figment. Not of the imagination, but something to disguise hate. And while hate broke her apart, being open allowed her soul to be free.

But jealousy would seep through the cracks. Kara's openness would be derailed while she defended her heart. She would close it again, a vicious cycle, allowing Kara to feel vulnerable.

When she felt like this, she wanted to remind herself that the honesty she entrusted her heart to feel was timid and fragile. She wanted to find hope, to soften the barriers to her darkened world. Kara wanted desperately to believe she could mend the broken parts of herself if she was open.

Honesty frayed the fragile fibres of Kara's idea of hate. She was now willing to try and push hate away, to share an openness with Val that would no doubt be uncomfortable. She wondered how the conversation would start and end. How much should she divulge? And how would she feel when he left?

There was an inevitability to it. Once Val heard everything, he was bound to leave. Kara had to prepare her fragile heart. It was an unwelcome feeling. No one had ever gotten this close to her;

no one had made the effort. Never had anyone shown her the tenderness Val currently did.

Memories of Val storming through Ray's office had her preoccupied. She remembered the way his chest heaved with determination, the way his eyes roamed around the room and his relief when he saw her sitting there, looking back at him with confusion. Perhaps Val thought he would find her in a compromising position. The old Kara would have been caught like that on purpose, and she would have laughed, believing it was hilarious. But now she wanted to try and make whatever she had better. She knew the shitty life she had been living would do her no favours. She wanted to believe she and Val had a chance. And it wasn't even a second chance, because whatever they had together was only the beginning.

Val was holding her hand. The subtlety of it was not lost on Kara. He had gone from possessive to protective, and she tingled with the feeling. They walked through the busy streets of Brunswick passing eclectic shops. They said nothing as they headed in the direction of Edinburgh Gardens, then towards a big oak tree. The branches hung lazily overhead, sheltering them. The sun cast cinematic shadows on the ground, inviting them to sit. Kara sat on the floor and began pulling on the grass as she thought of how to start this.

Fortunately, Val beat her to it.

'I'm sorry for barging in on you like that. I felt like I was going to go out of my mind if I didn't find you and try and explain,' he said, looking past Kara.

'I'd like to say it's okay, but I'm pretty sure you violated all sorts of privacy back there. Ray wanted to call the police. You can't barge into places and not expect people to be pissed.' When he didn't say anything else, she took a deep breath and kept going.

'Val, there are things you should know ... things that will change your mind about me. If someone told me what I'm about to tell you, I would want to run far away and not look back. So, I'm giving you the option right now.'

'You're asking me to leave without knowing anything?'

'Pretty much.'

'Does he help?' At first, Kara was confused, but then she realised what he meant.

'Who, Ray?'

'Yes,' he said.

'I didn't think he would but yes, he does.'

'That's all I want to know.'

He stopped speaking, suddenly deep in thought. After a pause, he looked at Kara as if a fog had lifted.

'The way I look at it, Kara, is there are two types of people in the world. Those who piss in the shower, and those who lie about pissing in the shower. Which one are you?'

'That's a pissy analogy, don't you think?' she asked him, trying to lighten the mood. She turned her head, a flush creeping up her neck and settling on her cheeks.

'I don't care if you piss in the shower, Kara,' he said. 'I asked because it shocked you. It was written all over your face. But the truth is, we've all done things we aren't proud of. But you,' he picked a blade of grass and let the wind carry it away, 'you went to help yourself. And that's more than I can say. I left and didn't care. I never went back to explain. Hell, I still haven't explained anything.'

She didn't know what it was he was trying to tell her. She believed Val was one of the most honest people she ever met. There was something in the way he was looking at her that showed his vulnerability. He stared at her as if he really wanted her to hear what he had to say and not to misconstrue or twist it. He seemed contrite and ashamed, emotions Kara recognised.

'Maybe I should explain first. I've been seeing Ray for a while now,' she began to tell him. 'I'm not exactly a nice person.'

'What is the definition of nice?' he asked her.

'Someone that isn't me.'

'Given the chance, would you change any of it? If all the not-so-nice things you've done had a re-do, would you want anything to turn out differently?'

'I don't know,' she said quietly. 'People say life doesn't always turn out the way you planned. If I was shown how my life was going to be, maybe I would have been different. But then I would never have met you and, right now, I don't think I'd like that.'

Val reached over and wiped a stray tear Kara didn't know had fallen. Desire hummed between them, and she was glad all her roads led her to him.

He leaned in and kissed her, his tongue entering her mouth. She found herself whimpering like a lust-sick teenager, instantly moaning at his absence when he pulled away.

'I'll never tire of kissing you, Kara. I knew the first time I met you there was something between us. I can feel it. It sits here.' He grabbed her hand and rested it on his chest. 'I feel it here.' His hand went to his head. 'And I want it more than anything I've ever wanted before.'

'Even Alexis?'

And like that, the moment was lost. Kara felt him disconnect. She wanted to apologise, to reach out and move the bit of hair on his forehead out of his eyes. But, more than anything, she wanted to take back Alexis' name, which tarnished their moment.

'Sorry,' he said.

'I'm the one that's sorry. I shouldn't have mentioned her.'

'You have every right to mention her name. You have every right to ask questions. I don't want any secrets between us. I want us.' He gestured between the two of them. 'I want us to work. I want it more than anything I had with Alexis. I thought I had it all with her, but I was wrong ... so wrong.'

His admission left her heart feeling like confetti drifting to the ground. She wanted to pinch herself, to scream from the top of her lungs that she felt the same way. But doubt bubbled up within her, and Kara didn't believe she deserved what she had.

Sensing where her thoughts were going, Val grabbed her by

the hands. 'Stop! 'You are one of the most amazing people I have ever met. Stop hating yourself.'

She loved him.

Kara was in love with the man who barged into her world. She loved him for being relentless and not giving up on her, even if she thought he should. And she loved him because he didn't want to know. All he wanted was the Kara he saw before him. He forgave her without knowing anything more than what she told him.

'I piss in the shower.'

He tilted his head back and laughed, his laughter scattering the birds. When his breath evened out, he told her, 'I also piss in the shower. Now we have one less secret.'

It felt liberating for Kara to have this moment of honesty. Val made her want to separate her hate and her reality.

'I'm worried about the feelings I have for you,' she told him. 'I'm worried about a lot of things, but what I feel for you terrifies me.'

He smiled at her, and it was radiant. 'What I feel for you is terrifying as well. I feel like you could ruin me. But I'm willing to risk it, to feel all of it, as long as you're there with me.'

Kara wanted to remind him he didn't know the real her, but he already told her it didn't matter.

'Alexis and I were going out for a very long time, almost three years,' he started. Kara knew not to interrupt. 'In the beginning, it was wonderful. She was funny and kind, and we instantly clicked. But after a while, Alexis started to change. At first, it was subtle, but then it was like I was seeing two different people ... one minute she would be pleasant, the next she was mad. And I'm talking lunatic mad. So, one day, I decided she needed help. We went off to our doctor, who sent us to see a psychiatrist. She was diagnosed with bipolar disorder which explained the highs and the lows. With medication, Alexis became a new version of herself, so we gave it another try.'

Kara wondered if she and Alexis were similar. But, despite her flaws, Kara knew she didn't need to be medicated. Maybe Val thought differently.

'I don't need medication,' she told him. 'Ray is all the help I need.'

His brow furrowed in confusion. 'I know you don't need medication.'

'So, what happened?'

'About six months later, I came home to find my house kitted out with balloons and streamers. Alexis sat me down and told me she was pregnant. I was overjoyed, over-the-moon ecstatic. I couldn't believe I was going to be a father. I thought the mother of my child should be my wife, so I asked her to marry me. She said yes, and that's when everything started to fall apart.'

The shock of what he told her sat heavily on Kara's chest. All she heard was that Val was a father. The dishevelled woman on his doorstep was the mother of his child. How could Kara be a part of a relationship with that kind of connection with someone else? Such a long-lasting commitment? Kara's chest hurt with a weight she had never felt. She wondered if this was what heartbreak felt like, because all the things they said earlier, now disappeared like ash in the wind.

'So you're engaged? And have a baby?'

'No.' It was a complete sentence. She opened her mouth to ask him more, but he stopped her, putting his hand over her lips. 'I'm neither engaged, nor do I have a baby.'

Kara didn't understand. Val recognised this and seemed to sense Kara moving like she was ready to run.

'Alexis made it all up to get me to marry her. Our relationship wasn't going anywhere. We'd been trying to patch things up for a while, and she could sense me pulling away. I loved her, but I wasn't in love with her. The only way she could keep me around was to lie. If there's one thing I can't stand, it's liars.'

So Val's question about the shower was to see if Kara would lie. She breathed a sigh of relief knowing that, for once, she hadn't lied and ruined everything.

'How did you find out?'

'I knew something was up, but I couldn't put my finger on it. She went to all her appointments by herself or booked appointments when I couldn't go. She rarely stayed over at my apartment and didn't want to be intimate because she felt sick all the time. You would think, as a doctor, I would have realised what was going on. She came home with pictures of her scans, and soon enough we started to buy things for the baby. I was thrilled and, to be honest, I wanted to trust her. But then she broke that trust.'

Feeling incredibly sad for him, Kara took his hand.

'We got married.'

And there it was. While they were caught up in their bubble of truth, she hadn't noticed the sun disappearing behind the full clouds. The heavens also decided to open up and pour on them in sympathy. Kara felt the rain weep for her, washing away all her dreams of happiness. He was married. The whole time they had been together, he was married. The word repeated in her head. She remembered the ring on his right hand the night they met, how he twirled it like he was nervous. She hadn't seen the ring since, he hadn't worn it again.

His secrets outweighed hers and, for the first time, she felt dirty and cheap, like she had been used. She had been manipulated.

She stood up, ready to bolt, but he grabbed her arm and pulled her back down into his lap. They sat face to face, dripping wet, the rain pounding their truth into the ground. He looked broken. Not just into fragments but decimated beyond oblivion.

'Listen,' he said, not letting her go. 'The day of the wedding, I went looking for her after the ceremony because the photographer wanted to take some photos. I knocked on the door, and with everything blaring in the background, Alexis didn't hear me. When she didn't answer, I opened the door to find her adjusting one of those pretend pregnancy pillows under her dress. I've never felt more stupid. The minute she knew she was caught, I left. I could hear her calling after me, screaming my name, but I never went back. I was done, and a small part of me felt relieved. I went wandering around the city thinking this couldn't be my life, asking myself how I let it happen. I found the closest bar because I wanted to annihilate myself. I wanted to drink so much that, when I woke up, it would all have been one big nightmare.'

She hung on to every word, torn between belief and disbelief, thinking no one could be that cruel. She couldn't believe someone like Val could be so easily manipulated. Alexis must have known he would give up his entire world to be with her and the baby.

But then she remembered Larn and Ethan and her stomach churned. She was equally repulsive.

'You see,' he continued, unaware of Kara's turmoil. 'That day, I hated everything. When I walked into that weird, secluded bar, I had zero expectations. I had nothing to lose because I'd already lost it all. I had a ring on my finger that didn't belong there, a wife I didn't love, and a baby that wasn't real.'

His anger was desperate, rattling his voice like windows in a cyclone. Alexis ruined him. As Val sat there retelling his story, Kara shrank a little inside, knowing she would never be able to tell him everything.

'I have never experienced hate so strongly before, especially towards a person. She managed to take everything I ever wanted and destroy it, all because she was scared of losing me. But, that day, everything happened, and I know it happened for a reason.'

He turned towards Kara, his brown eyes shimmering with unspent tears. There was now relief in his voice.

'Regardless of what happened before, I have been grateful ever since I spotted a pushbike hooked on a wall that told me the bar upstairs was open, because that was the day I first met you.'

MANIA

Kara knew mania was the byproduct of madness. Madness alluded to a mental illness. It meant the mind disconnected from the body, throwing the soul into chaos. It altered reality, making the tangible unreachable. Mania did not recognise love or lust and diminished hope for the two. It could leave you bitter and brittle, fractured and bruised, never allowing anything to flourish.

Time ticked along while Kara's madness set its own pace. It never ran with haste nor was it sluggish. She found when there was no concept of time, the distance between light and dark was altered. When light and dark didn't exist, her mind covered her thoughts like a blanket of dust.

When she could no longer distinguish whether a dream was real or not, her mind withdrew. She hoped those dreams would never blend with her reality.

Kara met reality when she woke. Sand settled in her eyes, a gritty resin when she blinked. A bright and remarkable starkness stunned her every time she tried to open them. It hurt to keep them open, so she would quickly shut them tight, trying to dull the shine that remained.

In the distance, she could hear a clock ticking. It

reminded her she was alive and breathing. Memories flooded in. She remembered clutching her chest and pleading for help. She sat bolt upright, ignoring her pain. Kara pulled at the cord that dangled from her nose and gagged as it continued out. The plastic stretched long and slimy until the tip came out, black and grainy. She wanted to vomit, but nothing came up or out. Her stomach ached as if it had done the same thing numerous times in the recent hours, only, the feeling was vague, and she thought she may have imagined it.

Alarm bells rang, and the doors swung open. A woman walked in, unhurried, and turned the offending monitor off. She pressed some buttons and eventually addressed Kara. 'Hello, I'm Natalie. Welcome back. How are you feeling?'

Kara tried to adjust her eyes, but every time she moved, her whole body hurt.

'Where am I?' she asked, even though she already knew the answer.

'The Royal Melbourne Hospital. You were admitted last night. Any memory of coming in?' Natalie asked, judgement in her voice.

Kara stayed silent for a while then looked away from the woman's accusing stare. 'I don't know how I got here.'

'You were brought in last night. You're lucky you have good neighbours. If your friend J hadn't found you, you and I wouldn't be having this conversation.'

J. The irony. The person who sold her drugs was the same person who had come to her rescue. 'Is he still here?' Kara asked, hopeful he was still outside.

'He left a while ago. Said to let you know he had to go and see a *Sally*... he said you would know what he meant. He waited until he knew you were feeling better and then left.'

Kara was surprised. She hadn't pictured J as someone who would care, but maybe he was covering himself in case she said something to the police. But Kara would never say anything. She had been a willing participant when she went into his home and knew what she had handed her money over for.

'When can I go home?' she asked, hopeful she would be cleared soon.

'I'm afraid it'll be a while. We need to make sure there are no residual side effects before we can let you go. And Dr Peters will want to see you as well.'

Natalie was matter of fact, as if her job required a level of nonchalance because of people like Kara.

'I didn't do it deliberately, you know,' Kara said, as if she needed to explain herself.

'Honey, it's not for me to judge what you did and why you did it. I'm here to make sure you're better so you can get out of here. But, once you're out, I don't want to see you back here again. Hospitals are for sick people, not for people who want to throw their lives away.' And there it was, the judgement.

Kara felt ashamed of herself. She felt dirty and violated. She knew whoever looked after her last night saw her in the grips of despair, clinging to the last fragments of a life she knew she came close to losing.

'Who is Dr Peters?'

'He's our resident psychiatrist. He comes and sees people like you.'

'People like me?' Kara repeated, like she was hard of hearing.

Natalie looked uncomfortable for a second, and Kara wondered how many times she'd had the same conversation with other patients. She took a deep breath and exhaled, as if it was the last thing she had to give before her shift ended.

'When people come in near-dead from drugs, they need to be assessed to make sure they are safe,' she said as she fussed with the drip in Kara's arm.

'Whatever everyone is thinking is wrong. You can let me go now,' she said, begging.

'You'll have to argue with Dr Peters,' Natalie told her. 'In the meantime, someone will be here to transfer you to the ward.'

'To the ward?' Kara echoed.

'Yes, Dr Peters will want to do a full assessment and make sure you're better. After that, if you can keep food down, we can discharge you.'

'Great,' Kara mumbled. 'I take a little speed, and I get treated like I'm a lunatic.'

'Kara!' Natalie voice softened as she approached the bed. 'You had a lot of drugs in your system last night. We had to sedate you and put a tube up your nose so we could pump your stomach. Your heart almost stopped twice. This isn't something we can overlook because you tell us to. Too many people come through our doors and don't listen. Maybe you can be one of the few who can change that.'

With that, Natalie walked out as if the argument was over. Kara closed her eyes again to stop the light from feeling like it was creating a fissure in her brain, but relaxation was short-lived when someone knocked on her door.

'Hi Kara,' he said. 'I'm Jason. I'm here to take you to the ward.'

'Great,' she groaned, but didn't argue any further.

The activity of the department ticked and mingled with beeping monitors and hurried conversations about people in other beds. Kara closed her eyes and tried to pretend the nightmare wasn't real. But it was the voice from the next bed that had her tilting her head to see who had disturbed her.

'What you in for?' the man next to her asked. 'Suicide? Overdose? Acopia?'

Everything in her screamed to ignore him. If she didn't engage, then he would get the hint and leave her alone long enough for her to close her eyes and get some rest. But instead, Kara laughed at his absurd choice of word. 'Acopia?' she asked him. 'Did you just make that up? I'm pretty sure that's not even a word.'

'Acopia,' he continued, 'the absence of the mechanism of

coping. We all have it in varying degrees. For example, if we put it in a sentence, the young lady in the bed next to me suffers from acopia, so she was admitted to the hospital and given medication to alleviate her symptoms. Acopia.'

'What are you, an expert?' she mocked. 'You're wearing the same prison gown as me.'

'Funny and observant, but does not baulk at the ideal use of acopia to describe her present predicament.'

'I don't have acopia,' she told him. 'I have a-life-ia, the inability for someone to live a normal life.'

'We all do, in varying degrees.'

'Some of us more than others, it seems.' She grimaced. Everything hurt.

'I like you,' he told her. 'I think when we leave here, we can be friends.'

'Just what we both need, two people on a ward like this becoming friends.'

'This isn't any ward. This is the psychiatric ward. We are beyond special in here.' He laughed. 'And you assume there is something wrong with me?'

'The gown gives you away, buddy.'

'It's a current fashion phase for me. I think I look good in it. The blue stripes bring out the colour in my eyes, no?'

Kara didn't answer him, hoping he would disappear. But he didn't and, when she didn't respond, he spoke again.

'I'm Michael.'

'Kara.'

'I'm hoping they'll let me go today as well. I've been in and out all week. I can't wait to go home and sleep in my bed. But I must admit I've enjoyed the bed baths ... expect from Jones. Be wary of him, he's a dirty bastard.' Michael didn't elaborate, instead he laughed like it was the funniest thing he had ever said.

The absurdity of the situation was not lost on. Twenty-four hours ago, all she wanted to do was obliterate herself to find happiness, and apparently she had done such a good job she ended up on a ward next to someone who liked to overshare.

Her curtains were pulled back, and a short, stocky man with wire-rimmed glasses pulled up a chair next to her bed as he sat down.

'Good luck,' Michael whispered.

Either the man sitting down didn't hear Michael or ignored him. The man's tie sat a fraction below his protruding belly, and the pants he wore looked like they had not been washed in a very long time.

'I'm Dr Peters, the resident psychiatrist here at the Royal Melbourne Hospital. I've been asked to have a chat with you before we can arrange your discharge. Do you remember what happened?'

Kara shook her head because she didn't want to open her mouth. She worried the curtains around them were not enough protection from Michael's prying ears. Kara wanted to ask whether there was somewhere private they could go, but she didn't want to be in the hospital any longer than she needed to be. This was going to be like ripping off a band-aid, quick with a lingering sting. Once she was done, she was out.

Dr Peters asked Kara all sorts of questions. He told her he was interested in talking about her past, and Kara told him she was not. He asked if she had ever seen a therapist before, and she answered no. He went on to ask why she took the drugs, and Kara knew he was trying to pry into her life. She told him it was for fun, and she knew he didn't believe her even though it was the truth. No matter what she said, he wouldn't listen, so she resorted to saying what she knew he wanted to hear. She was also very conscious her words were being broadcast straight to Michael. All she wanted to do was go home and get into her bed.

When he finished quizzing her, he said he was going to refer her to a drug and alcohol unit. He said she would need to attend for a few months and that the sessions had to be marked off. She tried to argue with him, but he told her she only had two options: to tell the police where she got the drugs from, or attend the seminars, and there would be no further backlash. Kara reluctantly agreed to go.

'And Kara,' he said, before he slid the curtain back. 'Drugs will only lead you to a path you don't want to go down. I can't tell you to stop, but I can tell you, you may not be so lucky next time.' Then he left as quickly as he appeared.

'Is that not the most odious man you have ever met?'

'Odious?' Kara laughed at Michael's description of Dr Peters. 'I don't even know what that word means.'

'Would you like me to use it in a sentence?'

'Please. How else would I ever understand?' she asked, unsure why she was encouraging him.

'Dr Peters is unpleasant, almost repulsive. And, if you let him get close enough, that breath! Ayayaya!' He pulled a face while he fanned himself. 'It's faecal, I tell you.'

And that was how Kara found herself laughing harder than she had in years. The stranger next to her, turned her sombre room into something that made her forget where she was, if only for a brief minute.

'I didn't let him get that close, so I'll never know. Hopefully, I won't have to find out because I'll be out of here soon.'

'Oh Kara, nothing fast ever happens in public hospitals. It will be a while before they discharge you. I've been waiting since I got up this morning. And Nurse Bitchy over there keeps walking past me, avoiding eye contact. I'm not sure what she's doing, but she better hurry the hell up.'

Kara knew then, in the brief moment her bed was next to his, that she liked Michael. She hadn't expected any of this, but she was glad to have connected with someone, even it was through a flimsy curtain in a dull, sterile ward.

'Sounds like you're lucky,' he said as if they had known each other their whole lives. 'From what Nurse Bitchy said earlier, if your boyfriend hadn't brought you in, it would have been curtains for you.'

He was straightforward and matter of fact and nothing in his tone suggested any sympathy. It didn't matter to him why Kara was there or how she got to be in the bed next to him. He sounded genuinely like he was grateful Kara had made it.

'He's not my boyfriend,' she said, feeling the need to explain who J was.

'Oh,' was all he said, but looked relieved by her answer. He smiled. Kara knew at that moment Michael would be her friend.

'I don't have time for any of that. Who needs boyfriends if I end up in places like this with tubes up my nose?'

'Well yes,' he said, then contemplated his next answer. 'I've also seen you at your worst.'

'Are you telling me the stripes don't bring out the colour in my eyes?'

'On the contrary, I think the colour makes you coruscate.'

'Sentence?' she asked, feeling like they were playing their own game.

'Of course.' He looked up at the ceiling to think. 'Kara's gown helps her sparkle and gives her eyes beautiful flashes of light.'

'You know I'm going to look these words up when I get home and call you out if they're a load of bullshit.'

'Please do.'

Kara knew they wouldn't be. The words he used were chosen carefully and deliberately. And while she had no idea why he was in the next bed, she also never asked him what was wrong because it didn't matter. Kara had a feeling the man in the bed next to her was like no one she had ever met.

She decided to be forward with the stranger she knew nothing about. Perhaps she relinquished the hold she had on herself and accepted the failure of her life as a shadow in a distant memory. Perhaps people like Michael came into her life when she least expected them and tried to help right her wrongs. Perhaps someone like Michael who had no expectations would be a balm to soothe her soul. Perhaps she gave him her number in a moment of madness. Perhaps Kara was still in the throes of mania when she said yes to seeing him again as a friend. Perhaps mania never left anyone. Perhaps Kara had always been mad and refused to see it.

18

SHATTERED

Kara wondered if she was like shattered glass. If she was, would she ever look the same if she put herself back together? Or would she fall through the cracks?

The pieces she left behind were lost forever. Like glass, she too could shatter beyond recognition and crumble into nothingness. Maybe she could float away like whispered bits of irrelevance. Only then could those fragments be brought back together, tempered and recompressed. Either way, Kara knew she would never be whole again.

Circulating through Kara's head were all the ways she wanted to shatter Alexis. She darkened the light Kara found with Val. Kara's anger towards Val softened and, she wanted to be present with him.

Alexis was pinning after a man who no longer wanted her. But what Alexis didn't factor in was Kara, and Val's intentions towards her. Val decided to not know about Kara's past, wanting to make a clean start. Together, they were determined to find new shapes in their glass house, where they could glue everything back together, if need be. Which made Alexis an afterthought, especially now Kara knew her heart belonged to Val.

Kara and Val walked back through the streets of Brunswick.

Kara felt someone bump into her shoulder as they walked past and, when she turned to apologise, she heard a voice that stopped her in her tracks.

'Kara?' The woman began to walk back towards them. 'Is that really you?'

Kara gaped at the woman she thought she would never see again. She looked the same as she had all those years ago, only older. But the bitterness behind her eyes still cut through Kara.

'Sweet lord! It really is you,' she continued. 'How many years has it been?'

Kara cleared her throat. 'It's been a while. Since high school.' Her voice was strained.

'Oh you remember high school, do you?' The woman sneered at her, her voice dripping with malice. 'Funny how you don't forget some things,' she laughed. 'Oh, I'm sorry.' She extended her hand to Val as if she suddenly realised he was standing there. 'I'm Larn. I'm sure Kara's mentioned me.'

'I'm Val,' he replied. 'And I'm sorry, but she hasn't.'

'Well ....' She smiled. 'That's surprising. Maybe one day she'll tell you all about our wonderful time in high school. So much fun, wasn't it Kara? Tell me, do you still keep in touch with Ethan?'

'No,' Kara stuttered. 'I haven't seen anyone from high school.'

'Such a shame. You and Ethan were so close,' Larn mocked. 'Maybe we should exchange numbers? Perhaps call Ethan? I'm sure he would love to see you. You certainly loved seeing him.'

'I don't know where Ethan lives,' Kara told her.

'Shame. Anyway, I'd say it was lovely running into you, Kara, but we both know that's a load of bullshit.'

When Kara turned to walk away, she heard Larn call.

'Oh, Val. Be wary of that one. She really isn't what you think she is. She'll break your heart if you have one and then she'll laugh while she watches the pieces shatter all over the floor.'

Kara stood there, her head hanging low.

'Want to tell me who Larn is?' Val asked.

'Not really.'

'The past?'

'Yes.'

'You hurt her?'

'Unforgivably so.'

'Are you sorry?'

'I am now. I wasn't back then.'

He didn't ask or push for any more from Kara. Larn and Ethan were the past, a past she shattered without a second thought.

They walked through familiar streets, a heaviness with each of their steps. Val's pinkie remained linked with Kara's. Now and then, his thumb would slowly run over her palm as if reminding her that although she gave him his hand earlier, he would still be willing to take whatever she offered.

When they got to her place, a sense of dread came over her when she saw the front door of her apartment wide open. Kara remembered closing it before she left, and she wondered if her mind was playing tricks. There had been times when she thought she heard things in the middle of the night, or when she had seen cars parked on the side of the road, idling with no immediate intention. Val looked at her curiously.

'I locked it before I left. I'm sure I did,' she said, with an undercurrent of self-doubt.

'Let's go in, but don't touch the door, just in case,' Val walked in before her.

Kara wanted to believe her front door was open because she had forgotten to close it. But what awaited them through those doors was beyond belief. Every inch of Kara's tiny apartment was shattered, ruined almost beyond recognition.

Pictures she collected throughout the years lay splintered on the ground. Glass sparkled dangerously in jagged shards in the carpet. The sofa she sat on every night was shredded, the foam inlay exposed and torn. The television was turned upside down, and the speakers lay close by. Val whispered 'breathe' in her ear. Following that one word required all the effort she had.

They walked through the mess into Kara's bedroom, which hadn't fared any better. Her mattress lay skewed on the floor. The room's upheaval was unhurried; whoever was here had taken their time going through every inch of Kara's life then turning it upside down.

Kara stepped over the pillows that cluttered the entry to the bathroom doorway and stopped when she saw the message on the mirror. In deliberate red were the words, '*HE'S MINE! STAY AWAY SLUT*'.

'Alexis.' The name left Kara's lips like the final breath of a corpse.

No one else could have possibly left Kara such a personal message. Val tensed behind her, exhaling.

'I think we should call the police,' Kara told him.

'I don't think that's a good idea.'

She was beyond exasperated when she turned to glare at him. He was obviously in denial even though he knew exactly who had done this.

'She has broken into my house and trashed it. She needs to pay for this!' Kara's face felt like it matched the colour of the lipstick on her mirror. She could feel a panic attack coming on. She felt violated. Alexis had been through every drawer in Kara's place and thrown them around.

'She's deranged!' she yelled.

'You don't know it was her.'

Kara stormed out of the bathroom, back into her bedroom and stopped in her tracks. She was a believer that most things could be replaced, but some things were irreplaceable. She owned one thing that kept her grounded, a physical reminder of the person she never wanted to become.

Kara stood in front of the chair then sank to her knees. Her mother's chair was ruined, sliced straight through the middle. Kara stroked the wood in apology and lay her head in the middle of the torn cushion before she cried. Even though the fabric could be replaced, the chair would never be the same.

'Call her!' Kara all but yelled at Val. 'Call the bitch and find out where she is.'

'I don't think that's a good idea. What would I say? "Hey Alexis, did you trash Kara's place?"'

'That's exactly what you should do. She's come into my space and ruined everything I own. Why would she do that?' Spittle flew from the corner of her mouth. 'Either you call her, or I find out where she lives, and *I* go over there.'

Val obediently pulled out his phone and dialled Alexis' number, which rang out.

'Call it again, and don't stop till she answers. If she doesn't pick up, message the bitch and tell her to get back here or I'll call the police. And I mean it.'

He did as Kara asked and kept calling her phone, which continued to ring out. After the fifth try, Val resorted to typing her a message.

'I'll help you clean up,' he told her, putting his phone in his pocket.

'I don't need your help. I think you've done enough.'

'That's not fair, Kara. I didn't know she would do something like this.'

He walked off and she could hear him moving things in her tiny kitchen. He came back with a broom and Kara's vacuum and told her to go find somewhere to sit while he vacuumed up the glass.

'I don't want you to cut yourself,' he said in apology.

Too exhausted to argue, Kara went to find a part of the lounge that hadn't been desecrated. She noticed the door was still open. As she went to close it, she saw Alexis standing on the side of the street. She was dishevelled, worse than she had been on Val's doorstep. Her eyes were pure hatred aimed at Kara, who stood defiant, undeterred by the woman trying to destroy her. She heard

Val asking a question, and somehow managed to mutter, 'front door,' to him.

When he saw who Kara referred to, long strides carried him to the woman across the road. She reached out a hand to touch him, and he shrugged it off. Alexis looked at Val for absolution and, when she saw that it failed, her demeanour fell. Her head hung down, her face curtained by her hair.

Kara couldn't hear what he was saying, but Val pointed back to Kara, then her apartment. Alexis didn't flinch through any of it.

Before Kara knew it, they walked towards her. Her fists rolled into balls by her side, and she had the urge to punch Alexis in the face, to break her perfect nose. The closer they got, the quicker Kara's breath became. Alexis saw Kara's face and stopped mid-stride, too afraid to move forward. Val didn't give her that luxury, dragging her like a petulant child the rest of the way to the front door.

He walked past Kara and sat Alexis on the shredded lounge. Kara followed them both, unsure of what to do. Part of her wanted to call the police so they could deal with her, and the other part wanted to destroy Alexis in true Kara style.

An awkward silence lingered between the three of them.

'What the fuck were you thinking?' Kara unleashed on Alexis, reaching for her, trying to grab her hair. 'This is my home, and you come in here and destroy everything I own. What's the matter with you?' She felt crazed, unhinged, all the things she didn't want to be.

'Kara!' Val reached for her, holding her back.

'Have you seen what she's done to my place? There are things in here I can never replace. She needs to pay for it. Either you call the police, or I will.'

'I'm sorry,' Alexis whispered, as if those two words would be enough to fix the damage. 'I just ... I got so angry. I didn't know what to do when the papers arrived, and then I saw you, and I ...' She started to cry. 'I lost it.'

At the mention of papers, Val exhaled and started pacing the limited space of the floor. Kara wasn't sure what papers she was referring to, but given the frustrated look on Val's face, it was safe to guess Alexis showed up at Val's house because she received divorce papers.

'How did you even know where I lived?' Kara yelled at her again.

It was suddenly all too much to take in. Val, his marriage, Alexis, the lies, Kara's house, the destruction, all of it.

'I followed you.' Her admission was barely a whisper. 'I followed you home one day when you were leaving Val's.'

'You've got to be kidding me!' Kara yelled. 'You're a stalker too.'

'Kara,' Val finally weighed in. 'Calm down. Yelling isn't going to help anyone.'

'Calm down? Not only has she completely ruined everything I own, but she has been stalking me. Anything else you need to tell me about Alexis? Because now would be a good time.'

Rage didn't have Kara seeing red immediately. It began as something tepid and yellow then transformed. It pulsed between fragmented beats of anger, intensifying and boiling orange before it escalated to a searing hot red. And when it got there, it touched surfaces like a hot iron and burnt any reason in its path.

In the haze of confusion, no one noticed Michael walking in looking stunned. It was only when he swore they all turned towards him, his head darting back and forth between the three of them. 'What the fuck?'

'Michael,' Kara exhaled with a relieved breath.

'Who is this?' Val asked, an edge to his voice.

'This is my friend, Michael,' Kara said, walking over to him.

As they embraced, he leaned in and quietly asked, 'Are you alright?'

'Yes. What are you doing here?'

'I tried to call you earlier and your phone was switched off. Thought I'd drop in and see if you wanted to go to New Gold

Mountain. But I see there are more pressing, or should I say, destructive issues at hand?'

'You could say that.' Kara's tone was sour.

She heard Val clear his throat when Michael's arm draped itself protectively around her shoulder.

Kara didn't move his hand. Michael was the only thing she could make sense of at that moment, and she was not fazed by what Val thought.

'I'm Val,' he said, offering his hand in an attempt to release Kara from Michael's hold.

'Michael,' he offered, shaking his hand without releasing Kara. 'Does someone want to tell me what the hell is going on around here?'

'I don't think this is any of your business,' Val asserted.

'As her friend, I say this is my business.'

Kara huffed, exasperated by Val's rudeness. He had no right to speak to Michael in such a way. Meanwhile, Alexis sat, not saying a word, with her head bowed.

Kara took Michael's arm off her shoulders and walked towards Val, deliberately knocking into Alexis' knee on the way. Her head shot up, and Kara glared a warning. She wanted her to know she had every reason to be frightened. Alexis let out a sad sigh, and Kara stopped menacingly in front of her.

'You have no say in whose business this is. As my friend, Michael has every right to be here,' Kara told Val. 'He is a guest in what is left of my house. So if either you or Alexis,' she sneered, 'have an issue with it, I suggest you both see yourselves out. But not before the police come and take her away.'

Val was seething. His face was tense, and the veins on the side of his neck bulged. He only nodded in agreement.

'Good, now that that's sorted ... sorry Michael. Alexis here thought she'd redecorate my apartment.'

Kara pushed Alexis' foot away and walked towards Val. 'We have a few options here. We're all adults, and I want full disclosure. And, if I don't get it, you will be explaining this to the police. Understand?'

'I can leave,' Michael told Kara.

'No. You stay. I'd like to have someone I know by my side to help look after this *frippet*,' she said, pointing at Alexis.

Michael smiled, knowing Kara used a word no one else in the room would know.

'Would you like me to put it in a sentence?' she asked Michael.

'No,' Michael told her. 'I'll be here guarding the frivolous flight risk, if that's what she is? I doubt she has any other moves to show off in your house.'

'I'll stay.' Alexis' timid voice cut through as she looked between Val and Kara, then to Michael.

The four of them stood strangled by each other's presence. Val reached out, offering his pinkie, and Kara took it because she wanted to prove to Alexis that Val no longer belonged to her.

'Can we go talk?' Val asked breaking the silence.

'We'll be here,' Michael told Kara. 'You do what you need to. I'll be here waiting when you're done.'

Kara knew it was a lot to ask of Michael given he still had no idea what happened. Michael agreed to stay because that was the type of person he was. His kindness was unquestionable, and Kara knew he would bend over backwards to make sure the people he considered his friends were well looked after.

'Make sure she doesn't fucking move.'

Michael nodded, his stare going back to where Alexis was sitting. 'I'll see if I can find some tea in this austere abode.'

'You know where everything is,' she threw in, even though Michael only came over occasionally.

Part of her said it to let Val know she also had secrets. She also knew it would irritate him. His whole demeanour changed once Michael showed up. Val was the type of man who did not like to be challenged.

'Have you slept with him?' he asked before the door shut.

'Yes,' she lied. 'Does it bother you that his hands have been all over me? To know he's touched me in places you have? That he's made me scream his name, like he's God?'

There was pain in Val's eyes as he shut them to block the visions of Kara and Michael. 'How does it feel, Val? To know someone can come into your life and try and destroy you?'

'Stop!' he yelled. She saw her words had sliced through him, exposing his vulnerability. He looked tortured, his hands twisting into fists to hide the repulsion he felt. Kara wanted to tell him to stop squiggling, to accept her truth. The old Kara would have kept at him, tearing him down to nothing, not caring what the ramifications were. But something stopped her, and she reached for his hand, unravelling the tension in his fingers. She found his pinkie and linked it with hers.

'No,' she told him. 'I haven't been with Michael.'

Val's eyes opened to see the truth in Kara's. He exhaled and pulled her in for a hug.

'Are we too broken?' she asked him.

'What do you mean?'

'Whatever this is. I feel like it hurts too much. We both have so much history, and I'm not sure either of us are prepared for it.'

'Alexis needs help,' he told her. 'Today only proves all the things I've been thinking about. I knew she was struggling, and I ignored her.'

'Why are you so kind to her?'

'Part of me feels like I'm the reason why she's like this. And, if I'm not, I wonder if what happened between us actually tipped her over her edge.'

'So now what?' Kara looked at Val as if he had all the answers.

'Maybe we try and offer her help? If she doesn't want it, then you have every right to call the police.' He looked at Kara, asking her for his forgiveness. The day felt turbulent and had definitely lent itself into the past and the mistakes they made. Maybe the run in with Larn had been a catalyst for the forgiveness they all needed.

They sat and talked about Alexis, and how the papers were something Val should have told Kara about. But Kara hadn't known anything about his marriage until a short while ago, so she couldn't hold this secret against him. Kara wanted full disclosure, and she got it, even if it was uncomfortable. They agreed they would get Alexis the help she needed and that while Kara's apartment was a shambles, she would pack what she needed and move in with Val.

Before they left, Val turned to Kara and said, 'I don't want to lose you. I meant what I said earlier.' He leaned in and kissed her and, for a moment, she forgot about everything.

Dreams. Shouting. Therapy. Trees. Truth. Carnage. It all vanished in the hope.

None of it mattered as Val gave her everything she needed in that one kiss.

When they exited the room, they heard laughter from the lounge and saw Alexis was engrossed in whatever it was that Michael was telling her. Alexis' face was tinged pink like she had been blushing.

'There you are,' Michael said to Kara. 'Alexis has something she wants to tell you.' He nodded towards her, giving her permission to speak.

'Michael has encouraged me to find help,' she said. 'I'm sorry for what I did, Kara. I'll pay for whatever damage I've caused.' She smiled softly back at Michael, who Kara noticed was gently squeezing her hand. She found the gesture unnerving, like a betrayal of their friendship. Michael smiled back at Alexis, and a moment passed between them that Kara couldn't describe.

It was at that moment Kara knew things would never be the same. As if fragmented shards of shattered souls were now permitted to be whole. Where a friend such as Michael could knock on your door, enter with positivity and polish the fractures in your life.

19

SILENCE

Silence was like a desolate seed. It grew in Kara's thoughts and nagged at her like a child asking for extra time. Kara woke one morning shivering, her skin crawling with a frightened chill. She felt on edge, like the world owed her an explanation for the way she was feeling. She was distressed and angry at nothing in particular, but she recognised a feeling that had interrupted her day.

The phone by her bedside sat like an ominous beacon. She dialled her mother's number, and it rang out. She tried again, knowing her mother neglected her phone. A part of Kara wanted to not care, to go about her day and not be fazed if she didn't answer. But Kara knew that no amount of forgiveness would absolve her of neglecting the signs she had clearly seen.

Memories of the last time she had seen her mother circled in her head. She had shown signs of suffering as she cowered in her corner, sitting in her favourite chair, staring into a great expanse of nothingness. She made idle chit-chat with Kara, then told her to go home. Just before she had, her mother hugged her and told her how much she loved her. Kara remembered wanting to see her smile, even a slight one, like the one she remembered, but her mother's happiness was long gone.

This morning, something she couldn't put her finger on sat heavy on her shoulders. Something was off. It sat in the pit of her stomach, a horrid premonition, and she was sure it had something to do with her mother. She made her way back to the beige suburb where she spent most of her youth, recoiling at the memories that flooded in.

She stared at her door, not wanting to touch the handle, a fear in her she didn't want to acknowledge. Kara wanted to walk into the house to find her mother sitting with a steaming cup of coffee, reading her paper and laughing at something innocuous. But there was a silence.

When she walked inside, she noticed the house had a distinct smell, like soured whiskey. The windows were holding all her mother's secrets inside, nothing escaping. There was stillness that bordered on eerie. But it was the silence that settled on the surfaces that she could feel the most.

Kara called to her mother and waited for her response. She wanted to believe she was in her bedroom and couldn't hear her. Perhaps she had fallen asleep, and the intrusion would wake her. Kara waited before she approached her room and called her name again, but there was still no response.

With dread, she walked into the bedroom to find the bed neatly made, and everything around it untouched and undisturbed. A fan hummed in the bathroom. She knocked on the door and called 'Mum' with no response.

'Mum, it's me. I'll wait outside for you,' she told her.

Silence.

She closed her eyes, as if it would make the inevitability on the other side disappear. When she opened the door, she found her mother lying motionless in the bathtub. Her eyes were wide open and there was a serene smile on her face. Death filled the room with its final silence.

Loss echoed within Kara. She didn't yell or scream. She was mute as she stared at her mother's lifeless figure.

The first thing she did was gently place her hands over her

mother's eyes, closing them. She sat on the floor for what seemed like forever while she held her cold, hard hand. And, when she eventually exhaled, she let everything out.

She wept for what felt like an eternity. She cried for all the times she was there but never present. She cried for the times she should have said more and didn't. She grieved all the times they should have spent together but instead squandered … the hours that frittered into nothingness because neither of them wanted to try harder. Kara wondered if she should have fought harder for her mother, knowing she deserved better. But, most of all, she cried because her mother was all she had left. Now she was gone, Kara would be alone.

She succumbed to loneliness for what felt like hours before she finally got up and pulled the plug. The water gurgled down the drain. She couldn't look away from her mother's face, wanting to memorise every detail. She stared at her intricate lines, especially those around her small mouth. She wanted to remember her smiling, looking as if she finally reached the place that meant she could exhale all the ugly she had been holding inside.

'Go find your peace, Mum,' Kara whispered before she walked out the door.

She picked up her phone and dialled the one person she knew wouldn't ask any questions.

'Mum's dead,' she told him, her voice flat.

'I'm on my way.'

From there, people went in and out of the apartment all day. Words like autopsy, funeral arrangements, flowers and burials all came at Kara at once and, when she thought she couldn't breathe anymore, Michael would answer for her, as if he had known her mother his whole life.

He made tea when Kara didn't need it, opened the windows to free the whiskey-sour air, and never left her side. He sat through it all as if it was his duty.

When the overwhelming feeling of finality arrived in her heart, Kara doubled over in agonising grief.

Michael reminded her to breathe, to inhale and exhale, as if it was the most natural thing for him to say. He tucked her hair behind her ears like she was a timid child as she shook with sorrow. She wanted to feel her mother's soothing touch, for her to cradle her and hold her close to remind her she would be fine.

She wondered if she would always remember the way her mother touched her face and stroked her hair and held her when she was frightened. She wondered how she would save those memories. Now her mother was gone, she would never be able to get them ever again. She mourned for her, weeping.

The bag zipped and woke her from her preoccupation. She stood in front of the gurney and the bag that covered her mother's body and whispered 'I'm sorry' before they took her away.

Michael stood by her side, taking it all in, never saying any more than he had to. He gave her the space to process it all. Grateful for his presence, Kara hugged him when he left a while later muttering 'thank you,' over and over again.

The days that followed were hollow. Kara decided no church ceremony was necessary, as no one apart from her would show. A quiet graveside funeral was all she would have wanted, and Kara wanted to grant her one last wish.

She also thought about her father and whether she should let him know. She wanted to contact him ... try to hurt him the way he had hurt them. She looked him up and eventually found a number that she believed was his. She held onto that number tightly for days before she found the courage to call him.

'Hello,' a female voice said.

'Hi, I was wondering,' she said, then stopped herself. Should she ask for Dad? 'I was wondering if Joshua is there?'

'Yes,' she said. 'Can I ask who's calling?'

'Can you tell him it's ... Kara. He'll know who I am.'

Before she knew it, his voice drifted through the phone. It warmed all the cold places in her heart, but she didn't want to feel any of it.

'Kara.' He sighed her name like a breath he had been holding for eternity. 'Kara, is that you?'

'Mum's dead,' she blurted.

She didn't want to give him any time to reconnect. She wanted to hurt him with two words. He didn't deserve anything else from her, and she didn't have anything else to give. He abandoned them when they needed him most, and Kara blamed him for everything, for all the times she cried when she should have laughed. For all the times her stomach grumbled for food only to be met with an empty fridge because her mother didn't want to leave the house. For all the schemes she thought up to make people notice her. And there he was, after all these years, and all Kara wanted to do was tell him how much she hated him.

'I don't want anything from you,' she told him. 'I wanted you to know.'

'Kara,' he said pleading. 'Please don't hang up. How did you find me?'

'It doesn't matter how I found you. I shouldn't have called.'

She hung up the phone then threw it across the room, hoping the screen would shatter. It had been a mistake to call him. She hadn't needed to hear his voice, it's familiarity reaching to her through all those lonely years. She fell to the floor and sobbed, thinking of all the things she had lost in her life ... the things she would never have again. She hoped he felt that loss too.

On the day of the funeral, rain pattered slowly down her window. Michael snored on her lounge; he had slept there all week refusing to leave her side. He went home to get clothes then came straight back. Kara told him he needn't come back, but he was insistent. A part of Kara was grateful for his presence.

That morning, she woke thinking of her mother's last thoughts. How does someone process their last day on earth? Did she count down the seconds before she took her final breath? Was she thinking of all the things she would never see before she died? Would she miss Kara? Did she love her?

'Stop,' the voice behind her said. 'It won't do you any good.'

'How do you know what I'm thinking about?' she asked him. 'I could be sad because it's raining.'

'Because your tears are falling like the rain outside,' he told her. 'There's no point asking questions. You know that even if you *had* asked her, she wouldn't have told you anything.'

'I know,' she cried. 'But I can't help thinking I should have tried harder.'

'Kara, how many times did you try? Your mother made her choices. Her final one was truly her own. You have to believe whatever she felt for you was genuine. Don't do this to yourself, not today.'

'I didn't cry,' she told him. 'When I first saw her in the tub ... I didn't cry. I felt relieved. What kind of a person thinks that when they see their dead parent?'

'Kara, you've told me before, your relationship with her was strained. Shock has a way of making people feel like they can't truly express themselves.'

'You don't understand!' she yelled at him. 'I was glad she had chosen death over life. She didn't deserve to be miserable because my father threw her aside and moved on. She wasn't living this life. I hope she lives in the next one.'

Michael didn't say anything else. He didn't try and correct her, nor did he try and placate her. He quietly went about his business, helping Kara with whatever she needed.

The rain stopped when they arrived at the cemetery. A familiar, uncanny feeling slid over Kara's skin and she shivered. Michael noticed and offered his jacket.

'I'm not cold,' she told him.

The sun was peeking out behind the clouds, trying to offer a hopeful ray of sunshine. The grass beneath her feet was dewy and yielding, soft and ready to accept her mother's death.

The coffin sat proud and alone, draped in roses. The priest stood at one end, smiling to offer comfort as Kara walked towards her mother. They told Kara she wasn't allowed to have a church service, even if she wanted one.

Suicides aren't allowed in the church.

Excommunicated for going against God's wishes. Nothing was said about her mother's wishes. Perhaps she felt God failed in his plan and decided to take matters into her own hands.

Kara didn't hear much of what the priest said about her mother's life; it all felt like lies anyway. The coffin rested with a quiet dignity in her final moment. When they began to lower it, the heavens opened up, and Kara cried with the rain. She wanted to believe heaven wept for all the moments she would never have. When the coffin reached the bottom, the rain stopped, the sun peeking through as if it had won its own fight.

Michael didn't say a word the whole time. He allowed Kara the space to navigate her grief. When he saw Kara stray, he gently guided her back to the present, never interfering with her time. As they walked to the car, Kara looked back and noticed the quietness of the cemetery.

A person appeared from the trees not far from where they stood. He was looking directly at Kara. She stopped, not believing what she was seeing as he slowly walked towards them.

'Stop,' she told Michael, nodding her head towards the man. 'It's my father.'

He walked towards them with an air of uneasiness. He had aged, his skin leathered by time. There was a pepperiness to his hair, especially around his ears. And he smiled, like that was appropriate. He didn't deserve to smile while her mother lay cold and motionless in her grave.

His hand reached out to touch Kara. When she pulled away, he flinched as if he had been burnt. Michael hovered, ready to pounce if needed.

'You look just like her,' he said, as if no time had passed at all. Kara stared at him, confused, not knowing what to say.

'How did you find us?' She gestured to the cemetery behind them.

'It wasn't easy,' he said. 'But I called the local cemeteries until I found the right one.'

'Well, you're here.' Kara all but spat at him. 'You've seen where she sleeps now, so you can leave again.'

He tried to hide his pain, and Kara hated that she wanted to do something to make him feel better. She hated that she still felt a connection to him, to the man who left and never said goodbye.

'I'm sorry, Kara,' he started to tell her. She cut him off. She refused to let him apologise, especially not today.

She was no longer the confused little girl he left behind. The woman who stood before him was strong because she carved her path out of the pittance thrown her way.

'You made your choices. Now I get to make mine.'

'Do you really believe, after all these years, she wouldn't want me to know she's dead?'

Kara stared at him, trying to understand what he said. Then, fed up with him and his presence, she turned and headed towards Michael. Her father's footsteps hurried behind her, and he grabbed her by the arm, swinging her around. Michael noticed and started to walk their way.

'Why do you think I left, Kara?' he asked her. 'What do you think happened between your mother and me?'

'It doesn't matter,' she told him. 'She's dead. As far as I'm concerned, you're dead too. Go back to your precious life and forget you had a daughter all over again. Is it any wonder she killed herself? Her heart stopped beating after you left her.'

'Is that what you think happened? That I left? Is that what you believe?'

Kara didn't understand why he was saying these things. Michael appeared, asking if everything was alright.

'Yes,' she told him. 'Joshua here is going back to his family, where he belongs. I'd say it was a pleasure seeing you, but I'd be lying. Goodbye, Joshua.'

Tears fell down his cheeks, and he bowed his head. He was broken.

'She told me to leave. I wanted to fight for her, but she told me to go. I should have fought harder, but she ruined me. I loved you, Kara and I'll always love you. Please take this.'

He reached into his pocket and pulled out an envelope. He held it out and waited for Kara to take it. When she didn't, he looked to Michael. Michael reached out and took it, and a silent thanks passed between the men. Kara baulked at his betrayal, but she also knew he wouldn't do anything to hurt her. She knew, deep down, she would have regretted not taking the letter.

'Read it, Kara. And if you don't want anything to do with me after that, then I'll stay away. Please,' he stopped to wipe his tears. 'Just know I tried.'

Kara shook her head in disbelief, as if he hadn't turned her life upside down. But she felt connected to him and felt his pain. It radiated through her and pierced her already bleeding heart. His silence spoke of the depths of his despair.

Kara wanted to hear his voice once more, to remember it in case she never heard it again.

'Joshua,' she called out as he walked away. 'The girl who answered the phone ... who was she?'

'Amy?' he asked like she should have already known the answer.

'Is she ...' she didn't finish her question because he was already shaking his head.

'Amy is Claire's daughter. Claire is the woman I've been living with. We never married, and I never had any other kids. You and your mother were it for me.'

With that confession, he turned and headed back towards the cemetery to kneel in front of her mother's grave. The rain heaved down again, pelting him where he sat, but he didn't flinch. He sat there in his silence. The last time she looked back, Joshua sat there a broken man. She should have felt relieved that this was the last image she would have of him, but it was something in his silence that resonated loudest within Kara.

HISTORY

Kara delved into the pits of reflection to justify her curiosity. It was here her history became more than reflections of her past, it had the ability to stretch thoughts creating volumes of annotated tales.

Kara immersed herself in the past. She tried to forgive herself in the present and hoped to change her future. For so long, she failed to realise how entrenched her history was, how formative her history was in her alienation.

It allowed her to genuinely forgive herself and those around her. Forgiveness gave her the ability to rationalise her actions and gave a reason to create her own history moving forward.

More than anything, Kara wanted to move forward. She wanted to believe the past didn't have to define who she was now, that she had control of the path she chose and could forge ahead with it.

This was how she found herself sitting in Ray's chair, willingly telling him what was left of the lies, treachery and heartache that were her history.

'Ray,' she told him, 'Today I need you to just sit there and listen. I don't want any of your psychobabble. I don't want you to tell me how I'm going to fix this, how I'm going to fix my life. So much has happened, and I need to let it all out. I'm so tired, so ... so tired.'

So Kara spoke for more than her allocated time and told Ray everything. As if her twenty-odd years were ever going to fit into the box of an hour. Ray sat there. He never interrupted or asked questions. When Kara finally drew breath and looked up at him, tears she hadn't noticed fell like drops of relief. She felt buoyant, relieved she could finally release all the demons in her heart. Ray casually pushed the tissue box her way, and Kara took one, smiling with gratitude.

'I'd ask you how you feel, but I think I can already tell. Can I ask something?'

'Only if it's not to repeat everything I said so you can record it and use it against me.'

'I'd never do that,' he told her. 'But why now? After all this time we've spent together, why the need to tell me everything now? You've been very private about your life, only giving me snippets of things you've done.'

'Because I love him,' she told him honestly and without hesitation. 'I want to do what's right and not mess this up. He tells me what we have now is all that matters. And I want to believe him, because I really don't want to share my past with him. We've both done things we aren't proud of.'

'And what about the situation with Alexis? How is that being handled?'

Alexis was indeed a situation. She catapulted herself into Kara's life, and now she was like a stain that couldn't be removed.

'She's there.'

'What does that mean?'

'It means Val has decided to get her help, and Alexis is ... there.'

'How do you feel about her being helped by Val?'

She wanted to tell him it hurt he helped her so much. But Val carried a lot of guilt from Alexis' life falling apart when he walked away. Val helping Alexis was his way of alleviating that guilt.

'She's not only got Val,' Kara said. 'Somehow, Michael is involved in all this, and he won't leave her side. So, now my boyfriend and my best friend are in this woman's life.'

She felt angry and jealous Michael was helping Alexis. Michael was Kara's friend first, and it felt like she was losing him to Alexis. She had no right to feel the way she did, and she should be happy for her friend. Kara would have been happy if it was someone other than Alexis. But the two of them had connected, and that bond was difficult for Kara to understand.

'If I remember correctly, Michael is the man you met when you were unwell?'

'I wasn't unwell, Ray. I was off my face and nearly died of an overdose.'

He smiled at her candid response. There was no more tiptoeing around the night Kara was admitted. She had willingly experimented with drugs and, when it had gone horribly wrong, it nearly ended her life.

'How much do you remember about that time?'

'When I was in the hospital? Not much. I remember waking up and Michael was there. He hasn't left my side since.'

Kara thought back to the pompous man in the striped gown in the bed next to her. He had been there to support her every step of the way, until she met Val. Now, Michael was there to support Alexis, and whether she wanted to admit it out loud or only to herself, it stung.

'Do you remember being brought in?'

'Not really. I remember trying to call the ambulance and someone calling my name. Apart from that, everything else is blank.'

'Who found you?'

'I called triple zero. But somehow, J, the dealer got involved and stayed with me. He came to the hospital but left pretty quickly. I assume he didn't want to answer any questions. Please don't tell anyone ... J would hunt me down if he knew I was talking about him.'

'Have you seen him since?'

'Only once,' she said.

Kara recalled coming home one evening. J had been waiting by the lift. He looked towards Kara as she stood there, neither of them sure what to say. He nodded towards her looking her up and down. 'You good?' he asked.

'I'm good.'

'Don't ever come knocking ever again.'

Kara had seen J in and around the building, but they never spoke again.

'When I was training as a psychologist,' Ray said, 'I was involved in a staff debriefing that involved a woman who over-dosed. She bought pills from someone at her university and swal-lowed them all at once. Her heart stopped and she wasn't one of the lucky ones. Some stories stick with you for a long time. That one did for me.'

'I'm sorry,' Kara told him, as if it was enough to make the memory better.

'There's nothing for you to be sorry about. She wanted to overdose and unfortunately succeeded.'

'I didn't try and overdose,' she said. 'I wanted to forget for a while, and it went wrong.'

'I'm not trying to accuse you of anything,' he told her. 'I wasn't sharing the story with you to try and take away what you told me. And I didn't tell you so you could justify the reason why you took drugs. You have been very open with me today and I wanted to share something that has stayed with me for a long time. That young woman didn't want to get better. But you should be proud of what you have done for yourself. Except for the part where you owe me a few boxes of tissues.'

'Thank you.' She smiled at him.

'It feels good to be honest, doesn't it?' That thought lingered between them.

They sat for a little while longer, and let everything hang in the air. Kara found the courage to stand up and hug Ray. He hugged her back, and she knew, whatever happened in her life from now on, she had people who would help her if she needed them. Like a proud dad, he walked her to the door. When she opened it, Kara saw brown eyes she had come to love looking directly at her.

'Ready?' was all Val asked.

Kara walked out, feeling lighter than she had in years.

'Michael and Alexis want to have lunch with us, if you are up for it?'

'Sure,' she told him. She wanted to believe that it was. She didn't care about Alexis, but she really wanted to see her best friend.

Val linked his pinkie finger with hers and they headed down Brunswick Street to the bar. There Kara found an immaculately dressed Alexis smiling at Michael, who was sitting opposite her. She faltered a little, seeing Alexis there. She hated that she had to welcome her into her life after everything she had done.

Kara forced a smile towards them, and Val must have sensed her hesitation because he gently squeezed her hand. It was his way of letting her know they were good, and that he was sorry.

When she looked up, Val was smiling. She smiled back without saying anything. Michael got up to hug Kara, lingering a little longer than necessary. She squirmed out of his embrace, suddenly uncomfortable with her friend. But it was Alexis who had her attention and, when Kara only smiled at her, Alexis knew that was all she would be getting.

Alexis sat comfortably in her beauty. She appeared timid, and Kara sensed she was waiting for some form of absolution. Michael sat close to her and, when she looked down, she noticed his hand gently resting on her thigh. Alexis looked at Michael, her doe eyes sparkling. Kara couldn't believe what she was seeing.

'Want to tell me what the hell is going on here?' Kara asked Michael.

'Kara,' Val warned her.

'Don't, 'Kara' me. What is this? Don't tell me this is you helping her.' She spat all the venom she tried to conceal earlier.

'Kara,' Michael started to tell her. 'Alexis and I have been getting close, and we ...' he stopped, and looked at Alexis then smiled. 'Well, we just clicked.'

'Just clicked,' Kara repeated, like she needed to say it to believe it.

'Yes,' was all he added, lifting Alexis' hand up to gently kiss it.

'Back the hell up!' Kara yelled, the volume of her voice rising. 'This is the same person who, a month ago, tore through my apartment like a woman possessed, and you're telling me that after a month,' she gestured towards them as if they were something unfathomable. 'This is what?' She glared at Alexis.

'We all need a second chance, Kara. You know that better than anyone,' Michael said. 'Sometimes things happen, and you have no control over them.'

He shrugged as if that was the only thing she needed to know, as if everything made perfect sense and now she was supposed to accept it. Michael turned towards Alexis and gently tipped her chin up so they were looking directly at each other. He leaned in and kissed her softly on the lips and whispered, 'We've got this.'

She smiled back nodding in agreement.

'Did you know about this?' she asked Val. He shrugged and shook his head at the same time.

'Well, this is *just* fantastic,' she told them all.

There was a bitterness to her voice that shouldn't have been there. Kara shouldn't care who Michael saw. And if Alexis was with someone else, then she wasn't focusing on Val. That should have been a good thing, but it wasn't. There was something about her Kara couldn't put her finger on.

Perhaps it wasn't Alexis that was worrying her, but rather that Kara saw herself in Alexis, as if Alexis' mind games were something that should have come from Kara. It was unsettling she could relate to her so much.

'If you hurt him,' she told Alexis, 'I will come for you.'

'I won't. I've been getting help. To be honest, I don't think I could have done it without Michael's support.'

'You had help before. Clearly, that didn't work.'

'Hey,' Val admonished her. 'That's not fair. We all need a second chance.'

'And you gave her that. She only gets one more shot. If she hurts him, I promise you I will hurt her.' It was a promise she knew she would keep.

She knew she should be grateful Alexis was getting help, but trepidation sat like a stone and Kara couldn't let it go. A fake smile formed on her lips. She had no choice but to pretend and go along with this newfound relationship.

'Reticent,' Kara said to Michael.

'Big word,' he said. 'Put it in a sentence.'

'Michael was reserved with his thoughts.'

They sat there, neither friends nor foes, not saying a word to each other. Kara knew Michael was serious. Never one to willingly give anything away, she knew his reluctance meant he was genuine.

'You've been warned,' Kara said pointing her finger at Alexis.

'Duly noted,' she replied.

Kara knew this woman wasn't the same Alexis she had seen standing on Val's doorstep, dishevelled and ready for destruction. This Alexis had clarity about her that radiated honesty. It was hard to disconnect the now from the before. But Kara took stock of her own life and reminded herself of everything she and Ray had spoken about and knew she had more important things to worry about.

Together, they sat for what felt like hours listening to Michael and Alexis talk about her therapy and how her medication had been changed. She told them during her sessions she had spoken about her past along with what happened with Val, and it made her want to get better.

'I'm sorry,' she said to Val. 'I know it can't undo all the things that happened between you and me but, if we're going to move forward, then I need to start somewhere.'

The sincerity in her voice startled Kara. There was no sarcasm or malice. Kara was desperate to pick up on something, anything, that would give her charade away.

'And you, Kara, I'm sorry. I needed help. What happened at your place was the tipping point. It's inexcusable,' she said. 'And I'm sorry for all the things I've ruined. Michael told me about your mother's chair. For that, I will never forgive myself.'

Alexis looked between Michael and Kara, as if apologising to both of them at the same time. First for Kara's chair, then for the fact she and Michael had spoken about Kara. The memory of the chair churned in Kara's stomach, and she downplayed how much it hurt her.

If they were to move forward from this, the chaos of their lives, they needed to be mindful of their combined history. They needed to try and navigate the future without any interference from their pasts. Michael sensed the discomfort. He had been quiet while Alexis spoke, but he exploded with an overcompensation of his thoughts. He kept talking as if there was a need to stop anyone else from saying anything. Kara couldn't decide whether he was nervous or whether he was trying to prove to Val that Alexis was salvageable. Either way, her discomfort grew such that Kara squeezed Val's hand under the table, it was time to go.

As they stood to say their goodbyes, Kara leaned in, and whispered to Michael, 'We need to talk about this.'

'There is nothing to discuss,' he replied, dismissing her.

Val and Kara walked back to Val's place without saying anything. Kara was lost in her thoughts. She had never felt as far from Val as she did at that moment. She wanted desperately to reconnect with him. When they got back to his apartment, she kissed him with all the conviction she had. She wanted to show him they were going to get through whatever it was, and that Michael and Alexis could not come between them.

Later as she lay satisfied in his arms, she broached the subject. 'Are we going to talk about the elephant in the room?'

'What's to talk about? It's none of our business.'

'You don't think it's strange? Michael and Alexis? It's not weird for you?'

'Why should it be? They're two grown adults, they can do whatever they want. It's got nothing to do with us.'

'What do you mean it has nothing to do with us? She's your ex-wife and he's my closest friend. And she's deranged,' she said, exasperated.

'And they are making their own choices, like we have made ours.'

'There's something about this that doesn't sit right,' she said.

'Kara, you told me you've done some terrible things in your life, did you not?'

'Yes, but ...'

'No buts. She's trying to turn her life around, and he wants to support her. All we can do is be accepting of it all. If things don't work out, that's different. But, for now, repeat after me.' He kissed her, making her forget what they were talking about. 'Not our problem. Now say it, "not our problem".'

'Not our problem,' she repeated between kisses, trying to convince herself.

But Kara felt like she was waking from the nightmare in the cemetery all over again. She felt strangled, trying to breathe through this new ordeal. It was unsettling, yet she was being told to settle. Michael and Alexis were forging their own path together, making their version of history. Kara was reluctantly learning things do not always end the way you thought they would. While Val and Kara created their little cocoon of reality, they had to accept the reality of others close to them as well. They had to believe in a world that could change the course of their history, so they could settle into a nebulous form of living.

LONELINESS

Kara had no comprehension of the depths of grief until her mother's death presented itself to her like a weeping phantom. Only then did she recognise her loneliness as an insidious eggshell. She too was fragile and wanted to protect herself against the sadness that followed.

Despair cried out deep and strident, like the mournful notes of a melancholy cello. Days blended into hours, never allowing her world to stop. Time did not sit still for Kara. It drummed like a tormented heartache, which echoed in her newfound hollowness.

For days after the funeral, she wouldn't leave the apartment. Kara couldn't fathom her anguish. She couldn't comprehend this was her reality. She stayed in vacant state of lucidity, performing menial tasks, repeating motions with their newfound unfamiliarity. The hollowness couldn't be translated into words, and she grieved for everything she lost.

Finally allowing herself the space to accept her situation was real, she prayed this wasn't happening to anyone else but her. Slowly, she returned to her bleak reality.

Kara was unrecognisable even to herself. The thought of showering hurt. Even the idea of water felt like a hammer against her skin. The idea of food churned her stomach like soured cream. Empty bottles of wine lay scattered all over the floor among the scraps of paper with words such as 'lonely', 'hate', and 'why'.

It happened without any effort at all. The most frightening part was she allowed it. For the first time, Kara understood her mother. It pained her she hadn't done anything to help her.

She didn't want to admit that it was grief she succumbed to. It wasn't until she wrapped herself in a blanket and sat in her mother's chair that her exasperation became evident. That chair was the only thing she took from her mother's home. The green velour chair had been in a corner near the window, where her mother sat and watched the world go by.

The chair was the only thing Kara felt had a connection to her mother. She touched every surface of it, trying to understand. Perhaps it was in the threadbare fabric where she could sense her, smell her, feel her.

She lay her head back and wished she was a small child again, wanting her mother to play with her hair. To feel her mother's love in the strokes of her hand. To giggle as she peppered her cheeks with kisses, until she thought she would burst. But all that was gone. Now, the only remnants were the words her father had said to her. He was a message in the bottle that washed up, unexpected and disruptive.

Kara couldn't let go of the things Joshua said. His words sat heavily, and she ruminated on them. There were so many questions she wanted to ask him, yet she was terrified of knowing the answers. Her life shattered when he left. His actions were unforgivable. Kara's mother never recovered, her heart eventually stopping because of the sorrow she never overcame. But his words were like a web, and Kara found herself caught in his trap. She wanted to stop, to only think about her mother, but eyes that looked so much like hers kept on resurfacing.

There were days when she would pick up the phone and dial his number. Kara wanted to hear his voice, the familiarity she knew when she was a child. When he would answer, she would hold her breath, as if he could recognise her through her exhalations.

One time, Amy answered and Kara pretended she was calling from a telemarketing company. She gave Kara information freely: height, weight, eye colour, everything except her banking details. Kara scribbled them down ruthlessly on a scrap of paper, thinking it was all she deserved. She hoped her relationship with the man Kara once called Dad, was strained and on the cusp of breaking, like it had done for Kara.

One morning, Kara picked up the phone and dialled again. She was going to hang up, but then she heard his voice.

'Hello.' He was quiet, like he had recently woken up. 'Hello, can I help you?'

She thought about how polite he was on the phone. She tried to remember if he had always been that way.

'Hello,' he repeated. 'Is anyone there?'

Just as she was about to put down the receiver, he said, 'Kara?' He was desperate, quickly adding, 'If it is you, please don't hang up.'

So Kara waited and let herself be known by her silence. She held the phone for what felt like hours as the seconds of silence ticked by.

He finally broke. 'I'm so glad you called. I would love to see you again.'

She didn't acknowledge what he said. Her breath was the only thing letting him know she was listening.

'You don't have to say anything. Please give me a chance to explain everything. Then you can make up your mind. Please ...' The desperation in his voice sounded genuine.

But Kara also knew she didn't owe him anything. Joshua was still the man who left. Anger replaced curiosity, and she yelled at him down the line.

'The time for explaining should have been before you left. I don't care what you want to tell me now. Mum is dead, and you don't care.' She sobbed.

She let out all her anger, and he didn't interrupt her. He waited till she stopped crying, then spoke to her as if she was a frightened child.

'Kara, I care. I care so much. Please,' he begged. 'Just hear me out, I promise. After that, if you don't want anything to do with me, then I'll leave.'

'Again?' she spat the words.

'Please hear me out.'

She went against her better judgement and decided to let him in, to allow him to finally give her the goodbye she needed when she was a little girl. Perhaps it was the closure Kara was looking for.

They decided to meet at her apartment the following day. That way he could leave, and she could fall apart in her own space.

'You finally spoke to him.' Michael's voice snapped her out of her thoughts. He walked over to where she stood and threw his arms around her. He lingered a little longer than necessary. When Kara went to break free, he took her face in his hands and whispered, 'God, Kara.'

There are moments in life that feel completely out of your control and, with Michael standing so close, Kara felt this was one of them. He was probing her eyes, trying to get close to her soul. When she blinked and looked away, closing herself off, his hands dropped, and he stepped back.

'Don't,' she warned him. She knew exactly where he wanted this conversation to go. Michael needed to be her friend and nothing more. They had been through so much since their days in the hospital. She didn't need Michael turning into a therapist.

'Maybe you should hear him out?' he suggested.

'Why? Because he says I should?' Her voice full of scepticism.

'Because it might give you answers you need.'

He was right, but admitting it out aloud would mean confronting the truth.

'What if I don't want answers?' Her denial was unconvincing, even to herself.

'Then take what you need and, do with the information as you wish.'

'Whose side are you on?'

He walked towards her and placed both his hands on her shoulders. 'Yours. Always yours.'

'It doesn't feel like that right now,' she admitted.

'Quakebuttock,' he said.

'Do I even need to ask?' she laughed, but her smile didn't reach her eyes.

'The Kara I know, is most definitely *not* a cowardly person.'

'Maybe I am, and I don't want to admit it.'

'I never thought you would be the type of person to shy away from something. Especially something as significant as this.'

'It might be the only way I can go on,' she said.

'You know you can't go on like this.'

But she didn't have the capacity to entertain anything other than getting through the day.

'Please don't make this hard.'

'This is already hard. I am not going to say I understand, because clearly I don't. But what I do know is my friend is suffering and will not leave this house. It's been three months since your mother died, and I feel like you haven't seen daylight since. When was the last time you went out for a coffee or to hang at the bar? You need to start living again, Kara. Staying trapped inside will do you more harm than good.'

Kara knew everything changed after her mother's death. She couldn't understand why Michael wouldn't let her grieve in the loneliness she found comfort in.

'I need my friend right now. The one who challenges me with words I have no intention of learning. You're my only friend, Michael. So please be that and nothing else. You are the one genuine thing I have left in my life.'

'I knew you secretly loved my philavery,' he told her.

'Let me guess.' She smiled at him. 'Michael loves the use of words?'

'Something like that.'

He leaned in and hugged her as Kara cried, wetting his shirt. She wondered where the tears continued to come from or whether they would ever stop. At the end of the day, it didn't matter how much she cried, because she knew Michael would always be by her side, trying to make her laugh and forget about her troubles.

'I promise to be your friend and not your therapist. But I must say, I would love to get inside that head of yours one day ... find out who Kara was before I found her looking so glamorous with a tube stuck up her nose. Maybe I can ask J for some help?'

'Maybe I can ask J next time you are there to find out why I met you wearing pinstripes,' she laughed back at him. When he didn't say anything in response, she knew she had overstepped her mark. Michael had never given her the details of why he ended up in the bed next to her. He had only told her it wouldn't happen again.

'Rantipole.'

'Put it in a sentence,' she told him.

'Michael is a young, wild person who is going to see J.'

He got up to leave. Kara wanted to beg him to stay so she could tell him everything about her dad. Instead, she gave him a broken smile as she closed the door.

Exhaustion settled in Kara's bones, and her bed called her in comfort. As she lay her head down, dreams tormented her. The years were all condensed into hours, their vividness leaving her gasping for air when she woke.

There was a knocking at her door. It stopped for a second only to start again.

'Coming!' she yelled to the door.

She opened it to see familiar eyes reflecting back at her, and his tears stopped her heart. Her father was standing on her doorstep, desperation in his eyes. He looked as though he hadn't slept since they had spoken. His hair stood upright as if he had been pulling at it in frustration. But it was his eyes that startled her because they were looking for forgiveness.

Kara stepped aside without a word, letting him into her apartment. She laughed at the made-up conversations she had practised in her head for this very moment. But reality had a way of catching you unaware, those practised lines fading into jumbled words and afterthoughts.

He stood in the kitchen, rubbing his hands together while looking around Kara's apartment. When no one moved or said anything, she walked over to the kettle and turned it on to make coffee.

'I'm sorry for showing up, but I couldn't sleep after we got off the phone. I wanted to come and see you.'

He sipped on his coffee and blew into the steaming cup. When she couldn't stand the silence anymore, she broke and slammed the cup on the bench. All the bottled-up hatred she'd had over the years started to spew out.

'You left!' she yelled. 'You left and you never told me why. Mum pined away after you and never went back to being who she was. She tried so hard to make up for both of you, to love me without making me feel like I was missing out. But you broke her, and I had to try and pick up what you left behind. Why are you here?'

'You called me!' he said. 'You called!'

'And, if I hadn't, you'd still be there with the perfect family that you have now.'

'It's not like that. It was never like that,' he said.

'Then what was it like, huh? I get up one morning and you're gone. Mum was a shell of a person sitting there, waiting for you to come back. Then I find out you have this family you've been with while we struggled to live.'

'There's so much you don't know, Kara. I don't know if you'd believe me if I told you.'

'Then try! Tell me everything I need to know so you can go

back and live the life you chose … the life that *you* left us for.' Her chest heaved, hurting with anger.

Part of her wanted to throw him out, to tell him to leave and never come back. But the other part, wanted to know what was so good about the other family that he chose them over her.

'She made me go,' he whispered.

'Who made you go?'

'Your mother. She threatened me. They threatened you. I didn't want to leave you. I should have taken you with me, but …' he stopped. His head hung with shame, and she knew whatever he was about to say was going to crush her.

This man, who had been absent from her life, was about to change everything Kara ever knew. His truth was about to make her question her reality, and she wasn't sure how much she wanted to believe.

When he didn't say any more, Kara headed toward the door.

'I'm not leaving Kara, not until I've said what I need to say,' he told her.

'You've had plenty of chances. I wasn't a kid my whole life,' she said. 'You could have found me.'

'I knew where you were,' he whispered. 'I made sure she wasn't going to leave with you.'

'You knew?' She was stunned into silence.

He had known exactly where she was, where she lived, how she lived, yet he had done nothing.

'I don't know what's worse,' she told him. 'The fact that you knew where I was, or the fact you did nothing even though you could have. You never even sent me a note, not a single thing. A letter, anything that said, *Dear Kara, I love you, I miss you, I'm sorry,* but all I got was silence. Mum's dead, she's not here to defend herself, so I don't know what you want me to believe. But coming here and telling me all these half-truths, not giving me any answers, doesn't cut it.' She pulled the door open. 'Don't let the door hit you on the way out, Joshua.'

He jolted at the mention of his name, and she knew she hurt

him by not calling him dad. He lost the right to that title when he decided not to return. Reluctantly, he got off the barstool and walked towards the door.

'You have her smile.' He was trying to placate her.

'You had her heart.'

He looked at the envelope with her mother's distinctive writing on the coffee table.

'It's all there, Kara. Let me know what you decide after you read it. She loved you, but they loved her more. I had no choice.' With that, he whispered *I love you* then walked out the door.

As he walked, she was reduced to that small child once again, waiting by the window with the hope her father would come back.

The envelope felt heavy with secrets. Trepidation had her stalling to open it up. She knew that letter would change the course of her life, she wasn't sure how.

In the weeks that followed, she willed the envelope on the coffee table to disappear. She hadn't heard from Joshua again, a reminder he was willing to give Kara some space to understand what he left behind. Michael called throughout the week, sounding edgy every time she mentioned the envelope and her father.

He asked her why she was reluctant to open it, and she told him it was because it wouldn't change anything: her mother would still be dead, and her father was gone from her life. Except she knew he wasn't.

A month after it had been left there, Kara sat down and traced her ink-stained name on the envelope. When she opened it, a photo dated 1989 fell out. There in glorious colour was a photo of her mother and father, smiling, on their wedding day. She looked inside and a few more photos fell out, some of her mother and father a few years before that, then one of them surrounded by three men Kara didn't recognise. There was another photo of an older woman who looked just like her mother and a stern-looking man with a moustache who wasn't smiling.

She flipped the photo over: *Me, Joshua, Antonio, Matteo, Franco, Mum and Dad, Adelaide 1986.*

She looked back at the photo and a memory flashed: a vision of her twirling in a dress before a party. She swore she could smell tobacco, then recognised the people in the photo as *Pi* and *Nonna*. But they were vague memories. She knew her mother told her once her grandparents were dead, that they died when she was little, but she couldn't recall the rest of the family.

There were no more photos, only a heavy letter inside.

'Ready,' she told herself.

Pouring a glass of wine, she nestled into the couch and pulled the papers out. There in the boldest writing was her name: Kara Collins. It contained her full birth certificate declaring her **KARINA LUCIA BENETTI COLLINS**.

Behind it was another page with her name in her mother's beautiful cursive writing:

Kara,
The truth lies within these pages.
I did what I had to do. I'll always love you.
Love Mum x

Lonely drops fell from her eyes before she even turned the page. There was a sense of nostalgia in seeing her mother's writing. But life is like a rolling boulder that smashes through your world. Kara's life was about to be ruined, and she feared she would never be able to come back from it. *Dear Kara ...*

2 2

LETTERS

D*ear Kara,*

I'm sorry. Children are meant to feel safe because that's what their parents are supposed to provide, and I failed to do that for you. Forgiveness isn't just a word but also a gesture that should be offered to you by the people who love you most. I've been unsuccessful with both. There was little in this world that I wanted more than anything: your father was one of them and you were the other.

There are so many things I should have said, and so many things I should have told you. While it saddens me to know you'll find things out by reading this, it also means I've finally been liberated and allowed to fly free.

Firstly, don't be sad about my death. You owe me nothing. I don't want you to surround your days with grief because you have so many days with joy to live for. And I want you to live them, Kara. Go find your true happiness and never let anyone steal it from you, because people will.

By now, I'm hoping your father has found you. He is not to blame for anything that happened in our lives. I know this most likely doesn't make sense, but hopefully, by the time you finish reading, it will.

I hope you will be able to find your father and freely live the life that was destined for you. When people try and control your life, they take everything you have and use it to change your intended path. Forge your way forward and do it with everything you have. Don't leave anything behind, and don't go looking for it if you do. Don't let fear get in the way and, most importantly, don't run. You and I have been runners our whole lives. You've inherited the need to distance yourself, putting up walls, escaping through lies and believing you aren't worth it. And I know this, Kara. I know who you are, even if you think I never saw you. And I loved you, knowing what you were trying to do.

The truth has a way of exposing itself regardless of how well it's kept. And this truth is not only part of who you are, but a heritage I've tried to contain for as long as you've been alive. I made choices that didn't end well for anyone. I chose to distance myself and disengage from my family, and the consequences of my actions were something I had to live with. But I will suffer all over again, knowing I did it all for us.

In the envelope, you would have found some photos. You may have a few questions about who some of the people in them are. There is also a birth certificate that has your original name. We all had amended birth certificates drawn up when your father and I decided it was time to change. Your full name when you were born was Karina Lucia Benetti Collins.

You are a Benetti by blood, the granddaughter of one of the biggest mafia bosses to migrate to Australia from Sicily. Your grandfather Pi, Piero Benetti, was born and raised in the village of Montalbano where he met your grandmother, Amelia, when he was nineteen. They married shortly after and had the three uncles you see in the photos, then they had me.

I was the only girl in the family and my protection was something they took seriously. Not long after I was born, your great-grandfather was gunned down in the middle of the street when he and your great-grandmother were coming home from the market. The bullet that killed him ricocheted and hit your great-grand-

mother as well. She died a week later in the hospital, and no one knows if it was from the bullet or a broken heart.

Panicked the rest of the family would be targeted, your grandparents decided to leave Italy and come to Australia where they could start a new life. Your grandfather was still engrossed in the family trading business and, not long after he came to Australia, he sought out the local community in Melbourne. People were frightened of him. He was known for his ruthless dealings, but he also had a softer side.

Melbourne was such a vibrant place to grow up. Weekends would be spent with extended family, and we never questioned who they were. Your uncles worked for your grandfather and, eventually. Their wives were handpicked to provide a long line of heirs to be integrated into the family business.

Antonio was the eldest and lived not far from your grandparents with his wife Hannah and their two children, Angelo and Carlo. I watched them grow up and settle into the lives expected of them. Antonio had a ruthlessness behind him that was similar to your grandfather. But your grandfather ran the business with a sense of compassion, something Antonio did not have.

He was known for roughing people up, demanding payment if they were a day late, and being angry all the time. People grew to dislike him, and he had more enemies than he did friends. His wife left with his two children before your sixth birthday, fleeing the country for fear someone would try and harm her and the kids. I never heard what happened to her but I hope that, somewhere along the way, she found happiness and forgot the life she once lived.

When I was seventeen, your uncle Franco, my second eldest brother, married and he and his wife fell pregnant shortly after. Unfortunately, she suffered complications during the birth and died, leaving Franco with a son named Micha. The family rallied behind him and decided Franco and your uncle Matteo should move to Adelaide and join another family in the wine-making business. They settled on a large property in the Adelaide Hills and had little to do with anyone else.

As I grew older, I began to grow restless. I didn't want my family telling me what I should do. I wanted to be free from all of them. I didn't care what my father did or what he did with the business. I struggled to make friends, and the idea of bringing someone home that wasn't part of their circle was impossible. Everyone in the family married who they were told. It was all set in stone, a sacrifice you had to make for the family's sake.

But life has a strange way of showing you a different path.

The day I met your father, I was thinking about enrolling in university. I remember walking through Alexandra Gardens, thinking about all the classes I could enrol in. I desperately wanted to be a psychologist. I wanted to help people. I thought if I could help others, I could also escape my own life. Your grandfather had been hinting I should get married but, unlike your uncles, they hadn't chosen anyone for me yet. A part of me hoped they would change their mind.

We would argue, and I would remind them we were in a country where forced marriage was illegal. I told them if they demanded this of me, I would run away, and they would never see me again. They let me be for a while, letting me believe I was getting my own way, but it was only a matter of time. Then, one day, I bumped into a man who changed my life - your father.

He helped me enrol at Melbourne University, and only then did I tell my parents what I had done. They screamed at me, telling me women belonged in the family business but, as usual, I stood my ground and told them that this was what I was going to do. So, along with going to my classes, I managed to see your father every day, and it wasn't long before we fell in love.

I didn't tell him who I was or mention who my family were. We lived in a blissful bubble of university life. One day, your Uncle Antonio came to pick me up and saw me kissing your dad. By the time I got home, my parents knew everything about your father. Your grandfather called me every name under the sun. He threatened to send me back to Italy where they would 'fix' me. He told me

I'd have to marry a good Italian man and produce a big family for them to be proud of.

Only I didn't stand for it. Your father encouraged me to be strong and to fight for what I believed in, so I did. I invited your father over and didn't tell your grandparents he was coming. We walked into the kitchen to find your Uncle Antonio deep in conversation with your grandfather. They looked up, glaring at your dad, but he wouldn't have any of it. He walked straight up to your grandfather and introduced himself, telling him he was in love with his daughter and there was nothing he could do about it.

It took weeks of your father going over before they finally allowed him in. But it was always at arms-length. Your father wasn't bothered by their lack of acceptance and never shied away from showing them how much he loved me. I loved him as well. Know that I loved your father with everything I had. He was the sole purpose for my existence, the only reason I knew what love was, and the reason why I wanted to stand against my family and make my life my own.

After a year of us being together, your Uncle Matteo sent a message saying he was engaged to a woman called Gabriella Cartelli. She was the niece of Stefani Ricci. Gio Ricci was her husband, and he ran the local fruit store. Stefani had a cousin named Aldo, whose wife Julia sadly passed away from cancer about four years before Matteo's engagement, leaving Aldo to look after Gabriella and her much younger brother Domenic.

Your grandfather flew into a fit of rage. He told your Uncle Matteo he would not attend the engagement party because he and Aldo Cartelli had history, adding, no son of his was going to marry a Cartelli. Your grandmother tried to reason with him, telling him the union would be a good thing for both families, and to bury whatever bad blood there was between them. She told him she hoped Matteo would give them more grandchildren, and that grandchildren were always a way to bring families together. She was full of hope. She adored Gabriella, but more than anything she wanted your grandfather to end whatever it was with Aldo and accept Gabriella into the family.

The tensions between the Cartellis and your grandparents stemmed back to the village. I never understood them because I never wanted to get involved. I was ecstatic for your Uncle Matteo; and he truly loved Gabriella. Your father and I knew firsthand what it was like to have your grandfather stand in the way.

Gio listened to what your grandfather had to say and, for the sake of your Uncle Matteo and Gabriella, he rallied and pleaded to both families. He asked them to put aside their differences, telling them he hoped the union would bring everyone together rather than tear them apart. Your grandfather eventually listened to Gio, saying if Aldo would put aside their differences, he would too.

I was adamant that I bring your father to these meetings, but your grandfather told me he was not welcome at family events. When I argued he was my family, he said he didn't see a ring on my finger and that I wasn't bringing someone who knew nothing about the family.

Shortly after that argument, I drove to your father's place, sat down and told him everything about who I was and where my family came from. When I was done, I told him I would under-stand if he never wanted to see me again. But he told me he didn't run away from love. And much to your grandfather's disgust, that night I went home wearing your great-grandmother's sapphire on my hand. It was our way of showing them we were serious and there was nothing they could do to stop us. I didn't know how wrong we would be.

The following year, in front of a small crowd, we married in Alexandra Gardens where we first met. I was so happy I became Isabella Benetti-Collins. I finally found the freedom I craved. We were so happy. But in the shadow that was our life, there was also an element of fear. I worried my future had been written in stone and I would never be able to escape it.

The year after, you were born with a screaming curiosity I know you still possess. As a child, you wanted to be into everything and, the more you grew, the further away from my side of the family I wanted to keep you. Your grandmother would beg to see you and, when I would relent and take you, she would hug you and cry.

She would say, 'Isabella, take her and move. If your father heard me telling you this, my life would be miserable. But you must protect your family. This life is not for everyone, and Karina deserves a life away from all of it. Don't let the family consume you. Run now, take Karina and Joshua, and build a life somewhere. Don't tell us where. But send me photos of my precious principessa.'

But we didn't leave. We remained in our ignorant bliss, pretending to live our lives as if nothing mattered and the family business wasn't a cloud of troubled ruin.

Years passed. We tried for another baby, but it wasn't meant to be. We went to every doctor money could buy, but no one could help us. There were a few times when I would fall pregnant, but I could never make it past the twelve weeks without miscarrying.

A week before your sixth birthday, I woke from a dream panicked, thinking it had been real. Your father sat with me most of the night, reassuring me it was a dream and there was nothing to worry about. But we both knew it was a lie. Your Uncle Antonio was in a dark place, and his dealings with the other families were caught in a crossfire of hatred and deceit. Your grandmother only phoned occasionally, but when she did, she would tell me how much she loved me and to never forget her conversation about leaving.

We settled into our home, and we didn't want to leave. You were comfortable in your school, but you also had a twinkle in your eye that kept us all on our toes.

The night before your birthday, your Uncle Antonio met in secret with someone from the Cartelli family. Antonio was determined to up the amount of money coming into the family. The Cartelli family were well known for their influence in the drug trade, and while your grandfather's 'business' was clean, Antonio muddied it with the shake of his hand.

That night, Antonio was abducted and tortured. He crossed an invisible family line during the meeting. When your grandfather got word of what happened, he called an emergency meeting with other families. He didn't know Antonio had already been tortured to death. But he went in adamant with belief that forgiveness in the business was still possible. He wanted to make amends for Matteo and Gabriella's sake.

After the news of Antonio's death, your grandmother phoned me again and told me to leave. Your father was wary and agreed we should go. But I assumed I was too far removed from the business. I wanted to believe no one knew me or us.

With Antonio dead, your uncles wanted revenge. Your grandfather was adamant they stay - one dead son was one too many. He waited for it all to simmer down, grieving privately for Antonio while maintaining the façade that the family business didn't falter or change. It was, by all accounts, business as usual.

On the day of Antonio's funeral, your grandfather sat through the eulogy without a word. Your grandmother was broken beyond repair, and I knew she would never recover from her grief.

I cried that day. and it wasn't because Antonio died. I cried at the thought of something happening to you. I knew I could never forgive myself. When I came home, sombre and draped in black, reeking of grief, I surrendered the Benetti surname and became Isabella Collins, in case anyone came looking for us.

Months went by without any word from your grandparents. I worried for your grandmother. Antonio's death tormented her, but she also worried for the safety of her other children. While the boys were in Adelaide, they were protected by the families they lived with. Your father and I lived freely with little or no connection to anyone else, but there were always concerns that people already knew who we were.

Eventually, there was a call for calm from the heads of the other families. But your grandfather was Sicilian, and, where he came from, it was an eye for an eye and nothing less. He soon arranged that the brother of Aldo Cartelli would suffer the same as your Uncle Antonio. He was captured and tortured, and rumour has it he was sent back in a bag to his family.

Everyone hoped this was the end, that the families would go about their daily business, and nothing further would be said or done.

But, on a cold July night, two years after Antonio was tortured, someone broke into your grandparents' house in the dead of night and strangled your grandfather to death. They roughed up your grandmother before they left. She called Matteo to tell him what happened, and he put her on a plane. To this day, I have no idea where she is or if she is still alive. It pains me to think she grieved for all the things she lost in silence.

When Matteo called to tell me your grandfather was dead, I didn't cry, because I always expected something like that would happen. His body was quickly taken away from the house, and it never made the news.

Your father was livid. He told me we should have left years ago, and I was too stubborn to see any better. He said my family would be our downfall and he was tired of looking over his shoulder. He said we all deserved better. He worried someone would come and do the same to us.

I told him to leave, to go far away, but he didn't want to leave you. He threw himself into his work and would often stay late. I was angry and accused him of having affairs with women I knew nothing about. I wanted to hurt him so he would leave freely. If he went with hatred in his heart, it would be easier for him to let go. Terror made me do all sorts of strange things.

The night before I made your father leave, I received a letter: a warning I should be concerned about my family and your father in particular. The letter said:

'Retribution spills blood by slitting throats. There will be consequences for the slaying of brothers that will befall those who married outside families. Husbands who protect will be severed while they sleep'.

I was terrified. I called Matteo and told him about the letter, and he insisted your father leave, at least until things simmered down. I didn't know what to do. I wanted to call the police but knew I couldn't. They would ask questions I wasn't prepared to answer, and if the families found out, the consequences would have been worse for everyone involved.

I was frightened for your father and beside myself at the thought of something happening to you. I worried, if he didn't leave, they would come after me and after you. Matteo assured me I was safe, that the family was keeping an eye on us, but he was out of answers when it came to your father's safety. He couldn't assure his protection. The family would only extend its protection to you and me and, while I argued and told him it was unfair, he told me there was nothing he could do.

I was livid with everyone. I cursed the family over the phone, telling Matteo this had nothing to do with us. We were living our own lives, but it didn't matter. Your father was not a Benetti by blood. And blood was everything to the family.

So, when your father got home, I lied and told him I no longer loved him and that he should leave. I called him all sorts of names. I told him while he was at work, I'd been sleeping with Nick Sturni, a family friend. It was all lies. I had been faithful to your father since the day I met him. I was faithful to him until the day I died. I loved him with everything I had, but I needed to protect him and you.

When he said he was going to take you, I told him if he did, the family would come after him. There would be no coming back from what I did to him. He was humiliated and I broke him with totality. I needed him to believe it so he would go because if he didn't, I knew they would make good on their promise. So he left. When he did, my heart collapsed.

I longed for it to be over, for your father to be back with us. I thought about calling and asking him to come and get us, but the situation between the families was still too volatile, and I knew it wouldn't end well.

In the years that followed, your uncles sent word that most of the

Cartelli family was moving back to Sicily to escape revenge from another family. Their involvement led them to a darkness I pray still haunts them.

I'm sorry I failed to protect everyone. To be honest, without your father by my side, I didn't know how to survive. My misery consumed me, and I knew I could never tell you what was going on, especially when you started to work for Gio, and you told me that Domenic was working there. I worried for your safety. Perhaps if you had known all of this sooner, things would have been different.

Domenic tried to make some waves for a while, but Aldo inevitably put a stop to that. Grief and heartbreak can bring even the greatest of giants to their knees.

The families have been quiet for a few years now. I would love to believe that that will last, but given the history, I'm not hopeful. As a Benetti, you should always be alert but not alarmed. But, so you know, your Uncle Matteo and your cousin Micha have been keeping a close eye on everything. I'm hoping one day you'll be able to meet Micha. I think you two would get along very well.

I know you suffered because of me, because of the hurt my family caused. But don't blame your father. He was innocent in all of it. I pray you find the man I forced out of your life. Just know I did what I did to try and protect everyone.

I contacted your father a few months ago with the news of my diagnosis. I didn't have much time when I saw him, but I finally had the chance to tell him everything my heart hid. We cried for all the years we lost, and all the love we could have shared. I never stopped loving your father, and he never stopped loving me. He found a family he adores, but he never gave up hope of seeing you. Perhaps one day you could meet them all and be part of a family where you belong. I'm sorry it wasn't with me.

The doctor diagnosed me with stage four pancreatic cancer. I didn't have much time, and I didn't want you to see me deteriorate even more than I already had. I wasn't scared of dying, I was only scared of you not knowing the whole truth.

Go and live life, Kara. Do not disappear into the world without finding love. When you do, love with all your heart and tell them our story. Don't hide anything from the ones you love, and lean into them when you need to. Don't run from them.

Carry your strength with the determination I know you have. Embrace everything that you come across, because one day it might be too late. It's only then you will know what true heartache is. No one should ever have to experience what I went through.

Lastly, go to your father. He forgave me after all these years, and I needed that to go in peace. While I won't get my happily ever after with him, you have the opportunity to enjoy the years that are left. Don't let anyone stand in your way.

I will love you forever.

I'm sorry.

Mum

x

23

CHANGES

The changed patterns in Kara's relationships were complex. She tried to ignore issues only to find herself overcompensating for everything. She struggled to accept her new reality without casting judgement.

She also recognised she was flawed. She had reason to doubt herself and no idea how to deal with Val's past. No one prepared her for the reality of everyone's past impacting their united new present. Most importantly, when all of them came together, they cross-connected, which was complicated with more than one person. It was a process of change none of them saw coming.

They were hazy with their honesty. Fragments of Kara's truth filtered through only if she deemed them necessary. None of them wanted their present tarnished by their past, and it was justified while everyone ignored everything else. Alexis and Michael challenged her through their unfettered, open devotion to each other. It should have been no one's business. In another universe, their relationship would have been inconsequential.

She decided after a few weeks she should call Michael. It had been a while since they had spoken, and she wondered if they were deliberately avoiding each other now that their lives seemed a little more complicated.

'I believe you have a lot to say, no?' he said when he picked up.

'More like a lot of questions to ask.'

'Fire away,' he told her. 'There are no secrets here. Are there?'

Kara didn't know whether he was mocking her.

'You tell me. You're the one who only dishes out necessary things.'

'Necessity is the key to minimising harm.'

'So,' she laughed into the phone, 'who is doing us harm?'

'Kara,' he sighed. 'Just ask me what you want to know. Actually, I'll save you the trouble. I like Alexis ... really like Alexis. If this is going to be an issue for you, you need to figure out how you are going to fix it. I don't want this to break our friendship. You mean a lot to me.'

'But she means more?'

'That's not fair and you know it,' he told her, sounding exasperated.

'Sorry.' She genuinely meant it. She didn't want to pick a fight with Michael. It was Alexis she had the issue with.

'Second chances,' he told Kara when she remained silent on the phone. 'You more than anyone should understand that.'

'Thank you for that insight, *Ray*.' She had gone from sincere to bratty all over again. When Michael went silent, she knew she had overstepped the mark. She had come a long way, and she knew while she had issues with Alexis, Michael wasn't to blame. He had been nothing but a supportive friend to her.

'Misocainea.'

'Sentence.'

'Kara has a hatred for new ideas and things which includes Michael and Alexis being together.'

'I don't hate you,' she told him honestly.

'But Alexis?'

'I'll try,' was all she could offer. For now, that would be enough.

Kara wanted Michael to be happy, but she didn't want his

happiness to come at a cost. Alexis was the margin in a border that gave a lot to the narrative of their lives. But no matter how she tried to adjust with the change, it sat somewhere in Kara's heart, uneasy.

She worried Alexis would ruin Michael, and Kara would be devastated for her friend if that happened. He deserved to be happy, and she desperately wanted him to be in love. But she couldn't agree with him that Alexis was the right person to make that dream come true.

So, they all kept up their pretences of civility, and spoke fondly of their relationships. Months passed, and Alexis and Michael's relationship found its own niche, the justification theirs alone. Kara couldn't explain to Val what it was that annoyed her about the fact.

Kara felt protective of Michael and, after meeting Val, Michael was both accepting and happy for her. They formed a little quadrant as couples, often sitting together at dinner, flitting through conversations as if nothing was amiss.

Ray also questioned why she felt uneasy, asking her if she had any underlying feelings for Michael.

'I only want him to be happy.'

'And you don't think Alexis makes him happy?'

'Alexis didn't make Val happy.'

'Do you not think that people are capable of change?' Ray challenged.

'People are only as capable as they allow themselves to be. Isn't that what you told me?'

'I think we don't give people enough credit to show us that they have changed. You have worked hard to try and change who you are. Don't you think Alexis deserves that opportunity as well? They're adults and entitled to make their own decision, even if we think they are right or wrong. Michael has been very supportive of you. I think you owe him that much as well. No?'

Jealousy wasn't in Kara's repertoire, but caution was. So, she decided she would give Alexis the benefit of the doubt. Kara wanted to mellow towards Alexis, especially since she adored Michael.

Kara's relationship with Val was solid. They had been together for almost a year, and she hadn't moved out of his apartment back into hers. Kara still held onto her apartment, not wanting to lose her private space. They replaced all the furniture Alexis ruined, so it was neat again. Now and then, Kara would go back there, sitting in a comfortable silence, reminding herself of who she was and what she never wanted to be again.

A few weeks after she moved in with Val, he surprised her by bringing home her mother's chair. While the fabric wasn't the same, he found someone local who helped restore it. Kara would often find herself sitting in it, looking out the window, thinking about her mother … thinking about all the things she knew, and all the things she wished she had known.

Kara tried to find something, anything, in the chair that would bring her back, from the way the texture of the fabric felt, to the way the wood felt cold when she sat down. She wanted to believe her mother loved this chair. It was the only true connection to a woman who disconnected herself deliberately.

One night, Kara was a huddled mess, crying in the corner. When Val saw her, he didn't ask why or ask her to stop. He pulled up a chair next to her, and they sat in stilted silence. Her quiet sobs the only noise in the house. When she eventually stopped crying, she opened up and told him about her family, about her father, her mother and everything that had happened to them as a couple.

She gave Val the same out her mother had given her father, knowing there was the possibility they would never be left alone. The burden of carrying the name was a new challenge. Her name was a link to the evil that ran through her blood. Giving Val the opportunity to leave terrified her, but it was necessary. He had the right to make his own choices.

Later, when they were both tucked into bed, he whispered, 'I'll always love you, regardless of your family's past. What they have done is not a reflection on you. You may have your flaws, we all do, but you are Kara, not someone defined by their surname.'

'You want to stay after everything I've told you?'

'Why is that so hard to believe?'

'Because ...' she stopped, not wanting to compare Val to her father.

'I'm not him,' he answered for her. 'I love you, Kara. I'll fight for you. Don't ever doubt that.'

And she didn't. She had no doubt in her mind Val would fight for her if he had to. She knew he would scour the ends of the earth to find her because he loved her. And she loved him. She felt an overwhelming urge to love him harder than she already did. The gentle, caring man before her was everything she didn't know she needed. He would stay and fight her demons for her because he loved her.

The world carried on, rotating without flinging everyone off, but Kara's felt like it was off-kilter. For the first time in a while, it wasn't because of Alexis and Michael, who remained a constant beat in their lives. It was getting easier to see them together, and they appeared settled, and happy.

So, while they lived in their little bubble of bliss, everyone carried on as if no one ever had any issues with each other. Alexis spoke to Val, and Michael would often text to check-in.

How are you, little Incony?
Magic words again?
Just checking in on my delicate friend.
I didn't ask for a sentence.
Ha! When can we do lunch?
Just the two of us? By lunch you mean martinis??? NO??
Say when x

It was a strange change in their dynamic, but everyone seemed to take it in their stride, so Kara tried not to fret. She adjusted her smiles accordingly. But change happens quickly.

Kara came home from the supermarket one night and felt a sharp stabbing pain in her left side. Breathing through it, it quickly passed but left her unnerved. She assumed it was from carrying groceries that were too heavy. The following day, it happened again, only this time the pain lasted a little longer. In the days that followed, she was tired and could barely move.

The pain settled in her stomach and would come more often. She didn't say anything to Val because she didn't want him to worry, often turning away and grimacing when the pain was unbearable. She worried about what her mother had written in her letter, how by the time she had any symptoms and was diagnosed, it was too late. She researched all she could on pancreatic cancer.

The computer screen tormented her with all types of symptoms. By the end of her search, she felt like she had every one of them. It listed side effects, specific organs that would be affected, how those organs would be consumed by the cancer and, finally how her body would eventually deteriorate and fail her. She was convinced she had pancreatic cancer and accepted that her time with Val would be limited.

Her hands hovered over the keyboard and typed '*mortality rate, pancreatic cancer*', and her breath left her. She thought of her mother and how she had gone through all of it without anyone by her side. She must have been terrified to find out she was destined for an early death, her insides consumed by an insidious disease. Cancer didn't discriminate.

And now Kara's heart hammered as she realised this would be happening to her. Suddenly, she was back in the hospital gown, but this time the tubes that were up her nose would supply the food she couldn't eat. She could hear the beeping of the hospital machines, smell the bleach from the floors being cleaned … the smiles of the doctors and nurses, who tried to mask the sadness of her predicament.

She pictured Val holding her hand, frustrated he couldn't help her. She saw Michael sleeping in the chair in the corner of her room, refusing to leave her side. She thought about her father and felt his grief at never having the chance to make peace before losing the loves of his life.

Her search burrowed further into gloominess.

'*Funeral costs and arrangements.*'

It was all there. The forms she could fill in to '*take the burden off the family*' as one place put it. Oddly enough, Kara found some solace in knowing her final resting place would be somewhere she had chosen on her own.

Floral arrangements, playlists, churches, pastors, celebrants - the more words tumbled over her, the more convinced she was that she had settled into death's sureness.

Sadness enveloped her at the thought of compressed seconds that ticked away. She was not ready to accept death at an early age like her mother had. She expanded her search to look for treatments and cures: traditional versus alternative, treatment success rates, travelling abroad for stem-cell therapy, healing with crystals and light therapy. Pages of material dedicated to helping people accept inevitable change. The reality was that page after page spewed the same words she was reluctant to accept. She closed her computer, determined to look for more information once her diagnosis had been confirmed.

'I'm not waiting for death,' she whispered to herself. 'That arsehole can wait for me.'

With that in mind, she arranged an appointment with her doctor.

Uneasiness spread through her. Kara couldn't help but think the worst while she sat there waiting for her name to be called. Her leg bounced up and down, and she thought of all the things she had read about her disease, such as nausea and vomiting, pain in the abdomen, loss of appetite; she had it all. Now she was only a diagnosis away from finding out her fate.

Dr Curtis came out with his wire-rimmed glasses perched on his nose. He smiled as if in sympathy at Kara as he called her name.

She sat opposite him, and he asked, 'So, Kara, what brings you here today?'

Kara didn't hesitate to tell Dr Curtis all about her symptoms and how she was terrified her diagnosis would be like her mother's and that it was too late. He listened to everything she said, taking notes on the computer as they chatted.

'So, this pain you describe, has it settled or is it still there?'

'It's weird,' she told him. 'Because it comes and goes, but it leaves me feeling so tired. I don't think I've ever felt like this before.'

'Let's do some tests and take it from there. Are you sexually active?'

'Yes,' she answered, slightly embarrassed.

'And he's only with you and you with him?'

'Yes.'

'I'll need you to take this to the bathroom so you can give me a sample, then come back and we can discuss the results.'

Kara took the little yellow jar and walked into the bathroom. Anxiety had her in there for a while as she waited for her bladder to catch up to her brain. When she was finally done, she hid it from the others in the waiting room.

She sat back in the office while Dr Curtis dipped a stick into the jar then matched it against the bottle.

'No infection, which is good,' he said and disposed of the stick. He walked over to another cupboard and pulled out another test in a wrapper.

'When was your last period, Kara?'

'Um,' she said, thinking. 'The start of last month.' Then realisation dawned on her.

'That would explain it,' he said as he showed Kara the stick. 'You're pregnant.' He smiled. 'Congratulations.'

The shock started with a benign beat. It formed slowly, then crept with a steady rhythm, unnerving the very centre of her reality. In the seconds that ticked by with the news, Dr Curtis continued to speak, as if what she heard was normal and inevitable. But, it was the start of Kara's downfall. She knew it would not end well.

They never broached the topic of children. They never spoke about themselves as long-term, even though she knew they would be. She never imagined she would be sitting here, in a dreamlike state, terrified of what Val would say and do.

Kara thought about Alexis and how she had manipulated Val to try and keep him. She remembered what she did to Larn. In reality, Alexis and Kara were cut from the same cloth. But Kara wasn't lying.

Kara left Dr Curtis' rooms with pamphlets and instructions, slips for blood tests, further appointments, scans, names of obstetricians, and a head full of unbelievable doubt. She couldn't remember if Dr Curtis asked if she was okay, or if he asked any questions about Val. Never did he give her any alternatives. She knew in her heart it would devastate Val. It had taken him a year to settle himself after everything he had gone through with Alexis. Now Kara was about to go in and unsettle everything they had tried to make work.

She didn't go back to his place, instead finding herself sitting in her old apartment, wondering what to do. She opened her phone and typed in all sorts of things like *what to expect when you're pregnant, obstetricians in the area*, then *termination of pregnancy*.

According to Dr Curtis, Kara was about seven weeks pregnant. The website said she had time if she wanted to make any decisions. She was torn with all sorts of possibilities. Never had the prospect of raising a child entered her mind. But now, as she sat there by herself, she found her hand protectively guarding her stomach. Instinctively, Kara knew she would raise the baby. The only question that remained was whether she would do it alone or whether Val would be part of their lives. He needed to know, and Kara needed to tell him and face the consequences.

She knew Val was home because of two things: she could hear music and there was a strong smell of garlic and onions coming from the kitchen. It hit her as she walked into his apartment, and her stomach revolted at the smell, settling quickly with a newfound hunger. Now she knew what was going on, it felt as if her brain and body had connected, reassuring her she wasn't dying and everything was going to be alright.

His face lit up when he saw her walking towards him but fell quickly when he saw her red eyes. He turned the stove off and enveloped her in a hug, not asking what was wrong. Kara breathed him in, wanting to remember everything about him ... the way he smiled, the colour of his eyes, the gentle way he kissed her when she needed it, and the way he loved her with everything he had. He walked her over to her chair and pulled out one for himself, linking his pinkie with hers.

'I went to the doctor today,' she said, after a while. 'I've been feeling off for a few weeks now and didn't want to say anything to you. I was worried I had the same thing my mother did.'

'You know the chances of that are pretty rare. Why didn't you come to me?'

'Because you're my boyfriend, not my doctor. And I wanted to be sure before I came back to tell you I was dying.'

'What's going on, Kara?' His face froze. She didn't think he would take what she had said so seriously.

She didn't know how to tell him. She was worried he would throw her out. He had every right to do so. While Val had professed his love, she never said it back. He didn't demand she did; he knew it was something Kara needed to do in her own time. But this news was about to change everything and there would be no turning back from it.

'I love you,' she finally told him. 'I've never said that to anyone. I didn't come looking for you, but I thank my lucky stars every day that I found you. You saved me, Val. I don't know how else to explain it.'

'Kara, what did your doctor say? Whatever it is, I'm here because I love you. You know that, right?'

She let go of his pinkie and got up to walk to her bag. She

pulled out the test Dr Curtis had given her and walked back to where Val sat. Extending her arm, she let the test dangle between them. He reached out to get it, knowing what it was, the colour on his face draining.

His hands shook almost violently as he whispered the word *'pregnant'* like a chilling realisation. Kara's tears fell as she watched the man she loved slowly leaving the cocooned relationship they created. Neither of them had seen this coming. He sat there for what felt like hours. Kara stood, too afraid to sit because she knew she would soon be running away.

'I thought I had pancreatic cancer,' she said. 'I was showing all the symptoms. This wasn't something I was expecting. I've been very careful with my pill and never missed a day. I know this changes everything for us, for you, but know I didn't do this to intentionally hurt you.'

She rambled, trying to fill the void with words. She needed him to say something, anything and, when he didn't, she knew Val had checked out and she would be raising the baby on her own. Acceptance greeted her with relative calm as she walked towards her bag and the door.

'How do I know it's real?' he finally asked.

Her heart skipped a painful beat at how broken he suddenly looked. She knew he grappled with the memory of Alexis and the baby. The betrayal was mapped in the lines of his face.

'Because I have all the slips ready for my next tests. You can come with me to each and every one. I have nothing to hide. You can call Dr Curtis and speak to him too. I told him that you might.'

She didn't want him to think she was lying, but given her history and some of the things she told him, she knew there would be an element of doubt. And doubt hovered in their relationship because both of them had been broken. She turned to see him still sitting in the chair, holding the test, wide-eyed and in disbelief.

Kara decided Val deserved some time and privacy to process

the news. The shock of finding out she was pregnant was clearly overwhelming. She wanted him to believe her, to realise this was not a lie or something she was doing to trap him into marriage or staying together. Because, for all her flaws, and she had many, she knew one thing for sure, the mistakes of her past had changed her, giving her insight into her life and Val's. She may have been devious and deceptive once upon a time, and there would most likely be times where the old Kara would resurface, but not now. She knew she was not the same person who had once ruined Larn and Ethan. She was not Alexis.

'I think I should go. This is a lot to take in. I won't be upset if you don't want to have anything to do with me, or us. I won't be upset. I didn't plan this and I'm not trying to trap you into anything. I can come back for the rest of my things another time.'

She opened the door and headed towards the lift. She cried because, for the first time in her life, she felt like she belonged. And while it felt secure and comfortable, Kara knew she would have to learn to navigate a new normal. She was going to do this, and she would keep Val informed and involved along the way if that was what he wanted.

The door to the elevator opened and she quickly walked in, bowing her head in case someone saw her tears. She had a few seconds to compose herself before she faced the outside world. Reaching into her bag, she looked for her phone. She wanted to call Michael and tell him what was going on but, at the same time, she didn't want him to be in a position that meant he would be with her more than Alexis. After everything they had been through, she didn't want him to feel compelled to help her. She typed the only other number she thought of and was about to call it, when the doors opened. Kara was greeted by tormented brown eyes.

'Why do you always run? Why am I always running after you?' Val stepped into the lift and hit the stop button. 'This way you can't go anywhere.' He pulled her in for a kiss, breathing life into her saddened soul. She sobbed into his kiss and apologised, hugging him tight.

'I love you,' he said, smiling through his tears. 'I wasn't expecting this day to turn out like this, but I've concluded that life with you is full of stuff like this. You challenge me, Kara, frustrate the hell out of me. And you run. But,' he said, slowly lowering himself to the ground, 'I'll always run after you.'

Kara couldn't believe what she was seeing. The man she loved with everything she had was on bended knee, professing his love.

'Kara,' he said. 'This was supposed to be a lot more romantic. But I love you. I'll love you 'til I have no breath left in my body. And now, I'll love this little person growing inside of you too. It wasn't something I was expecting, but I feel a love for the two of you I've never felt before. Let me be a part of your life. Let me be a part of our baby's life. I want to cook food you won't eat, rub your belly as it gets bigger, and not miss anything along the way. You and me, we are meant to be. And this baby, while a little unexpected, is the perfect little addition to us. I love both of you. Marry me.'

'Why?' she asked. The absurdity of the day had her questioning everything. 'Why would you want to marry someone like me?'

'Because you are my someone,' he told her. 'Now you're *our* someone. I'm not scared of committing to you, Kara. I'm not scared of committing to our baby. I've been wanting to ask you this for a while. I don't know how many times I have to tell you. I love you!' He shouted in the lift as if wanted to tell the whole world. 'I LOVE YOU!' he screamed again as if he had lost his mind. And he had, for Kara and now for their baby.

'Yes.' She kissed him and sobbed. 'Yes Val, I'll marry you. I love you.'

The lift decided it'd had enough of the stop button and opened up to people standing at the door. But Val didn't care: he was in no hurry. He pulled the ring out of the box and slid it on Kara's finger.

'She said yes,' he told the people outside the lift. 'She's having my baby, and she said yes,' he repeated, as if they wanted to hear.

He managed to get up off the floor and smile at the patient people waiting their turn. They heard their congratulations still as the door to Val's apartment closed.

Val smiled at her, beaming with happiness. Kara placed her hands on her stomach, protective of the baby inside. He dropped to his knees and kissed her belly, and said, 'Hello little one, this is your dad. I love you and your mummy very much.' He looked up to see Kara's heart filled to the brim with love and happiness.

Changes can be unexpected, and this one would be a change forever. Val and Kara would be planning a wedding and having a baby. Their lives would be catapulted into a new strangeness. But reluctance simmered in Kara's heart.

She knew they wouldn't marry before the baby was born, but she knew she needed support. She didn't have her mother to lean on now, so she called the number she almost dialled earlier. His voice came instantly with a breath of relief.

'Kara,' he exhaled.

'Hi, Dad. I'd like to see you.'

REFLECTIONS

Kara wanted to believe reflections were like glassine filaments that protected the stillness of captured time. She wanted to store those reflections like personalised memories in an album.

She didn't want to shy away from the images that captured sadness in a wilted smile, nor the happiness that radiated with curiosity. She wanted every reflection, every memory to be etched in her heart so it twinkled in her eyes. She wanted those unguarded seconds completely unblemished by the frissons in her life.

The photo album lay open in her lap. Her mother had given it to her father before she died. Her fingers traced pictures she had never seen before, trying to memorise them. Her mother managed to store these moments in time, hidden away in her wardrobe as if the memory of them was too painful. And it was all there. From the beginning, when Kara came out wrinkled and crying, to the moment where you could see the light slowly fading from her mother's eyes. And her father was a constant, his arms encircling her mother protectively.

Kara spent hours flipping through the photos, backwards and forwards, peeling off the pictures from their backing, hoping there would be a hidden message. Each section held a frozen moment of time.

Karina aged 6 months. Karina aged 1. Karina's first camping trip. Karina aged 2. Joshua and Karina at the park. Joshua teaching Karina to ride her bike. Karina aged 3. Karina, Mum and Dad. Karina going to school aged 6. Then nothing else.

The photos showed a cross-section of their time together as a family. But it stopped so suddenly, as if it was inconceivable to think there was life after the last photo. As if the memories ceased, a little like the life her parents once shared.

Why had her mother never mentioned these photographs? But, more importantly, why had Kara never questioned anything until now? Was she so absorbed with hatred and anger she refused to see the little things blatantly in front of her? Her mother never displayed any pictures of Kara, yet she held onto the albums. Each picture was fragile last moment, protected by withered sheets.

She flicked through the album relentlessly, going back and forth between the pages, memorising each smile, each squint of their eyes, each look her father longingly gave her. And throughout it all Kara was there, ponytails and pigtails, ringlets and curls, cute little smiles and eyes that shimmered with mischief.

It was hard not to try and be saddened by what she was seeing. These were memories of happier times with her mother. These were the memories she didn't remember, the ones she told Michael she wanted to find. She wanted to erase the years she could remember and replace them with these newer happier times.

She rued the fact that happiness only existed for her in years where her memories felt insidious. She had no recollection of them, nor did she know whether this was on purpose or not. But these reflections were of a time where her family still existed and everyone coexisted.

Kara thought of her Uncle Antonio and wondered if they were cut from the same cloth. He was rebellious, always looking for deception and finding dishonour along the way. Had he still been alive, would they get along or would they be too similar and clash? Or perhaps she was like her other uncles, Matteo and Franco, who lived a quiet life. She wondered whether they would know who she was if she reached out to them. Maybe they knew nothing of Kara. Finding them would be hard, but it wasn't impossible. There were so many questions left unanswered that her mother could no longer help with.

Kara cradled her growing belly. Already vigilant of everything around her, she wanted to make sure no harm came to their little Peanut. Val was territorial and possessive of everything Kara did.

At first, Kara worried Val didn't believe her, as if everything she told him was a lie because his version of truth had been skewed. But as they settled and the doubts disappeared, Val opened his heart further if that was even possible, and it radiated a pureness that Kara couldn't describe.

Part of her wanted to flaunt it in front of Alexis, to show her this is what her life could have been if she hadn't been so deceitful. The other half of her remained tight-lipped. Kara remembered the things she had done, and she was no better. Alexis would smile at Kara with longing and regret. And while Alexis and Michael hadn't spoken about a future, Kara knew that somewhere in the recesses of Alexis' mind, a baby bump was something she craved. She hoped one day Alexis and Michael would find their own type of happiness, the kind that Kara and Val had.

Val came to every appointment and would often lay awake in bed, reading out loud to the baby.

'Never too early to learn. Perhaps he will be a doctor, like his dad,' he would say.

Kara would laugh with him and ask what if it was a girl? He would tell her it wouldn't matter as long as everyone was happy and healthy. While her belly grew, the plans for the wedding remained on hold. They wanted Peanut to be there with them on their special day. Apart from Kara's father, she had no immediate family. Michael the closest thing. Val and Peanut were now her new family.

Kara sat in the dewy grass, picking weeds from her mother's gravesite. The gold letters etched on the cold stone shimmered with words of love and memories for a woman she felt like she had hardly known. There was no photo, but now she had the album, Kara wondered whether it was too late to add a picture. Maybe she could find one of her smiling.

Regret filled her to overflowing. She had been so consumed with destruction she failed to see anything else in front of her. Kara knew she would never allow that to happen to Peanut. She would be a pillar of strength, guiding them through life's difficulties and answering questions as openly and honestly as she could. Eventually, Peanut would learn of Kara's family. But for now, Val and Kara would be a family, along with Uncle Michael and Aunt Alexis.

She sensed her father coming. He stood at the end of the grave for a while, taking a moment for himself. Kara didn't interrupt him. They stayed in the moment, existing in the silence of death that surrounded them.

He leaned over and gave Kara a little envelope.

'I thought maybe you'd like to put up a picture of her. I wasn't sure if you had one.' 'Thanks. I was thinking a picture would be nice. I wasn't sure if I could find one in the album.'

She opened up the envelope, and her mother's smile caught her off-guard. Kara almost thought it couldn't be her … it couldn't be the woman who sat in her chair and gave up on life. But it was, and she was smiling back at Kara, asking for forgiveness.

'I wasn't sure if you wanted it. I didn't want to tread on your toes or anything like that. If you don't want to use it, that's also fine. I understand.'

'No, it's more than fine. She needs to have her picture here. It's nice to be reminded she was happy once.'

He visibly retracted as if she had slapped him with her words.

The decisions her parents made affected Kara's life. Had the two of them stayed together, perhaps things would be different, but hindsight and reflections were not going to help with her current reality.

Kara's back was hurting, so she stood, supporting Peanut as she did. Her father's eyes travelled to her bump, and she could see his hand move wanting to reach out. Without saying anything Kara reached out and made contact with his hand, pulling it towards her belly.

His eyes instantly lit up, and he exhaled with happiness. They stood there unmoving, allowing the moment to be shared, while Peanut kicked as if acknowledging their grandfather.

'I wanted to see you after the last time you called. But I also wanted to give you the space to figure things out on your own,' he said.

'It was a lot to process … Mum, you, the baby, I needed to take it one day at a time.'

He took his hand off her belly, sat on the grass and placed roses Kara hadn't see earlier on her mother's grave. His head hung low, and he sounded as if he was saying something to her mother. When the moment passed, he stood up and leaned over the stone, kissing it. His tears fell on the gilded stone, and he lingered while.

'She loved you, you know.' His voice was strained, cracking through the painful words. 'She adored you. When we couldn't have any more children, she dedicated everything she had to you.'

'But it wasn't enough. She gave up after you left. I didn't know what happened and, no matter what I did, she was never the same. Trying to live through that was hard.'

'We all made choices we regretted, none more than me. I should have stayed, fought harder for her. But I didn't. I was so worried they'd hurt her … hurt you. I knew if I didn't leave, that was a possibility. They killed your grandfather, and who knows what happened to your grandmother or if she's even alive. Your mother and I lived in the shadow of their death. When they threatened us, threatened you, I knew there was no turning back from it.'

'I assume you knew everything that happened between the families?'

'I ...' When he didn't continue, she knew she had her answer.

'Tell me,' she whispered. 'How much danger was I in? How much danger am I still in?'

He took both her hands in his. 'I swear I'll do everything to protect you. I'm not going to lie, you deserve to know the whole truth. The families, they know you, they know about you, but so much time has passed, there's no need for anyone to come near you. No one has mentioned us for so long and, if they did, I would know. What your uncle did was a long time ago.'

'How would you know?' The she remembered her mother's letter. 'Matteo.'

His hesitation was her confirmation.

'He's always been in touch, hasn't he?'

'Not always ... just when it's been necessary.'

'How many times has it been necessary?' she asked.

'Only when Domenic's name comes up.'

She should have been surprised he knew about Domenic, but she wasn't. Domenic's name however, made her skin crawl, like it did when she saw his face flash across the screen.

'Last year when he was in the news, you knew about that too?'

'I did. I told Matteo.'

'Only necessary phone calls then? Nothing I should be concerned about? Nothing Val should worry about? My baby?'

'The situation with Domenic is being closely monitored.'

'Now he's a situation?' she yelled, instantly feeling bad for raising her voice in a cemetery.

'He's nothing for you to be concerned about.'

'You don't get to tell me what I should be concerned about.'

'I'm sorry,' he said.

She knew he meant it.

She wondered if he would feel the same way if he knew the true extent of her relationship with Dom. She chose not to say anything to him. Her family clearly knew more about Kara's life than Kara did.

'I don't think anyone has the right to tell me what to be concerned about, let alone now. My concern is Val and this baby ... everything else is irrelevant.'

'Of course,' was all he could offer. The intention behind Kara's statement didn't go unnoticed. She didn't want to be deliberately awful to him. He was trying to give her some insight, which is what she thought she wanted. Kara desperately wanted to tamp down the feelings that were resurfacing.

Hurt. Loss. Pain. Worry. Fear. Loneliness.

They were all there and they would serve no purpose.

But her heart ached for the man who also lost so much. She thought about Val not being in her life after Peanut was born, and it was a torment she never wanted to think about. But the agony her father had shared was very real. The decisions made at the time, were supposed to be for the better, but they were anything but that.

Ray would tell her forgiveness was the path to healing. She desperately wanted to forgive her father, it wouldn't be easy; a lot of time had passed, and too much had happened. While she still had lots of questions, Kara also knew she had a life she finally loved. It would take time to heal, and she would allow him in slowly and carefully so he could be a part of the little unit she created with Val.

As if on cue, Val was there. He wouldn't let her come to the cemetery on her own. He told her crazy people hung out there during the day. He also didn't want her to face her father alone. Secretly, she was also afraid the family were still around, spying on them from every angle. It was a new paranoia that settled like grit in their eyes.

'Val.' He extended his hand towards her father.

'Joshua, or Josh ... whatever you prefer.'

'Ready?' Val asked Kara.

'I think so. It was nice seeing you again, Dad.'

It was the first time she had called him Dad in a long time. Regardless of what happened, he was still her father. Now that the truth was out there, it was entirely up to Kara to voice how much or how little he was involved. She wanted him to have a relationship with Peanut, but it would have to be a gradual introduction.

'I'd love for you to come over one night with Val. Maybe you could meet Claire and Amy?'

He ruined the moment. She bristled at the thought of meeting the people who shared her father's life while Kara went without him. He sensed her unease.

'I don't think I'm ready for that yet,' she told him honestly. 'It's a little too early.'

'You tell me when you're ready. They know all about you,' he said. 'I've been very upfront with Claire about you and your mother.'

Kara wondered how much of the truth he told them, whether or not the truth he saw was the reality Kara lived. She could feel anger coil within her, and it replaced the calmness she felt only moments earlier. It was like whiplash, and Kara forgot about the niceties that had been exchanged.

'Did you tell them how I lived?' she snapped.

'Kara,' Val admonished.

'No, Val. I need to say this. This is all very hard to take in,' she started. 'For years, I didn't hear a word from you. Nothing. I broke, and no one was there to pick up the pieces until Val came along and fought for me. It's the first time in my life anyone has ever fought for me. Each day, I wake up and think I don't know why he does, because I don't think I'm worth it. And do you know why?'

He shook his head, appearing too frightened to say anything.

'Because for years, no one gave a shit. Not you or my mother. And do you know what the sad thing about this whole mess is?

Even though both of you gave up on me, I never stopped loving either of you. It hurts that you had a relationship with Amy. It hurts that while I was destroying my life deliberately, you were helping to keep hers together. So no, *Joshua,*' she emphasised his name with venom, 'I don't want to meet them. Not now, and maybe never.'

Forgiveness is a taut cord that never snaps equally in half. It relies on two important factors, forgetting and forgiving. Forgetting the past was easy. Kara could move on with her life with Val and Peanut and accept that her past life was not as it should have been. But forgiving all the people who had hurt her was hard. She wanted desperately to have her father in her life, but Kara also knew she couldn't welcome a family he accepted while he ignored one that he already had.

As if knowing what she needed, Val pulled her close and laid a protective hand on her belly, standing defiant in solidarity.

'Perhaps it would be better if you came to us instead, Josh?' Val told him. 'That way Kara might feel a little more comfortable.'

'Of course,' he told them. 'Whatever works for you.'

Kara walked over to her father. She thought about offering her hand for him to shake, but it felt cold and emotionless so, instead she put aside her anger. She leaned in to hug him, and his arms wrapped around her. They stayed like that for a while until the wind picked up surrounding them, as if her mother was embracing them with her spirit.

'I'll be in touch again,' she said when they finally broke apart and walked away leaving him standing next to her mother's grave.

In the weeks and months that followed, Kara would call, and he would go to their place for strained dinner and quiet conversations. At times, she didn't know what to say to him and was grateful Val was there to break the silence. Other times, she would ask him questions about when they were younger, and he would beam with stories about their love and their past. Kara cherished those moments the most. She wanted to believe her mother didn't die loveless.

During these visits, he never mentioned Claire or Amy, or anything about his life with them. He respected Kara's wishes, and she appreciated it. While she was sure Claire and Amy were wonderful, she doubted she would ever be ready to be welcome them into her life. Her loathing quietly simmered until she eventually accepted that love was hard.

They all settled into a comfortable routine. In the months that ensued, Kara's belly swelled, and her feet ached. Her back permanently hurt, and she could barely breathe after eating. Sleeping was uncomfortable, and she counted down the days and weeks till she could have the intruder out and her body back.

All the while, Val ran around for her like nothing was a bother, getting pickles if she craved them and cooking balanced meals she could stomach. They would sit at night, and he would read stories while leaving a protective hand on her growing midsection, letting them both know he was there. Michael and Alexis continued to be part of their lives while finding their own stability. She approached Michael one day and asked him if he would drive her on the day of the wedding.

'I'm no antithalian, you know. I intend to have a wonderful time at your party. I am not opposed to having fun.'

'I asked you to drive, not suck the life out of the party,' she said, laughing.

'I know. But as your best friend, I would be honoured to drive you.'

'No big word for honour?'

'Perhaps you can give me a new one on your wedding day.'

'Challenge accepted.'

Kara extended the invitation to her father, asking him if he wanted to meet her at the church. He didn't hesitate before saying yes. She didn't ask him to walk her down the aisle, figuring she would make up her mind on the day.

The wedding date was set for three months after baby Peanut was due. Val said it was too long to wait, and they should do it the day the baby was born. That way, he told her, there would be double the celebration with minimal fuss. Kara laughed and told him they had waited this long, and a few more months wouldn't change anything. She also desperately wanted to fit into her dress. It was their day, and she wanted it to be special.

Two days after her due date, Kara's membranes ruptured. Val went into full doctor mode, barking orders at people he felt needed to do better. Kara tried to placate him, telling him it wasn't too bad, but she had never experienced anything like the contractions. The pain was so intense she thought she would pass out. And, when she thought she couldn't take anymore, it would start all over again, making her scream like a drug-seeking banshee.

After a gruelling twenty-eight hours, the first cries of Sophia Isabella Kavalenko were heard. She was born with brown eyes deeper than Val's, and hair as fair as Kara's. Val cried when he saw her, his tears falling on his daughter's face. Sophia settled in his arms as if she had always belonged there, and Kara loved the two of them with an enormity she knew she would never understand. No matter how long Kara had, she knew it was never going to be long enough.

Kara had never known anything close to this feeling. She knew that no matter what happened in her life, this little girl would never have a day go by without being told she was loved.

2 5

UNRAVELLING

Maybe Kara was searching for a place where she could quietly unravel, a place where she could find freedom from the reality of the family's history and interference. She desperately wanted to know it wouldn't stand in the way as she forged a new path. She needed to create a space so she could be absent and present when necessary. It was her version of utopia, where Val and Sophia could also exist, cocooned and safe from harm ... safe from the reality that Kara wanted to deny.

The mirrors Kara collected from New Gold Mountain throughout the years had been decimated by Alexis. Not long after the break-in, Val had gone back to New Gold Mountain without Kara knowing. He walked up the stairs and without hesitation, peeled a mirror off the wall and walked out.

The mirror in the bathroom was a reminder of the old version of Kara created, the one who was always on the run.

Kara smiled at the reflection as if she finally welcomed herself. This new Kara was someone she could be proud of. And when she heard little murmurs in the background, coming from someone who never questioned who she was or what she was looking for, she loved what she had found.

Sophia stirred in her cot, and Kara walked over. She had

grown so much since the day they brought her home, and it was hard to remember what their lives were like before her. Picking her up, they sat in the corner in her mother's refurbished chair while Sophia nursed. Kara watched Sophia's eyelashes flutter against her fragile, new skin and wondered if she would ever realise how much Kara loved her. Sophia settled and was fast asleep. If Kara had more time, she would have happily sat there staring at her daughter while she slept.

A knock at the door pulled her out of her love gaze, startling her. She walked over to her crib and gently placed her down, smiling at the sleeping little girl, and whispered *I love you* before tiptoeing towards the door.

Her breath caught on seeing the familiar face and tattoos she hadn't seen since she was eighteen years old. His arms were braced up against the door frame, muscles bulging under the tight black T-shirt, and his smile was tilted to one side as if what he was about to tell her would change her life. Seeing him on television had made her want to run. Her mother's letter had been a warning. And the worried look her father had when he called Dom 'a situation' should have been alarm bells. She remembered what Domenic once told her, *'It's cute that you have no idea.'*

Except now she did.

She had seen him on television, remembering the words the reporter used. *Notorious* was one of them.

This was the same man who callously told her Gio was dead and to never come back. It was the same man who mentioned his father Aldo, implying he was sending a message to her mother, a message that held so much danger she wasn't aware of at the time. Kara thought about the day she left, grateful she would never see him again. How wrong she was. He stood before her after all these years, looking at her with more than the expectations he had all those years ago; now there was a threat in his eyes.

'Kara,' he drawled. 'I can't believe it's you.' He looked her up and down.

She stood there, staring at him, noticing how much he had

aged in the years since she left the fruit shop. His hair was peppered around his ears, and his green-grey eyes were unblinking and full of secrets, which she now knew held no mirth nor curiosity.

This slightly older Dom had an edginess to him that wasn't there before. Or perhaps she had been too young to recognise it.

There was something dark about him, predatory. He unnerved Kara, making her hug herself protectively. Men like Dom didn't resurface after years of silence to greet you with a casual hello. Men like Dom came to your door with intention. Given her family history she hoped this was an awful coincidence and he would disappear, and she would never see him again. But hope was a dangerous thought, and Kara knew she would be a fool to believe it existed.

'Dom,' she finally managed to say, her voice an octave higher than normal. 'I can't believe it's you. What are you doing here? How did you even find me?'

She raised herself on her tiptoes to try and see if there was anyone else there, but he appeared to be alone. Uneasiness settled all around her. She wanted to close the door on him, only she knew that when she opened it again, he would still be standing there, waiting, looking smug.

'I'm sorry for dropping in on you. I probably should have called ahead rather than just turning up. But I was in the area, and I wanted to surprise you.'

She could tell he was lying because Kara had lied most of her life. Dom showing up on her doorstep was no coincidence. Instinct had her immediately protecting herself and Sophia, who was thankfully still asleep in her crib and not making a sound. She didn't want to look back and alert him to Sophia. But, from the way he was looking at her, she could tell that Dom knew more than he was letting on.

'Surprise me? You've certainly done that.' She tried to make light. 'It's been years since I've seen you.'

'It has been, hasn't it? How many years has it been, K-aa-r-aa.' He mocked her the way he had all those years ago.

'It's been a few.'

'A few indeed.' His smile was lecherous.

She waited for him to speak again, but he didn't. He stood there staring at her, smiling like a predator cornering his pray.

'I'm sorry, Dom. I'd invite you, in but I'm kind of in the middle of something.'

'It's okay.' He nodded. 'If you don't have time, I know where you are now. I can always come back.'

His promise to return was threatening, and her skin crawled at his suggestion. She held her resolve, not wanting to unravel in front of him. This was not the same Dom she stole cigarettes and pleasure from as an eighteen-year-old girl. The man that stood menacingly on her doorstep was hardened. Kara knew whatever Dom wanted or was looking for, he wouldn't stop until he got it.

'I don't understand why you're here. Is there something I can help you with?' she asked, immediately feeling stupid.

'There's plenty you can help me with,' he said, running his finger down the side of her face. 'Perhaps we can go and share a cigarette like old times?'

'What the fuck, Dom?' she said, finding her voice and pulling herself away from his touch. 'I have no idea what you want, and I'm certainly not leaving to have a cigarette with you. I'll have to ask you to leave.' She said with zero confidence.

'Awwww, *K-aa-r-aa*. Come on, it will be like old times.'

'Leave Dom, or I'll ...'

'You'll what, Karina?'

She flinched at the use of her real name. He was not here to play. Something had changed. She didn't know what it was, but she knew one person who would: her father.

'So Karina or Kara, which is it?' When she didn't reply, he continued. 'I'm sorry to hear about your mother. My father sends his condolences.'

Her tears burnt at the mention of her mother. She knew he

could see them but she was determined she wouldn't show him how much she was affected. She stood there, never looking down, desperate for him to leave.

'Tell me, what has you all dolled up today? Special occasion? Meeting someone? Or perhaps you're seeing a friend?'

'It's ...' she stumbled, not sure how much she should tell him. She had a feeling he already knew but was waiting for her to confess. 'I'm getting married.'

'Married? Who would have thought? Anyone I know?'

'Why are you here?' she asked again, this time with more courage than she actually had.

'Perhaps I wanted to see it all for myself.'

'There is nothing for you to see. I think you should leave.' She stood her ground, wishing the man who stood before would disappear under the rock he crawled out from.

He nodded, like he understood, then smirked. She wanted to call Val or scream loud enough that J would hear, but she didn't do either because she knew it would aggravate him.

Alexis appeared then, dressed in her soft pink tulle gown, breaking Dom's stare.

'Kara,' she said, looking between her and Dom.

'I'll leave you and this beauty to it,' Dom told Kara. 'I'll see you soon, Kara. Maybe we can share that cigarette after all?' He smiled, looked Alexis up and down suggestively, then turned around to walk away. His departure rattled Kara more than she showed. She knew he would be back.

'Is everything alright?' Alexis asked, watching Dom's retreating figure.

'Yes, it is,' Kara lied, fixing a smile on her face. 'You look amazing, come in.' She held the door open to make sure Dom was gone.

'Who was that?' Alexis asked.

'No one important,' Kara lied again.

'Did he want something?'

'I don't know, and I don't want to think about it. You look incredible,' she told her, changing the subject.

'I didn't know you smoked.' Alexis said.

'I don't. I mean, I did once, but that was a long time ago.'

'You sure everything is alright?' Alexis asked again. Kara realised she must look rattled.

'Yes. All good.'

Kara shelved the thought of Dom and gave all her attention to Alexis, who stood in her apartment fidgeting with her dress. Alexis was stunning in her gorgeous gown, and Kara smiled at her, thinking the two of them had come a long way.

Alexis leaned over the crib and stared at Sophia with a longing Kara would once have despised seeing in her eyes. But while things unravelled, Alexis found herself, and Michael helped her pull herself back together. He had been there for her every step of the way. Their relationship was now an everyday occurrence, and Kara no longer hated Alexis. Hate was a useless emotion she could not devote time or energy to. Kara now had a new focus.

Sophia stirred in her cot, and Kara instinctively walked over to where she slept.

'I can do that if you want to keep getting ready,' Alexis told her, waiting for Kara's permission.

'Thanks,' Kara said. 'But she may vomit, and I don't want your dress ruining.' She held Sophia tight to her chest and smiled at the little girl Alexis looked at so adoringly.

Alexis tucked an errant curl behind her ear. A small tear formed in the corner of her eye, and Kara's heart broke for Alexis. Kara had everything Alexis once wanted, and it felt as if Kara was flaunting her happiness. She knew it wasn't the case but, no matter how they all tried, the past sat lurking in the background between the four of them, unspoken and ignored.

As if she read her mind, Alexis spoke up. 'Thank you, Kara. For your compliment, but more for everything else. Your forgiveness means a lot to me. I almost destroyed this for you. But I'm happy Val has you and Sophia. You both make him happy.'

Her apology was heartfelt, and Kara knew what Alexis said was true. Val was happy, and Sophia had brought them closer. They hadn't missed a thing happened since she was born. They shared every smile, every burp, every little noise, even down to the dirty nappies. Val was there with her every step of the way, and Kara relished the love he gave the two of them.

She now wished Michael and Alexis shared the same joy she and Val had. Every single one of them had come a long way, and each of them deserved forgiveness.

'Alexis, we can both be sorry. I've done some things in my life I'm not proud of either. Val taught me our past and our mistakes don't define who we are as long as we are willing to change.'

'I'm grateful you've all given me a chance. Especially Michael. I do love him, Kara. I know that, in the beginning, you were worried. Michael is the most honest person I have ever met in my life. His support has been amazing and, in a way, I should thank you. If he hadn't shown up that day at your house, who knows if I would have ever had the courage to try and get better.'

Kara was happy for Michael and Alexis. But even more so, she was happy Michael had found someone to share his life with. No matter what happened, Kara would still be there for him as she knew he would be there for her.

'His head would grow if he heard the two of us right now,' Kara said, laughing.

'It so would.' Alexis chuckled with her. 'Enough talking about the past. You need to get ready. I'm sure Michael will be here soon, and Val is no doubt pacing up and down waiting for you.'

'I can't believe I'm getting married!' Kara almost screamed, then walked over to Alexis to hand Sophia over. Alexis took a long inhale, smelling Sophia like she wanted to remember her scent, and smiled down at the little girl, who instantly smiled back.

Kara knew there was no point thinking about the past any longer, even though it had shown up on her doorstep not long before Alexis. She wanted to shake the feeling Dom would be back. It was her wedding day, so she could ignore it for a little while longer, then she would tell Val and her father everything.

Sophia burped in Alexis' arms. They both giggled at the little girl, thankful she didn't revisit her milk. Alexis swayed back and forth with Sophia while Kara fussed with her make-up, looking at her reflection in the mirror.

She stared, thinking the day was all a dream. Perhaps she would wake up and none of it would be real … that her final unravelling would come from a nightmare, and she would wake all alone in her apartment. She thought of her mother, and sadness flushed her eyes as she wished she was still alive to share her special day.

She wondered if she would have liked Val, whether they would have gotten along. Most importantly, she knew she would have loved Sophia. It would have been the spark that she needed to try and hold on, even if it was only for a short time.

'Do you need a hand with anything?' Alexis asked, pulling her from her thoughts. 'Getting your dress on?'

'I need to get a wriggle on. I'm not even close to being done,' she said, laughing.

Kara walked over to the bag she had packed and brought it towards Alexis. It was a big moment. Hesitation saw Kara holding back for a second, but she held the bag out for Alexis, who took it. The moment was huge. Kara knew Sophia would be undisturbed in the car for the short trip, but relinquishing control of her child was harder than she expected.

'Everything you need is in the bag. Do you want me to help you strap her in the car?'

'That would be great, if you could.'

Together they walked out to the car with the bag packed, and Kara helped Alexis strap her baby into the car. She kissed Sophia on the forehead and whispered '*I love you*' before she closed the door and turned to Alexis.

'I'll promise I'll message you as soon as we get there,' Alexis told Kara as they hugged.

'Thank you. That would be wonderful. It feels very weird letting her go.'

Nerves caused jitters within Kara, threatening to unravel her there on the footpath as Alexis drove away with her daughter in the back. The street was empty, as if everyone had been deliberately removed. And she could feel eyes, like the green-grey ones that appeared on her doorstep earlier, hiding somewhere around the corner. She looked both ways before retreating to her apartment to finish getting ready. Kara was rattled and now that Alexis had left, she prayed Michael would hurry up and get to her, in case Dom decided to reappear. She didn't want to think about him. She was getting married. The day was going to be special for everyone.

26

—————

MEMORIES

Some memories danced around Kara's heart purposefully. She cherished every one of them. Her memories now sustained her. They carried the reality of her presence, even if that presence was fractional. How much she had changed, and how much this change had impacted her life. It made an impression on her memories, and she embraced them so no one could try and take them away from her.

'Twirl, principessa, your dress is beautiful,' her mother laughed. They were holding hands, swinging around to face the sun so that it warmed them.

'Faster, Mumma! Faster!' Karina shouted, and they twirled together till they fell to the ground laughing.

Her father stood over them, blocking the sun, laughing and shaking his head. 'You two will make yourselves sick doing that one day.'

'Do you want to join us, Daddy? Let's go, Mumma, one more time,' Kara said, getting up and dusting herself off. 'Ready, Mumma? Ready Daddy?' she said, holding out her hand towards them.

'Ready, Karina,' they said together.

The memory made her smile. It was amazing how many memories she had unlocked of her childhood, and she wanted to remember all of them. She thought back to when she was little and was astounded to think how far she had come. Val changed the narrative of her life, and he never let her escape, even when she tried to run. Kara was grateful he fought for her, especially when she thought there was nothing worth fighting for.

She also thought about her father, who had been invited to be part of the day. She wanted to ask him to give her away when she got there, a surprise she would share with him later.

She was dressed and ready. Her gown hugged the curves she now loved, and her short veil hung delicately around her shoulders. The clip in her hair was something old given to her by her father. He told her, her mother kept it for her to wear on her wedding day. The clip was a heavy reminder that memories of her mother were ones to cherish, even if some of them were hard to process.

The noise at the door made her jump. Thinking someone was breaking in, she looked around her room for something to defend herself with and picked up her shoe, which she hadn't put on. She was poised, arm raised, ready to strike.

'What the?' Michael said.

'It's just you!' Kara let out a breath.

'Who did you think it would be?'

'Never mind.'

'What's going on, Kara? Alexis called and told me someone was here earlier, and you looked nervous.'

'Just someone who showed up unexpectedly.'

'Who?' he insisted.

'An old friend. I hadn't seen him for years and he said he was in the neighbourhood.' She lied and turned away from him so he couldn't see the truth.

'What did he want?'

'Drop it, Michael. He left. I doubt he will be back. And, if he comes back, I won't be here anyway.'

'What do you mean, you doubt he will come back?'

'It was nothing. He was nothing. Someone who showed up today out of all days for some reason.' She could hear the lie as clearly as he could.

'Kara. Is everything alright?'

'Yes, Michael,' she mocked. 'Dom won't be back,' His name slipped out.

'Dom?' he repeated.

'Don't worry about it. It's my wedding day and I have more important things to worry about.' She changed the subject but, for the first time ever, her friend looked rattled.

'What did he want?' he asked, something like fear flashing in his eyes.

'He wanted to catch up with an old flame,' she told him honestly. 'Seriously Michael, it's no big deal. He left. I doubt I'll ever see him again.'

She knew that wasn't true.

'An old flame? Kara,' he started, but she wanted nothing more of it. Dom could wait until after the wedding. There was no way he was going to ruin her special day. She wanted him to drop the subject, even though Dom's name still lingered like stale smoke in the air.

'Please, let it go. For me?' She reassured him.

She took a moment to look at her friend who wore a black tuxedo, which she knew would rob Alexis of air when she saw him. His hair was styled perfectly, and his blue eyes stood out like jewels on a crown. He was handsome; there was no doubt about that.

'Bellibone,' he whistled, as if finally noticing how she looked in her wedding gown.

'Sentence?'

'Kara is full of goodness, but more so today, because she is exceptionally beautiful.'

'Thank you,' she told him, holding back tears.

'We've come a long way, haven't we?' he said as he walked

towards her. He wrapped her in a hug, and she smiled, thinking how lucky she was to have her best friend, her only friend, with her today.

'To think the first time you saw me was with a tube down my throat. How embarrassing.' She laughed.

'Meh.' He shrugged. 'We all have a past, and we've all done things we're not proud of. But we got through it and look at you now.' He stepped back and held her hands, beaming as he looked. 'Stunning,' was all he said.

Kara was finally ready to leave as Kara Collins and return as Kara Kavalenko. She pinched herself as a reminder that this was real. Today was happening ... never in a million years would she have thought she would be standing in the gardens, pledging her forever to a man she didn't deserve. He loved her, and she promised to love him with everything she had.

'Got everything?' Michael asked, waiting by the door.

'I think so,' she said. 'Actually, I have something for you.' She handed him the wrapped present.

'For me?' he asked, taking the gift and unwrapping it swiftly. The book had taken a while to find, but she knew it was something Michael would love.

'*Foyle's Philavery,*' he read.

'Now you can give me new words I'll never know the meaning of.'

'I don't know what to say,' he told her, tears forming in his eyes.

'You don't have to say anything. It's my way of saying thank you. For everything.'

He knew what she meant and grabbed her, hugging her tightly. Her best friend was one of the most precious people on earth to her, and she looked forward to creating all sorts of skewed, warped memories with him.

They laughed as they walked out of the apartment together. When they got to the bottom of the stairs, Michael turned to Kara and whispered he truly was happy for her.

Kara noticed a parked car that was not Michael's. Turning to him, she wordlessly queried where the rusted piece of junk he owned was, and he winked like it was a big secret. People stopped and stared; no one had seen a red Ferrari in their street before. He opened the door and Kara slid in, wary she may scratch something with the beading on her dress. Michael walked around like a rat-pack legend, swinging the keys around his finger like it was the most natural thing in the world to do. He started the car, and the engine rumbled Kara's belly.

'You sure you're right to drive this thing?' she asked. 'Where on earth did you get this from? I would have been happy in your brown bomb.'

He smirked and eased the car out. He waved to people along the way as if he was some sort of celebrity, and Kara laughed at how silly they must have looked. But she also noticed he was heading in the opposite direction they were supposed to be going in.

As if reading her mind, he said, 'There's a protest in the street ahead, and they recommended people go around on the freeway if they need to get into the city. Don't worry, you'll only be fashionably late.'

She hummed in happiness while the engine roared on the freeway. When Michael missed the next exit, she turned to her friend, whose eyes kept going back to the rear-view mirror.

'That was the exit ... where are we going?' she asked.

He didn't answer, then she noticed they were speeding. Kara grabbed onto the side of the seat, like that was going to slow him down and asked again with a little more concern in her voice. 'Michael, where are we going? You've gone past the exit.'

'Shit,' he breathed as he swerved to overtake the car in front of them.

'Michael!' she screamed, wanting to grab the steering wheel. 'Michael! Stop the fucking car!'

But he ignored her and drove faster, his eyes going between the road and the mirror. Kara turned to see what it was he was looking at and noticed a sleek black car with tinted windows close behind. She wondered if this was one big nightmare and what she was seeing wasn't real.

Her first thought was of Sophia in her dress and tears in black streaks immediately ran down her face. Michael didn't pay attention to her distress, suddenly turning the car left off the freeway into streets she had never seen before. When it was safe, he parked the car and let out a long, steady breath. They were a long way from the gardens, and all Kara could think about was getting back to Val and Sophia.

'Who was that?' she yelled at Michael wanting answers.

'You know who it is.'

'What? I have no idea.'

'How much do you know about Dom?'

'What's this got to do with Dom?' she asked, feeling stupid that they were having this conversation.

'How much do you know?' he asked again.

'I worked with him at Gio's for a while, but I hadn't seen him since I left. That was years ago. Then I saw his name flash on the television screen after some thug was found floating in the river. And, after my mother died, she told me he was the nephew of someone called Aldo, who—' She didn't want to explain any more. 'What the hell is going on, Michael?' she screamed at him. 'Take me back to Val!'

Regret simmered in his eyes. 'I can't do that.'

'What the fuck? Let me out,' she said, grabbing for the handle only to find it locked.

'What did Dom want at your place earlier?'

'He said something about finally finding me and that we would catch up again. What's going on?'

'What's my surname?' he asked, ignoring everything she told him.

It was an odd question to ask. Michael once told her it didn't matter what people's surnames were because, if we knew them, then we knew everything. He said surnames removed the element of disguise, and they made it too easy to stalk someone.

'Why are you asking me shit like this?' she screamed. 'Michael! Turn the car around and take me back. I want to see Val and my little girl.'

But she didn't get a chance to beg or ask anything else. The black car from earlier hit them from behind, propelling the Ferrari forward. Kara screamed in terror while Michael recovered and straightened the car, flooring the pedal to make the car move.

'What's my surname, Kara?' he demanded.

'Farrino,' she told him, crying uncontrollably.

'How much do you know about your family?' he yelled, never taking his eyes off the road.

They were somewhere east of Melbourne and the roads were beginning to wind into the hillside following the landscape as they exited the suburban jungle. Michael weaved around corners, looking back at the car that was still relentlessly close. It dawned on her that Michael knew about her mother and her family. Terror seized her when she realised who was driving behind them.

'Dom,' she whispered, his name a memory she wanted to erase.

'Yes. Fucking Dom!' he yelled. 'Tell me everything he said. Fuck!' He slammed his hands on the steering wheel.

History had a way of drowning memories in the depths of an ocean but could also make them resurface. Her mother was terrified for her father, and she knew something could happen to Kara. That was why she made her father leave. She worried for all of them, and it was justified.

Family like that did not disappear into the crevices they crawled from. They lingered like cockroaches who could survive a nuclear blast, the ones that disappeared along the way replaced as they multiplied.

Michael was driving fast around the corners, as if being chased in a supercar was normal. Kara turned around and saw the black car was lagging around the corners. Maybe they had escaped.

'My real name is Micha Augusti Benetti. Your cousin,' he blurted out. 'Matteo contacted me a while ago to keep an eye on you after the Cartelli family started making noise again. It turns out Franco, my father, decided to follow in his brother Antonio's footsteps.'

'My cousin?' she asked in disbelief. She recalled the last lines of her mother's letter that suggested she hoped her and Micha would one day meet, she was sure they would get along. Memories of their time together flooded her, beginning with meeting in the hospital.

'That day when I woke up?'

'We knew the doctor on call. Paid him to let me stay.'

Kara thought back to when she met him, and how it didn't look like anything had happened to him. It all fell into place. He had been put there to protect her, the opposite of the hitman, but a dirty thug no less.

'All this time?'

'Here, just for you.'

It all started to make sense. The reason why Michael always told her to be wary. The reason why he never wanted anything more than friendship. The way he was over-protective of her relationship with Val, guarding her like a protective older brother.

But all she could feel was the anguish of another lie her family had told.

He kept driving, oblivious to the effect his words had on Kara.

'What the fuck is going on?' she yelled at him. 'I can't fucking believe this!'

'I wanted to tell you Kara, I swear I did. But so much was happening, and we decided it was best not to tell you.'

'Who the hell decided what was best for me? This is bullshit. None of you had the right and now my family is in danger.'

'I'm sorry ... I swear to you, I'm sorry.'

'Sorry ... You're fucking sorry? People want to kill me for someone else's shit, and you're sorry, like it's going to make a difference? You've known me all this time and it was all one big lie.'

'Matteo thought it was best not to say anything, especially after your mother died. He didn't know she left the letter.'

'Let me guess, my dear *cousin* told him all about it. I've been so stupid. So, so, stupid,' she cried, holding her head in her hands. 'This whole time I was so happy I finally found a friend I could trust, and yet here he is ... you're no better than the prick who showed up on my doorstep.'

She seethed at the person she thought was her friend. He was complicit in ruining her wedding day and her life with Val and Sophia. She wanted to hate him with everything she possessed. The man sat in the car next to her was a stranger to her, and he lived a life she knew nothing about. All of the secrets he kept, all the times he told her not to go looking for things she didn't need to find, now it all made sense.

But his eyes, that now looked so similar to hers, were shimmering with regret. She knew he was sorry for what he had kept from her.

'Just know everyone wanted what was best for you. We've all been keeping an eye on you, Kara. They know who you are.'

She tried to take in everything he was saying as they continued to swerve through the hills. Instinct had her looking back, and she noticed the black car was even further away, struggling to catch up. It was a momentary pause, and Kara blew a breath of relief. She reached for her phone to call Val, to tell him to get Sophia and meet her at the airport, like her mother should have done.

'You can't call him, even if you wanted to,' he told her. 'They know where he is. If they know you've called him, there's no telling what they'll do.'

It all churned in her head with a terror she couldn't put into words. Val was waiting, unaware of what was happening, and Sophia was too small to know. Kara cried at the thought of never seeing either of them again.

'Pull over!' she screamed at him. 'Stop the fucking car and pull over.'

'I can't do that. We need to keep moving, until they can't see us anymore.'

He drove, pushing the car to its limits as it gripped the corners. She turned again, and the black car was nowhere to be seen. There were so many questions she wanted to ask, but all she kept thinking about was Val and Sophia.

It was supposed to be a happy day, yet here she was, driving further and further away from them. Was everyone alright? Was Val worried? Sophia would be due for a feed. And poor Alexis; this whole time she was worried about how she would ruin Michael, but little did they know that Kara would be everyone's undoing.

She glanced across at the person she knew nothing about and wondered how it was she missed all of the clues along the way. Michael had appeared, adamant that she never learn anything about her past.

'Michael,' she pleaded. 'Let me go back, I need to see my baby.'

'No. They've slowed down, but they won't stop. I need to get you safe. Val will be okay. I have people watching him and Sophia. Matteo will make sure they're unharmed.'

'What about Alexis?' she asked, and regret lined his face.

'She will be fine,' was all he said.

She wanted to be 'fine' with everything he said. But the absurdity of it all was beyond comprehension. Until her mother's letter, she had no idea about the family or their sinister connection. She was blissfully unaware, living in a bubble that Kara loved. Now, she shook, terrified at the possibility of her family being hurt.

'Call Matteo,' she demanded. 'Tell him to get them. Fuck!' she screamed at him, 'FUCKING CALL MATTEO!'

'We need to keep going for a while, then we can stop.

Someone is telling your dad what is going on. He's aware of the situation.'

'My father knew who you were this whole time, didn't he?' she asked, already knowing the answer.

She couldn't believe how many people kept secrets from her, helping her make fake memories so she wouldn't know the truth. She felt sorry for her father and wanted to make amends with him, but he also knew everything and hadn't said a word. He disregarded her life, along with Val's and Sophia's, and that was inexcusable. Betrayal had her hating all of them. She hated being born into something she knew nothing of and didn't want to be a part of.

Michael eased around the corner, then slowed down and turned to look at Kara with pity. 'I'm sorry,' he told her. 'I couldn't say anything. Matteo wanted to make sure it all disappeared. We thought it had, but I guess we were wrong.'

'Wrong? How fucking funny you were sent to protect, and yet here we are! This would be funny if our lives weren't depending on you getting us out of this shit show right now. Fuck! Val!' she called. 'Sophia!' She wailed at the sound of her daughter's name.

'We fucked up. We know we did. We don't know why he wanted to come for you.'

Wrong. Dom had been keeping tabs on her the whole time. Dom wanted revenge for something that had nothing to do with her. He waited until her wedding day to come and make himself known, a day that was supposed to be filled with happiness but was now replaced with terror. But Kara already knew why he had come looking for her.

She was the easiest to get to.

She never stood back to stay in the shadows.

She once flaunted herself as easy prey.

She needed to destroy everything she touched.

She wanted to destroy herself.

She finally succeeded.

Michael looked back in the rear-view mirror and frowned before reaching over and grabbing Kara's hand.

'Everything will work out,' he told her with an assurance that didn't meet his eyes.

Everything was ruined. And Kara could only think of Val and Sophia.

As they drove further, the road looked as if it was about to clear. The problem with the clearing was it unravelled to a space that left everything exposed. And there, waiting on the side of the road was another sleek black four-wheel drive, idling ready for them.

Kara howled in terror and Michael swore, yelling, 'Hang on!' as the Ferrari ploughed through a wire fence going off-road. The car wasn't built for bumps, and they bounced around on the uneven road in doomed discomfort. Kara was hysterical as they were jolted around. The car that followed was made to go off-terrain but didn't miss a beat on the unsteady ground. She clung to the door handle, ready to open it and run if she needed to.

She kicked off her heels in anticipation, knowing she needed to be prepared, but it was no use. The Ferrari launched over a small hill and remained airborne for what felt like an eternity, then landed, rolling several times. The sound of metal crunching screeched in their ears as glass shattered all around them piercing their skin. Blood trickled from Kara's wounds and the seatbelt gripped Kara across her mid-section, depriving her of whatever breath she had left.

They landed on their side. She was disorientated, hanging in a weird position and in agony from her injuries. She looked over to Michael, whose head lolled to the side. He had a cut on his head. She wanted to reach out, but didn't have the energy to move. There was water all around them.

'Val,' she called out, as if he was there to help her. He was a doctor ... he would know what to do. He would know how to help Michael who hadn't opened his eyes. The car suddenly righted itself, and Michael's body slumped forward onto the steering wheel. Kara's feet were cold. She thought she was bleeding everywhere, but the smell of algae mixed with freshness made her very aware that it was not only blood.

The car rapidly filled with water. She tried to open the door to get out, but it was a mangled mess and stuck shut. Water was now up to her waistline. She desperately tried to undo her seatbelt. It was jammed and she screamed in frustration. She gathered strength and tried to shake Michael awake so he could help her, but he didn't move.

'Michael, wake up!' she yelled when the water was up to her neck.

The car would be fully consumed in a few seconds. She tried to bang on the windows to break them and failed. Holding her breath, she reached for her shoe on the floor and tried again. She failed.

Desperation had her clawing at everything else around her. It was amazing how time felt quicker when terror seeped in with water that you couldn't escape from. She took a big breath and held it for as long as she possibly could. The water invaded her nose as Kara tried the door again. It didn't budge, and she was stuck, weighed down by her dress and strapped in with a seatbelt she couldn't undo. She knew she would be met with certain death.

An eerie silence filled the cabin, and she felt calm. She thought back to when she believed she might have been dying. It was something she didn't want to accept at the time, because she wanted to fight and savour the little time she had left with Val. But now, as the car filled with water, she recognised the futility of her situation, and she accepted her fate.

Perhaps it was her way of believing her death would be the end of the vendetta between the families. Maybe it was the quietness in the cabin that silenced the voices in her head. Maybe it was the deep breaths she was no longer taking as the water rose. Either way, she accepted her fate.

She thought about Val and Sophia, and her heart began to

beat with a love that allowed her to succumb as the water rose. She thought about all the memories they would never make and the memories she would never be a part of. She was filled with happiness knowing she had known true love, a love she never sought out. No matter what happened, her heart would echo to let them know she would love them forever. Val and Sophia would be her final memory.

27

VAL

How do we dream of an ending if we thought it would be forever? A place where we wander through life, snug in our own cocoon protecting us from our vulnerable truths, where we allow ourselves the belief that happiness is eternal. In this space, we are unaltered, blissfully unaware of the chaos happening around us. We settle into oblivion and ignore the intricacies of our lives, and we fail to acknowledge our reality or our greatest fears. And fear is very real and very primal.

So, when death comes to greet us, its inevitability shocks us. We are unprepared for the aftermath. It does nothing to hasten our understanding of rational thought, or the slowness of each forlorn memory, or the passing of the grief that can stay with you, unguarded and always present. Sadness echoes in everyone's lives, and it lingers, lamenting and lost.

Belief allows us the understanding that not all stories end as they should. Perhaps logic and reason prevent belief from becoming something more than it should be, preventing anything from twisting the narrative and leaving it open for interpretation. Maybe it allows us a different point of view, a self-reflection through a broken mirror, that only allows the scattered fragments of self-recollection. Maybe you see yourself as an alternative to your own reality, a utopian distortion that you know was never real.

But reality doesn't always disguise the reflection that looks back. It echoes and reverberates, at times tragically. And, when this happens, forever becomes an unexpected berm that throws you off the path you thought was well established. And paths lead you to bridges that you've travelled over but never taken notice of.

Grief strangled Val from within. It was a sadness that enveloped him wholly, cradling him in a filthy grip. It touched his soul, tarnishing it. He felt as if it ruined everything.

The church started to fill with people. They wore black, and it surrounded everyone like an ominous cloud of grief. It was the colour of numbness. It was as a stark contrast with the roses draped over Kara's casket, the only hint of colour to counter the sadness. The smell of the flowers was a reminder that death lingered in the air. The mahogany casket gleamed as if hope radiated from the wood. It was a permanent reminder of light and shade, good and evil, love and hate. Everything Val lost.

There were people sitting in the church who had come with their own version of belief: where the greater good was serviced by something unseen, and their belief rested solely on the words of scripture. It was here their prying eyes could cast judgement in a place Val knew should welcome every wounded soul.

He watched on as the procession of condolences began with tears and unsteady words. He felt someone touch his shoulder. There was a nod of recognition and a steady stream of people who paid their respects as they passed Kara's casket, each person recognising this too would be them one day. Death had a finality that no one wanted to recognise. People feared it with everything they had, rather than accepting it for the gift it gave us.

Accepting finality meant acknowledging an end to his and Kara's forever. He had to relinquish everything he held close, including his dreams. When Val recognised this, he had to admit that forever was not something that anyone could attain, even if they wanted to. Val finally acknowledged this and, when he did, it settled with acceptance.

Death robbed Val of everything, leaving him feeling nothing but empty. If his breath was coloured, each exhalation would be grey. His tears that fell created their own private storm, and his feelings shattered the glass protecting his fragile heart. It kept beating, even as the shards fell around it.

He was unsteady on his feet, and the walk to the ambo felt as though it was further than it really was. The faces in the crowd stared back at him with renewed pity. They tried to sympathise, so they could connect with his grief. It was only then they could process how any of it was possible.

His heart ached its beat a sad melody that drummed him into numbness. He felt it was impossible to find the words to speak. How could he say goodbye, when he felt like he had never really said hello?

The church hushed around him. He wondered if truth could justify everyone's despair, that it would bring light to the darkness that hovered, that somehow, he could bring closure to everyone's suffering, while embalming his own feelings.

But it was moments like these when he felt his memories break through – he and Kara were sitting in a meadow laughing while the wind carried their truths. They would hear music in strangled chords, and it gifted him with words that reflected their time together. He remembered the comfort of being together, kissing each other one last time.

These were moments he once wanted to share, except now as he stood there, staring at the people he hardly knew, part of the life Kara never spoke of, he wanted to keep them as his memories and not share them with anyone else. Now there was only sadness, as people's heads hung in recognition of death. Death tattooed him with grief, profound and indelible.

He began the eulogy, not knowing where he drew breath from.

'There are a lot of things I could say right now, about love and loss and grief. And, to be honest, all of it would apply.' The crowd hung onto every word he said. He wondered if they were hoping to connect their grief with his. But he knew this would be impossible. He knew his words would fuel their emotions while they sat in the church but, once they left, they would only have memories of a day they spent at a funeral.

He felt angry. The people here didn't deserve to hear any words. He wanted the crowds to vanish so he could sit with his grief in the corner of the room and unpack the raw emotions that simmered.

'It really is hard to try and find something would signify goodbye, where time is stretched to the length that it needs to be, to say goodbye so you can comfort the people left behind. I wanted to read something poetic about death and grief, but no one can write how you truly feel. Each depiction is a sadness which reaches places where words feel fill something that can only be described as a void. How do you find the words that truly describe how you feel? I guess you never can.

'To be honest I didn't want to share any of our memories. I wanted to keep them private, locked away in my heart. Because I know that is where they belong forever. It sounds so selfish when I say that, but it feels like none of it matters now.'

Val noticed the crowd nodding in sympathy, acknowledging his admission. His knuckles gripped the edge of the ambo as if he could seal in his sadness, pressing into the wooden panels, imprinting himself there forever.

Sophia cried, breaking the silence. Alexis bounced his little girl on her knee, hushing her in the already stifling church. She looked up to where Val stood and smiled awkwardly, a broken apology, then excused herself, walking out with Sophia. The sound of his baby crying was a stark reminder not everything turned out as it should. Alexis found her light, and it transformed her and her life in a way that was beyond imaginable. But, Sophia's crying served as a reminder that even sadness did not stop life from moving on.

'I never went looking for love. Except fate had a different path for both of us. Our road to get to where we were wasn't always easy … just ask Ray.'

Everyone laughed as they turned to look at Ray. Ray ignored the stares, and Val noticed his gaze travelled to the casket. There was a recognition, a grief that reached everyone, and he saw it in Ray as his smile faded and he lowered his head.

'I was up late last night, pacing through the house thinking about today. I ended up staying up all night, writing on bits of paper only to throw them out. I didn't want to go through our photos because the memories made me sad. I tried to drink wine to help with my thoughts, but I gave up on that too. I know I wanted to do something that would be meaningful, that would be a true reflection of our love. But now I'm not so sure I want to share it. I want to keep all our moments private, all of our memories and the love we had. We are all tethered feathers, connected by something we believe we want to see. When death comes with a gentle hand, we want to believe it guides us into our final resting place. But instead it's a mirror that shares fragments of who we were, where fractured memories are seen through a broken light, and love flies with padded wings from darkness to light.'

'You will want that one moment all over again. To hold it close so your soul sings and whispers with love and then you laugh sadly at the cruel goodbye. You're mocked by the heavy tears that fall like lead and crash through your heart, where you remember all that was said and done with sadness. Death is a farewell, and sorrow is the end of your goodbye.'

He walked away from the ambo, stopping in front of Kara's casket. He leaned over, draping his arms around it, crying, uncaring that anyone was watching, hoping somehow she would be able to feel his grieving tears. He didn't know how long he stood there and only moved when he felt Joshua's hand on his shoulder. Joshua stood there, his eyes shining with unspent tears, and Val hugged the man who said nothing of his grief.

After the service, people stopped Val to give their condolences, saying how sorry they were and offering to help if there was anything that he needed. He smiled going through the motions, never taking his eyes off the casket that was resting in the back of the hearse. The driver sat there, idling patiently, waiting for everyone to say goodbye one last time. When the last of the mourners shared their sympathetic smiles, the driver finally left, taking Kara and her casket to her final resting place.

The gates to the cemetery were secured with wrought iron. There was a woman with wiry red hair sitting behind a glass window, and she got out to greet the driver of the hearse. She shook her head looking at the procession, acknowledging everyone with a look of sorrow. She told Val she was sorry for his loss, but Val recognised her sympathy wasn't something new. She directed the hearse and the cars that were following, instructing them to go over the little bridge and then to turn left. Just before she was about to leave, she stopped at Val's window and told him how sorry she was again. He noticed her nametag read Piper, and he thanked her for her help. He thought it an old-fashioned name, but it suited the woman who sat guarding the dead.

A big oak tree stood guarding Kara's spot. Just under it, was a fresh mound of dirt. Val wondered how long it would take them to return the dirt once everyone left.

The stillness of the cemetery was undisturbed. Sombreness was replaced with peace and ease, at Kara's final resting spot. Somewhere, Val could hear someone saying gentle words. And then they finished, and he found himself standing at the end of the coffin, the mahogany smooth and cold under his fingers. It was the final thing of hers he touched as he said goodbye. They gently lowered the casket into the ground, and he remembered hearing words that carried Kara down to her final resting spot. Ashes, dust, and then everything echoed in the wind.

Dirt fell through Val's fingers, and it created a dark shadow on the roses that lay on top of Kara's coffin. From there, people came and went, saying their final goodbyes, and it was only then he felt loneliness overtake his grief. Val knew his life would never be the same.

Ray approached him. He opened his mouth but quickly closed it. Sometimes saying nothing is more powerful than saying anything at all. It was a quiet moment where they both thought much and said little.

Standing side by side, staring into the ground, neither of them said a word. It was a moment condensed within the silence of conversations they would never have. Ray turned to leave, and Val pulled him back.

'I wanted to say thank you. For everything.'

Ray reached into his pocket and handed over a tissue.

'For all the times you think you won't need it, but you actually do,' he said and walked off.

The tissue was weightless. Val wondered how something so simple could have such a dramatic impact. Ray had known it was exactly what Val needed. The tissue was caught in the breeze and it gently landed on Kara's casket.

The significance of the gesture was not lost on Val. It was a reminder that this was the final goodbye: for missed chances, for the things that should have been said but weren't. For all the times when honesty allowed the rawness of their lives to be at the forefront. For all the times that vulnerability allowed a glimpse into how fragile they really were. Where they allowed themselves the ability to be open to love, to embrace it without hesitation. Because, when he and Kara had done that, they finally realised they loved each other enough, which gave them the ability to love someone else, equally and without judgement.

But, most of all, their goodbye was the final stop in a journey that no longer existed.

'For all the times you'll need it more. Goodbye.'

Unbound Wings (Book 2) by Liz Tolevski

*Memories in the beauty of the daylight wind are
where secrets are scattered through the embers of whispered words.
-Every story has darkness that hides in the light-*

ACKNOWLEDGMENTS

Who would have thought I would get here? Who could have imagined that being forced to stay at home during COVID-19 would lead to an achievement I never anticipated? When I first sat down to write this story on a cold winter's day, I had isolated myself outside with my computer. It all began with a single paragraph, which quickly led to two, and before I knew it, Kara and Val took shape in my mind and refused to leave until their story was fully developed. They have settled comfortably in my thoughts, and I have no doubt they will remain there for a very long time. From the highs to the lows and everything in between, writing 'Tethered Feather' has been a cathartic wild ride, and I wouldn't change any of it.

First, I would like to express my heartfelt gratitude to my husband Sam and my children Erica and Dean. Words cannot convey how thankful I am to you for your support, especially to Sam, who supported me on this journey, encouraging me every step of the way, reminding me that I could, even when I thought I couldn't. To Erica and Dean, who have patiently listened to me talk about Kara and Val as if they were real members of our family: thank you for celebrating every chapter I wrote, listening to me brag about how far I'd come, and for laughing at me when I finished writing the story and didn't know what to do with myself. I hope I have inspired you to pursue your dreams, no matter what stage of life you are in.

A special thanks to my Mum and Dad, Jane and Cveta. I thank you for always asking how the story is going, even though I've tried to translate it numerous times into Macedonian and you still ask in broken English, *'is story finish?'* To my sister Lila and her husband Matt, I'd give you some words in Macedonian, but I'm pretty sure Google will translate them, and we would be in trouble with Mum and Dad, none of us want that. To my nieces Grace and Lisa, remember when I said I'd write a book? Well look at me ... I've finally done it.

My manuscript wouldn't be where it is if it wasn't for my editor Rebecca Fletcher from Words on Words editing. You helped shape Kara and Val's story so they could shine on every page. When you said yes last year, I didn't believe that my story would be worthy of someone believing in it. But between the endless back and forth, to the final copy, I am forever grateful for you hard work and I cannot thank you enough.

To Hannah Smith, for casting a keen eye, pointing out my useless words such as 'that', 'had', 'own' and 'okay' and replying to my endless questions even while you were away on holidays. But more than anything I thank my lucky stars you knew what you were doing even though I still have no idea. With your help, Tethered Feather is finally complete.

To Murphy Rae, who saw my vision and helped create my cover. You knew exactly what I wanted and I thank you endlessly. I can't wait to see what you do with the sequel Unbound Wings.

And a shout out to the Josh and the crew of New Gold Mountain. Thank you for allowing me to use the bar as the constant backdrop for Kara. Here's hoping she returns there sooner rather than later.

But finally, this thank you wouldn't be complete without acknowledging my little village - my lady loves. To Briony, Ellie, Dana, Amber, Megan, Alana, and Chrissy. Thank you for keeping me hydrated with endless bottles of champagne. For the encouragement to keep going when I almost gave up, and for the praise that I still believe I didn't deserve. But more importantly, for a belief so strong none of you doubted me for a second.

It is the true definition of *Presence*.

ABOUT THE AUTHOR

Liz Tolevski is a contemporary fiction author whose writing captures the complexities of human relationships within everyday life.

Liz holds a Bachelor of Nursing and has over twenty years of experience as a perioperative nurse, specialising in orthopaedic and spinal surgery. She also earned a Bachelor of Arts with majors in English and Creative writing where Liz further honed her craft through her Honours in Creative Writing.

Over the past five years, she has embraced the written word as both an art and a refuge, breathing life into stories that reflect contemporary themes with depth and authenticity. Tethered Feather began during the quiet introspection of the COVID-19 lockdown, allowing her to intertwine the lives of Kara and Val. Liz is currently working on a sequel.

Liz balances her literary passion with family life. A wife and devoted mother of two, she lives in Melbourne, alongside two dogs who provide her with endless entertainment. Liz hopes her work resonates with anyone who has navigated the intricacies of love, loss and the everyday moments that define our existence.

Contact Liz:

liztolevskiauthor@gmail.com

 instagram.com/lizloves2write